The Falcon Soul

Amy Sumida

Legal Notice

More Books by Amy Sumida

The Godhunter Series (in order)

Godhunter
Of Gods and Wolves
Oathbreaker
Marked by Death
Green Tea and Black Death
A Taste for Blood
The Tainted Web

Series Split:
These books can be read together or separately
Harvest of the Gods & A Fey Harvest
Into the Void & Out of the Darkness

Perchance to Die
Tracing Thunder
Light as a Feather
Rain or Monkeyshine
Blood Bound
Eye of Re
My Soul to Take
As the Crow Flies
Cry Werewolf
Pride Before a Fall
Monsoons and Monsters
Blessed Death
In the Nyx of Time
Let Sleeping Demons Lie

The Lion, the Witch, and the Werewolf
Hear No Evil
Dark Star
Destiny Descending
The Black Lion
Half Bad
A Fey New World
God Mode

Beyond the Godhunter
A Darker Element
Out of the Blue

The Twilight Court Series
Fairy-Struck
Pixie-Led
Raven-Mocking
Here There Be Dragons
Witchbane
Elf-Shot
Fairy Rings and Dragon Kings
Black-Market Magic
Etched in Stone
Careless Wishes
Enchanted Addictions
Dark Kiss

The Spellsinger Series
The Last Lullaby
A Symphony of Sirens
A Harmony of Hearts
Primeval Prelude
Ballad of Blood
A Deadly Duet
Macabre Melody
Aria of the Gods
Anthem of Ashes

A Chorus of Cats
Doppelganger Dirge
Out of Tune
Singing the Scales
The Devil's Ditty

The Spectra Series
Spectra
A Gray Area
A Compression of Colors
Blue Murder
Code Red
With Flying Colors
Green With Envy
A Silver Tongue
A Golden Opportunity

The Soul Stones
The Hawk Soul
The Lynx Soul
The Leopard Soul
The Fox Soul
The Wolf Soul

Fairy Tales
Happily Harem After Vol 1
Including:
The Four Clever Brothers
Wild Wonderland
Beauty and the Beasts
Pan's Promise
The Little Glass Slipper

Happily Harem After Vol 2
Including:
Codename: Goldilocks
White as Snow
Twisted

Awakened Beauty

Erotica

An Unseelie Understanding

Historical Romance

Enchantress

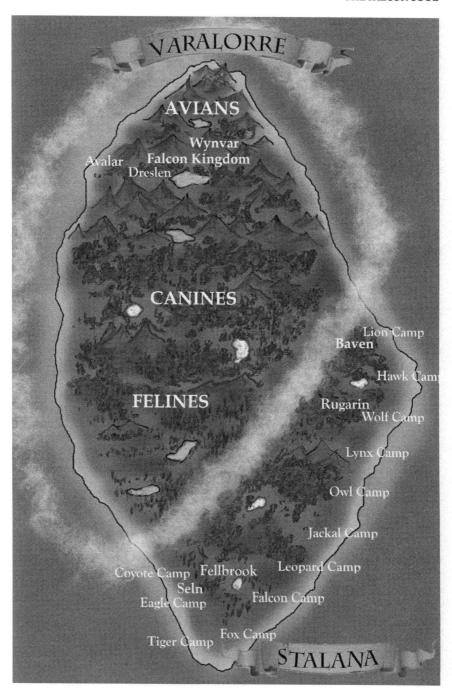

Chapter One

I took a deep breath of the crisp air and stretched my shoulders as I headed toward the baking pavilion. It was 5 AM, a time when most of the camp, even the early risers, was asleep, but I wasn't your usual soldier. I'm a baker; I make bread. It's my favorite thing in the world. Well, bread, pastries, crackers, anything with yeast or a lot of flour in it really. I loved getting my hands in the dough and transforming it into something delicious that could bring a smile to someone's face. Truly, is there anything better than freshly baked bread? The aroma, the warmth, the crispy crust and soft center. Bread is the foundation of food; a culinary lynchpin. No meal is complete without bread. And I make damn good bread. My plan was to open my own bakery, but that would be after I raised enough money and got out of the Falcon Army. For now, I was happy where I was. I got to do what I loved and serve my country: a win-win.

The Falcon Army that I'm contracted to is one of twelve armies whose ranks are composed of fae shapeshifters and human soldiers. We humans share a continent with the magical Fae, and that continent is continually attacked by monsters—the Farungal. Farungals are big, black, scaly, clawed, fanged, venomous things with barbs on the ends of their tails that can kill you with a single sting. In short, they're the stuff of nightmares, and they're also evil. I suppose evil is relative, and I shouldn't be classifying a whole race as such, but after fighting them, it's hard to think of them as anything else.

I couldn't imagine a baby Farungal sitting on its mama's lap, looking adorable. Nope, I think they were born nasty.

The Fae lands are called Varalorre and they're separated from our portion of the continent, Stalana, by a magical misty barrier that nothing but animals and faeries can pass through. So, really, the Fae didn't have to help us. They could have hunkered down behind their sparkly mist and hoped for the best. But they knew we were the last line of defense between them and the monsters, so they sent their armies to help us defend the continent. In addition to the twelve beast armies of shapeshifting Sidhe, they also sent twelve Unsidhe armies, full of faeries whose appearances can be as frightening as the Farungal. They'd previously kept the Unsidhe armies separate because humans could be skittish around the Unsidhe, but recently, that had changed. The Unsidhe Armies had joined the beast armies, moving their camps closer to ours and adding their soldiers to our training exercises. It was quite the thing and had the human soldiers all atwitter.

Most humans weren't scared of the Unsidhe anymore, not after fighting beside them on Alantri, the Farungal's continent, across the Bellor Sea. The general attitude was excitement more than anything, and from the few training exercises I'd been a part of, I understood why. Fighting alongside the massive Trolls and Redcaps and watching the stunning Leanan-Sidhe—all women, their men don't fight—whiz about with their blades flashing was quite thrilling. But, as I said, I'm a baker.

The chefs and bakers of the armies were, of course, trained to fight just like everyone else, but our training wasn't as hardcore as it was for the regular soldiers. We had trained in the craft of cuisine along with the art of war, and once we were placed in an army, our sword training was reduced to once a week. We spent most of our time cooking for the hundreds of soldiers in our army and didn't have much time for honing our fighting skills. You'd think the other soldiers would resent us for this, or tease us for always fighting in the back when we went to war, but no one teases an army cook, especially not a baker. Not if they want to eat, and every soldier loves to eat. An army marches on its stomach, as they say. Plus, chefs have sharp knives, and we bakers have thick muscles from working dough all day. You don't have to swing a sword to be a badass.

I was particularly fortunate in that my skill had been noted early on, and I was assigned to be the Falcon Lord's personal baker, the captain who runs his baking pavilion. The Falcon Lord is my army's warlord—the Sidhe man in charge of the entire Falcon Army, both the human and fae portions of it. All warlords were elite, the best warriors Varalorre has to offer, and they were also the only ones who possessed soul stones. At least *fae* soul stones.

The Farungal had started making their own soul stones with death magic, trapping hundreds of human souls in their evil amulets to give themselves great power. You see, the Sidhe, in addition to being shapeshifters, were great magic-users and could move objects, light fires, summon rain, and stuff like that, just with a wave of their elegant fingers. The Farungal, however, had that ability taken from them when they pissed off their goddess—a goddess who, it was discovered recently, is also the mother of the Fae. It's a long story, but to sum it up, a Farungal had the hots for a faerie who didn't want him, and the Farungal resorted to black magic to get her. Then he taught all his buddies the trick, and seducing faeries with black magic became all the rage. It ended horribly, with the Goddess taking the Farungals' magic, beauty, and wings in punishment. Yeah, they used to fly. I can't tell you how grateful I am that they can't do that anymore.

But back to the fae soul stones. Every warlord was given a soul stone connected to the magic of his kingdom. As a country, Varalorre is divided by the beast races of the Sidhe. In other words, the kingdoms of Varalorre—all run by the Sidhe —are each home to a particular sub-race of Sidhe, each sub-race being determined by the animal a faerie shifts into. For example, those who can shift into falcons are Falcon Fae and live in the Falcon Kingdom. The Unsidhe live in those kingdoms too, but they're not divided by their races. Technically, only twelve armies were sent to Stalana, one from each kingdom, consisting of both Sidhe and Unsidhe soldiers. But after the Fae saw how humans reacted to the Unsidhe, they divided their armies. That's how we ended up with twenty-four instead of twelve. Anyway, there are twelve kingdoms, then those kingdoms are grouped into three regions by their animal families— Canine, Feline, and Avian.

The fae soul stones draw upon the magic of those kingdoms, and what's used cannot be replenished, so the warlords only employ their soul stones in times of great need. *Or* to make a valorian. Valorians are humans who have shown such great valor that a warlord decides to share his soul with them. Yep, their *soul*. This doesn't automatically make the human a valorian, they could simply end up with an extended life. However, if the Fae Goddess decides that the human is worthy, she will add her magic to that of the soul stone and use the piece of the warlord's soul to change the human into a faerie. The human is reborn, his or her body altered into an immortal version of itself. They're also given nearly as much respect as the warlord himself. In other words, it's a *big fucking deal.*

Back at the beginning of the war, nearly forty years ago, the first valorian had been made, but then he'd disappeared into Varalorre, and we humans forgot about him entirely. Forty years may be nothing for faeries, but it's a hell of a long time for us. Anyway, it wasn't until recently, when there was a wave of new valorians made, that we remembered—or as was the case with most of us, heard about for the first time—that valorians were a possibility. I also heard that there's a prophecy one of the valorians made; it said that every warlord would have a valorian, and they'd all be needed to end the Farungal War.

Heavy shit. I was glad I was just a baker. Don't get me wrong, I joined the army to defend my country as well as learn my trade and earn money, but I'd rather be a little guy at the back than one of the valorians up front, facing down the Farungal with magic and faerie might. I wasn't a coward, but I wasn't a hero either. I'm just your average guy, trying to survive the war so I can live knowing that my family and I are safe. And right now, that meant starting the day's bread. This was why I was up at 5 AM; I kept baking hours. Chefs get up early too, but not as early as us bakers. We had to coax the bread to life and start the process of it rising long before the other soldiers rose from their beds, or it wouldn't be ready in time for their breakfast.

But I was good with that. I liked walking through the camp at this hour. It was as peaceful as an army camp could get. Even the soft murmur of soldiers on guard duty didn't carry to me. Everything was silent, the land asleep beneath its blanket of stars. I sighed as I strolled along the beaten dirt path, a soft smile on my face, and glanced at the Falcon Lord's tent as I passed it. I passed it every morning since my work area, a baking pavilion attached to the cooking tent, was just behind the warlord's sprawling tent. This was so his food was always hot. As I mentioned, my team was assigned to the Falcon Lord, but we also prepared food for his personal guard. Every warlord has a unit of knights who are responsible for his safety and wellbeing. They aren't technically a part of the army and hold no rank in it, beholden only to their warlord. And I had a crush on one of them.

His name was Daron, and he was big, buff, and blond. I have a thing for blonds. Maybe it's that whole opposites attract thing. My father's family came over to Stalana from Lek a couple of generations back, so I have a darker complexion than most Stalanians and different features, though I've got my mother's eyes—a hazel heavy on the green—and her blue-black hair. I use those eyes to my advantage. I'm told they look striking against my honey-brown skin, and many a man has fallen prey to one of my don't-you-want-this-in-your-bed looks. Many, but not Daron. I'd been trying to catch his eye for years, all to no avail.

I sighed again, this time in lament when I saw that Daron wasn't on duty. *Hold on.* I stopped and backed up. There were no guards at the front of the Falcon Lord's tent. None at all. I crept closer, gooseflesh rising on my arms, and peered around one fabric corner, ducking beneath a tent rope. Bodies. A pile of them. Oh, fuck. My heart started racing, but I could still hear a soft shuffle over its pounding. Someone was inside the tent, and I didn't think it was the Falcon Lord. Or rather, I didn't think it was only the Falcon Lord.

I went cold suddenly, in a way that only happens when I'm on a battlefield. My heart calmed and my hand reached for the dagger on my hip. Creeping back to the front of the tent, I pulled my blade and stretched my shoulders. I wasn't the best at hand-to-hand combat, but I knew just where to hit a Farungal to bring instant death. All humans were taught the skill because when we fight Farungals, we have to kill fast or get killed. If I could keep the element of surprise on my side, I had a chance of killing this invader, whoever he or she was. Hey, maybe it wasn't a Farungal. Maybe it was just . . . oh, who was I kidding? It had to be a Farungal. No one else was going to sneak into our camp and slaughter the Falcon Lord's guards.

I slipped through the tent flap and was instantly encased in darkness. But, at the back of the tent, a sickly green glow drew me forward. Along with the light, a soft gasping sound filtered back to me and set my teeth on edge. I wanted to race forward, but I knew the floorboards would creak and give me away. So I continued to creep down the main area of the tent, past dark passages to rooms defined by hanging panels, to the opening at the back. I edged into the halo of green light and had to bite my lip to keep from making a horrified sound.

There lay the Falcon Lord, his body sprawled between his latest lovers—a man and a woman, both dead from the look of them. The Falcon Lord, however, was still alive. His gaze, normally so bright, was dark and tainted by the glow of the Farungal soul stone that hung around the invader's neck. The Farungal hunched in his cloak, but not by design; all the Farungal have a hunch. The only time they lost it was when they used their soul stones to magnify themselves, enhancing their bodies and their magic. This one, although obviously employing his amulet, hadn't done that. I assumed he'd kept himself normal to make creeping through camp easier, but who knows why the monsters do what they do?

All I knew was that this particular monster was killing the Falcon Lord.

And the Falcon Lord hadn't managed to remove his soul stone—the Falcon Soul. It was glowing pale red on his chest, and I knew that its magic was being stolen by the Farungal before me. It was likely the only reason the Falcon Lord wasn't dead yet. A similar thing had been attempted recently, at the last big battle with the Farungal, so I knew that this monster wasn't just draining the Falcon Lord, he was also draining the Falcon *Kingdom*. The Falcon Lord's hand laid limply just below his amulet, as if he'd tried to remove it but had been weakened too quickly—likely in his sleep. His eyes shifted to me, and I saw the bleakness there turn to hope. A tear trickled down his cheek.

That tear nearly broke my cool focus, but at the same time, it also hardened me. Sharpened my determination. I couldn't let the Falcon Lord down. I didn't think about how ridiculous this was; that the magic of an entire kingdom depended on the knife skills of a baker. I just nodded to the Falcon Lord and stepped forward, my stare locking on the back of the Farungal's hood. Right above his hunch—that's where I had to hit him. The blade needed to go in right between the third and fourth vertebrae to sever his spinal cord and disable his tail so he couldn't sting me as he died. Too high or too low, and I'd still kill him, but there would be the possibility that he could get a strike in and kill me right back.

I didn't think about dying; I thought about his spine. Only that spine. I saw the bones in my mind, placed them by that hunch, and struck with as much strength as I could put behind a single blow. My blade went deep, miraculously sliding between the vertebrae just as I'd intended, and pierced the Farungal's throat to emerge out the other side. The Farungal didn't even have time to gurgle. He simply crumpled to the ground, dead.

And I was alive. *Holy shit, I was alive!*

I didn't have time to freak out. I left my dagger in the Farungal's neck and shouted, "Help!" as I ran for the Falcon Lord. "Someone help us! The Falcon Lord is hurt!"

I yanked the body of the woman off the bed so I could kneel on the mattress beside the Falcon Lord. He was gasping, but a smile of relief hovered around his lips. His hand twitched and his soul stone brightened as its magic returned.

"Are you all right, my lord?" I laid a hand on his chest.

"I'll live," he whispered. "Thanks to you, soldier. Well done."

Damn, he was beautiful. Now that the threat had been eliminated, I could appreciate that he was lying there naked. Gloriously naked and not an inch of him beneath the blankets. The Falcon Lord was even bigger than Daron, his body thick with muscles that still managed to look sleek—a fae trait. His chest alone was a thing of beauty. And you know how I love blonds? Well, this guy was like a blond supreme. His hair was a tawny blond that truly looked like spun gold, as if someone had attached gold threads to his head, but made them silken. Those metallic strands flowed around a face of such elegant and yet masculine beauty that it was hard to look at him. He was simply too stunning. Almost painfully so. Breathtaking in a literal way. Those plush lips, high cheekbones, and classically fae jawline were enough to make my knees go weak, but add to them a pair of eyes the color of amethysts and you have a face so enthralling that it became divine. And those amethyst eyes? They had gold striations in them. I'd never been close enough to see that before, but now, in the pale red light of the Falcon Soul, they glittered at me.

I finally managed to speak, "Thank God. And the Falcon Soul?"

"It's fine; the magic has been returned to it. Be at ease." He took my hand. "What's your—"

"Falcon Lord!" a man burst into the bedroom. It was Daron.

I looked over at him and felt the tension in my chest release. I hadn't even realized that I'd feared for him, not until I saw him standing there. But Daron barely glanced at me, only rushed forward and shouldered me aside. I moved back, off the bed and out of the way as the rest of the Falcon Lord's surviving knights flooded his bedroom.

Go figure. I saved the Falcon Lord and his kingdom, but get brushed off like an annoying insect. I shrugged. They needed to see that he was safe, and I wanted that too. I wasn't the kind of man who craved recognition. As I mentioned, I'd rather be in the back, supporting the heroes instead of being one. But I would have liked a pat on the shoulder or a smile from

Daron.

Oh, well, that's how it goes in the army; you might get praise from your commanding officer, but anyone above him won't even know your name. Why would I expect Daron to be any different? At least the Falcon Lord had thanked me; that was enough for me. He had seen what I'd done and praised me for it, and that left a warm feeling in my chest. Plus, I'd have a good story to tell at the campfire that night. I grinned as I thought about how my friends were going to react; they weren't going to believe this shit. Then I slipped out of the bedroom and wound my way through the sudden mass of people filling the Falcon Lord's tent. They could take it from there; I had bread to bake.

Chapter Two

"Did you think you could hide from me?" the deep voice of the Falcon Lord made me flinch.

I was on my second round of baking for the day, hands currently stuck in a lump of dough that was destined to become his lunch. Had I been trying to hide from the warlord? Perhaps. But, honestly, I'd thought he'd forget about me in the midst of the investigation into the Farungal infiltration that was, according to my assistant, ongoing. And then there was that confiscated Farungal soul stone. I assumed he'd be way too busy to bother with me.

"Uh, no, Falcon Lord," I said as I glanced over my shoulder at him and found my pavilion empty, my assistants all conveniently busy elsewhere. "That would be silly since I literally spend my days forty paces from where you sleep. Plus, with my Lekian heritage, I kinda stand out among all you pale-faces." I grinned nervously.

"Yes, you most certainly do," he drawled appreciatively as he stepped up to my worktable.

The Falcon Lord cocked one hip against the table, glanced at my hands, then brought that incredible stare—even more incredible out in the light of day—up my body slowly. Consideringly. My hands clenched in the dough and my throat went dry. *What the fuck is happening right now?*

"Your skin is stunning. I imagine you have a lot of fae

lovers."

"Uh, no. Why would you say that?"

"We faeries prize darker skin tones," he explained, looking me over again. "They're so rare among our kind, and when they do appear, they're usually a true black, not this deep, golden-brown shade. Like coffee with the perfect amount of . . . *cream.*"

The Falcon Lord stroked a finger over my bare bicep as if admiring the shape, and I flinched but in a good way, tingles running down my spine as the breath caught in my throat. There I was, sweaty and covered in flour, while the Falcon Lord was fresh-faced and gorgeous. He wore a pair of brown leather breeches that molded to his shapely legs, a sleeveless tunic similar to mine except that his had a deep V neckline to show off his sculpted pecs in addition to his bulging biceps, and his hair was brushed into a straight line, held back by two tiny braids, one at each temple, the one on the right with a falcon feather attached to the end. I don't know why that feather was so sexy, but it was, especially with the tip caressing his chest.

I determinedly brought my stare back to his face, but the way he was staring back didn't help to calm my racing pulse. Doran was incredibly handsome, but the Falcon Lord was on a godly level. His features were sharper than those of most fae males, making those sensual lips look even more luscious, and those amazing eyes were framed by thick lashes and brows that arched like wings. In short, he was *way* out of my league, out of my fucking universe, and I couldn't deal with it.

Most men would be thrilled to have the attention of the Falcon Lord, even straight men, I'd wager, but not me. I like to stay within my hotness range. If a guy is too far above me on the sexiness scale, he makes me nervous, and I'd never be able to have a real relationship with him. Sure, I could do a one-night stand, but I doubt I'd even enjoy it; I'd be too worried about what I looked like compared to him and what he thought about it. So, instead of smiling at the Falcon Lord or blushing at his shockingly basic innuendo, I looked away, down at my dough, and went back to kneading. It hadn't been a compliment, not directly, so I didn't feel as if I had to thank him, or say anything at all.

His opinion differed; I saw him scowl out of the corner of my eye.

"I'm sorry, are you busy? Am I interrupting you?" the Falcon Lord snapped.

Oh, fuck. If I rebuffed his advances, was he going to get pissed at me?

"No, my lord!" I dropped the dough and turned to face him, coming to a parade rest, my sticky hands clasped behind my back and head lifted.

The Falcon Lord sighed deeply. "This is not going how I expected."

"How you expected?"

"Why did you leave my tent so quickly, Captain Ruhara?"

Oh, shit, he knew my name. Why did that send a zing of pleasure through me?

"Because I wasn't needed anymore, Sir," I said. "You were alive and in good hands. Doran, uh, I mean, your knight, moved me aside, so I figured I should go."

"Did he now?" The Falcon Lord cocked his head in a distinctly avian way. "And you didn't hear me call for you?"

"No, my lord." *He had called for me?* "Uh, did you need something else?"

"Did I need something?" The Falcon Lord chuckled. "Yes,

Captain, I needed to thank you for saving my life."

"Oh. I thought you did that already. You even gave me a 'well done' which was appreciated. But, uh, you're welcome, Falcon Lord." I flushed and looked down. "I just happened to be where I needed to be."

"I think you happened to be *exactly* where you were *meant* to be," he said softly.

The Falcon Lord's tone was so surprising that I lifted my head and met his stare. His eyes were hypnotizing; I could have blissfully stared into them while a band of Farungals tore me apart and counted it as a happy death.

"Wash your hands, Shane," he shocked me by using my given name—by *knowing* it. "You're coming with me."

"I, uh, I'm making bread for your lunch, my lord."

"Someone else will do it."

"But why, my lord?"

His eyes widened at my brazenness. "Because I gave you an order."

"Yes, Falcon Lord!" I saluted and splattered flour and bits of dough over us both. "Shit! I'm so sorry." I moved to brush off his tunic, then realized that I'd only make things worse. I yanked back my hands as my cheeks heated.

The Falcon Lord burst out laughing, making him even more divine. I could only gape at him.

"It's all right." He brushed the mess away, then reached out and flicked the flour off my hair. "You have beautiful eyes." His hand lingered at my temple, then stroked the line of my hair back into its tight ponytail.

"You don't owe me anything!" I blurted.

The Falcon Lord blinked in shock, backing up a step with it. "What?"

"I, uh, if you, um, if you're being nice to me because you feel as if you owe me something, you don't. I was just doing my job."

"Are you suggesting that I would *whore* myself to you out of some kind of obligation?" the Falcon Lord snarled, his expression shifting immediately into fury.

"Oh, fuck," I whispered. "No, Falcon Lord! No, Sir! I was just so shocked that you'd flirt with me that I . . . *fuck*, I'm sorry. I didn't mean it that way."

The Falcon Lord took a calming breath and nodded. "Forgiven. You shouldn't sell yourself short, Captain. I was flirting with you because I find you attractive, no other reason."

"I'm not attractive enough for you."

The Falcon Lord lifted a brow and smirked. "So, you think I'm attractive. More so than you?"

"Well, yeah," I huffed as if that were a simple fact.

He chuckled softly, sensually, and my stomach clenched in response.

"Well, maybe I can even things up a bit, so you won't feel so nervous about me flirting with you," the Falcon Lord suggested.

"I'm sorry, my lord, but what are you talking about?"

"I want to give you a piece of my soul, Shane," he said. "I believe you're meant to be my valorian."

Chapter Three

I stared at the Falcon Lord, trying to come up with a polite way of refusing him. Yes, I know a lot of soldiers would have done nearly anything to be given a piece of a warlord's soul, but not me. I didn't want immortality. Living forever sounded like a really bad idea to me, especially if I'd have to pay for it by becoming a valorian. What good is immortality if it's likely to get you killed? No, thank you. I just wanted to bake my bread and maybe fall in love, then get out of the army and move to Lek where I could be openly gay without people trying to murder me. You know, just an average man's dreams.

I finally went with the old standby, "No, thank you."

The Falcon Lord's slightly wicked smirk faltered. "What?"

"If it's all the same to you, my lord, I'd rather not. I'm happy as I am."

The warlord blinked. Gaped. Looked me over. "Are you straight? If that's the case, I'm sure we can work something out. Being my valorian doesn't automatically put you in my bed. I admit it was my intention, and most valorians do wind up with their warlords, but—"

"Please, stop." I held up a flour-coated hand, flakes of dough still falling from it.

He had intended to get me in bed? Seriously? It was nearly enough to make me want to accept. But then I thought about how that would work out, or not, as would be more likely. This guy wasn't gay, he was bi. That's fine and all, but in my experience, bisexual men don't settle on one person for long. We'd have a good time for a few weeks, and then he'd move on. Probably with a woman. Or he'd want me to share him—something I don't do—which meant a quick death for our relationship. And one look at this man told me that I'd never recover from being dumped by him. If I landed in the Falcon Lord's bed, I'd never want to leave it.

That didn't work for me. I don't like being that vulnerable with a lover. It's the very reason why I don't fight outside my weight class, if you know what I mean. As I mentioned earlier, I'd be too nervous—first about being good enough for him, then about being good enough to keep him. I don't need that kind of stress in my life, especially not my sex life. Give me a moderately attractive man, on my hotness level, who I won't feel insecure around, and I'd be blissfully happy.

I wouldn't be happy with the Falcon Lord. Oh, I'm sure I'd have moments of bliss, but then he would destroy me, and being destroyed isn't worth any amount of bliss. Mama didn't raise a fool.

"Excuse me?" the Falcon Lord growled.

"I'm gay, and I think you're divinely attractive; that has nothing to do with my refusal."

"Then what does?" He looked as if he couldn't decide whether to preen or pout.

"I don't want to be a valorian."

"What?!" he snarled.

"I don't want that kind of pressure." I shrugged. "I don't want the responsibility, and I sure as shit don't want to be immortal."

"You *don't* want to live forever?"

"No. I don't know about you faeries, but I think humans were made to live and die for a reason." I brushed off my hands and went to a nearby basin to wash them off, continuing to speak to him over my shoulder. "Life is more precious when it has an end. What would I do with forever? I think it would get old even while I didn't." I dried off my hands and turned back to see him gaping at me. "Besides, I thought a human had to be dying to be made a valorian?"

"No," the Falcon Lord murmured distractedly, as if trying to speak while also trying to figure out a massive quandary. "Sharing our souls can heal all wounds shy of death, so it's been used to save humans, but the process doesn't require you to be injured. It's a reward; it can be given at any time."

"Oh. Well, then find someone else you think is worthy."

"That's just it, Captain," his tone hardened. "There is no one else. I've been compelled to choose you."

"Compelled by who?"

"The Goddess and the Falcon Soul."

I blinked, then lowered my gaze to the triangular jewel that hung around his neck on a thick, gold chain. Its rosy color seemed brighter now, more vibrant than it had been in the tent earlier, and I swear that it winked at me.

"The soul stone told you to choose me?" I whispered, as if it could hear me. "It speaks to you?"

"It's connected to my kingdom and also to the Great Falcon—the God who birthed my race with the Goddess," he explained. "In that way, it has sentience. It urged me to share my soul with you."

"Well, fuck," I huffed.

The Falcon Lord chuckled, probably thinking that had done the trick.

"Now I really feel bad about saying no," I went on.

The Falcon Lord's face fell. "Are you fucking insane?" he snarled. "You don't refuse the chance to become a valorian."

"Why not?"

"Because . . . it's . . . it's an honor and you're made . . ."

"Fae?" I lifted a brow at him, suddenly angry. "Are you saying that no human would pass up the chance to become fae because you guys are so much better than us?"

The Falcon Lord blanched. "No, of course not. I just meant that it comes with certain perks. Not only do you become immortal, but your body is also made stronger and you'll get to go to Varalorre."

"All things that I don't care about, Falcon Lord," I said, not unkindly. "I'm sorry, but I'm not your guy. Your soul stone made a mistake."

The Falcon Lord clenched his jaw, lifted his chin, and stalked away.

"Fuck, I'm so fired," I muttered.

Chapter Four

Chefs and bakers tend to stick together in an army camp —outside of one too, come to think of it. In the camps, it's because we keep different hours than everyone else. Up earlier and asleep sooner, but we also got done with our day sooner too. Work for me was over by 2 PM, and I was out, lounging on the beach with my friends exactly 20 minutes later. The chefs weren't off for the day, but they had a long break between lunch and dinner.

"No fucking way," Rupert—who we call Ru because no one can say Rupert without laughing—declared. "You're so full of shit."

"I'm serious." I gave him a look to convey my honesty.

Our group was mainly composed of chefs, only Evan was a baker like me, and chefs are on the crazier end of the culinary spectrum. I don't know what it was, if it was working with fire and knives all day that did it, but they are some hardcore freaks, and it takes a lot to freak those freaks out. Me saving the Falcon Lord did the trick.

"No way," Rachel whispered.

"Yep. And he came to talk to me this morning in the baker's pavilion," I said.

"One of my cupcakes mentioned something about the Falcon Lord visiting the baking pavilion," Evan confirmed, nodding to the others. "He kicked all of Shane's cupcakes out so they could speak privately."

The cupcakes Evan referred to weren't delicious baked goods but our baking assistants; it's what we call them. Evan baked for the masses, so we didn't work in the same pavilion, but my assistants often went back and forth between his and mine, fetching supplies for me from the stock Evan kept. They must have gone straight to Evan's tent when the Falcon Lord booted them from mine. And cupcakes talk to other cupcakes.

"The Falcon Lord hunted you down and kicked everyone out of your pavilion to talk to you?" Tod asked in amazement. "What did he say?"

I cleared my throat, knowing they wouldn't take this well. "He wanted to share his soul with me. You know, try to make me a valorian."

"I thought you had to be dying for that?" Vanessa asked.

"Yeah, I did too." I waved a hand toward her in kinship. "Evidently not. The process heals most wounds, so it can save someone who's dying, but it doesn't have to be done when a person is on death's doorstep. Or so he told me."

"You asked him?" Tod gaped at me.

"Hold on." Evan held out his arms to stop everyone. "If he offered to make you a valorian, why aren't you one? Are you one of those duds that only got extended life?"

"No." I cleared my throat again. "I told him no."

"You what?!" They all shrieked together.

The guards in the nearby watchtower looked over at us with scowls.

"Shh," I hushed them. "I don't want all that, okay?"

"All what? The immortality, a hot body, or the Falcon Lord?" John, the only other gay guy in our group, asked in amazement.

"Yes," I said.

"Are you fucking out of your mind?" John shrieked. "Fuck, tell him I'll take your place. Sign me up for a fae make-over and the hottest guy in camp."

Everyone laughed, but it was in a horrified way.

"Really?" Evan asked me. "You told him *no*? The fucking Falcon Lord?"

"Think about it; sure, I'd get immortality, more muscles, and, possibly, him for a little while. But that guy isn't going to settle down with anyone. I've seen the soldiers stumbling out of his tent in the morning, and they're always different from the ones the night before. *And* half of them are women."

"So what?" Evan asked. "Make the guy fully gay. Win one for the G-Team. I believe in you."

"That's just it." I nodded toward him. "I don't. I'm not that good."

"Says Mr. Sweet Eyes with his guitar," Rachel teased me. "Just sing him one of your songs, and he'll be eating out of your hand."

"For a few nights. Maybe a week." I shrugged. "Then he'd be right back to eating pussy instead."

"As if that man has to eat pussy," Vanessa huffed.

"We don't do it because we have to." Tod smirked at her. "We do it because we *want* to. Hell, I'll lick you right now, baby. Spread 'em."

"Fuck off!" Vanessa exclaimed as she laughed and

pushed Tod's shoulder.

"So, Shane, you're saying that you gave up immortality because you don't think the Falcon Lord can be faithful to you?" Evan asked. "Seriously? Like, who gives a shit? Take him while you can, then go on your happy immortal way."

"If I made it through the war." I gave him a heavy look. "You've heard about the prophecy; the valorians will be needed to end the war—all of them."

Tod chuckled. "Yeah, and you prefer to fight from the back of the army."

"Hey, I'm not a coward," I said defensively. "I'd fight at the front if I had to, but I'd rather not do it as a fucking target."

"Fair enough, man." John slapped my shoulder. "But as a faerie, you'd be more likely to survive, not less."

I sighed. "I don't agree, but that brings me to another point; I don't want to live forever."

"Yep, he's a fucking lunatic," Vanessa declared. "You should have been a chef."

"Fuck, I'm not that crazy," I huffed, and everyone chortled.

To a chef, the term crazy was a compliment.

After the laughter died down, Rachel asked me, "You think he's going to let it go?"

I thought about the way the Falcon Lord had stared at me just before he left the baking pavilion and admitted, "I don't know. We'll see if I still have a position in the Falcon Army tomorrow."

They went silent and pensive with me. No one tried to brush aside my worry; we all knew that warlords were the ultimate power in the beast armies. The Falcon Lord could do as he pleased with my contract, including tear it into tiny bits and send me packing. And with it would go my dreams of moving to Lek and opening a bakery.

"Last one in the water's an idiot who doesn't want to be immortal!" John shouted and ran for the ocean.

Everyone else whooped and ran after him, me included. If I only had one more day in the army, I intended to make it a good one.

Chapter Five

When I got back to my tent, I found Daron standing outside it, looking grim and fucking handsome as all hell. I swallowed past the dryness in my throat and approached him.

"The Falcon Lord wishes you to dine with him tonight," Daron said, his expression annoyed.

I wasn't sure if his annoyance was with me or the fact that he'd been sent as a messenger.

"Please, tell him, no, thank you for me."

"You fucking piece of—" he cut himself off with a snarl. "What the fuck is wrong with you? You could have immortality, or at least a longer life, and *him*. Do you know how many people—how many *faeries*—would kill to warm that man's bed?"

That's when I realized that the guy I had a crush on, had a crush on the Falcon Lord. Fuck, of course, he did.

"Really? I never would have guessed." I crossed my arms, trying to hide my disappointment. Part of me had thought that Daron had come to apologize for brushing me aside that morning. That maybe he'd thank me for saving his warlord. Maybe he'd actually look at me and see me for once. Instead, it looked as if Daron was a bit of a prick.

"You ignorant, ungrateful asshole," he hissed at me. "You're afraid, aren't you?"

I went still, my expression falling into a blank mask. My father had taught me that when you get mad, really mad, it was better to hide it. To wait like the lions in Lek, stalking their prey silently. And then, when the moment was right, you release your rage and tear out their fucking throats. So, instead of punching him in his beautiful nose—the one he had lifted in distaste—I calmly asked, "Do you seriously think you can convince me to become a valorian by calling me chicken?"

Daron's hands balled into fists and his face went red. His father obviously hadn't taught him to get angry like a lion. Nope, he was an Avian, and they get all puffed up and squawky. Birds have no subtlety.

"Frankly, I'd rather you didn't accept," Daron sneered as he looked me over. "You're obviously not valorian material. Valorians don't shirk their duty. You got lucky and I'm grateful for that. You did well and saved a man worth twenty of you. So, thank you, Captain. And thank you for not allowing the Falcon Lord to waste a piece of his precious soul on the likes of you."

I snorted and smirked. "Now, you're trying to use reverse psychology on me."

"I don't give a shit about your human mind doctors either," he said imperiously. "I don't bother with games. I say what I mean. So, don't try to read anything else into my words when I call you a piece of shit. That is *exactly* what I think you are."

You're a lion, lying in wait. Be the lion. Don't let your prey see you, I heard my father in my mind.

"Right back atcha." I grinned, more of a baring of teeth.

"You little—" Daron launched himself at me.

Oh, yay. I didn't have to wait after all. My prey was attacking me.

I slipped to the side, clasped my hands into a ball, and bashed Daron in the back of his head, using his anger and momentum against him. He went sprawling in the dirt. Soldiers who were just returning from the bathhouse after a day of training stopped to gawk at a human taking down a faerie knight. A crowd started to form as Daron jumped up and spun to face me. His head cocked sharply, in that Avian way, and he sprung again, this time more carefully. He caught me right in the jaw. My head snapped back and I fell into my tent, landing on the floorboards hard. Shaking the ringing from my ears, I rolled, and as Daron came lumbering in, I bent over and rammed my shoulder into his stomach. We fell to the ground outside my tent, and soldiers started to cheer.

Rolling, punching, kicking, we fought like a couple of teenage boys, both of us knowing that we couldn't give it our all. No matter how mad we were at each other, this fight wasn't like our usual battles; we weren't trying to kill each other. But we were trying very hard to injure.

I grunted as Daron's fist found my belly, then he shrieked like a bird when mine met his nose. Blood sprayed and dirt turned to mud on my slick skin, still wet from my swim. I grabbed Daron's pretty hair and used it to shove his face into the dirt; it wasn't fair that I was the only filthy one. Plus, I only had on a pair of shorts, while he was fully dressed. Nope, not fair at all. I kneed him in the balls, earning another shriek from. Instead of curling up as most men would after such an assault—one most men wouldn't resort to, but let's face it, I was outmatched and had to fight dirty in both a literal and figurative way—Daron just got meaner. His hands went to my throat and began to squeeze.

"That is enough!" the Falcon Lord's voice cut through the cheering.

The crowd went silent as the warlord stepped up to

Daron and me. Daron let go and surged to his feet, leaving me gasping and covered in muck at the Falcon Lord's feet. Not that I cared about looking like a mess in front of him. Much. Fuck, all right, I was really embarrassed.

The Falcon Lord reached down and helped me up, his gaze softening on me briefly. "Are you all right, Captain Ruhara?"

"Yeah, thanks. I was holding my own until he went for the kill," I muttered.

"You kneed me in the balls," Daron growled.

"You're a faerie; I had to even the odds."

"You little—"

"I send you to extend an invitation and you *attack him?!*" the Falcon Lord cut Daron off.

Daron paled. "My lord, he refused and was being disrespectful."

"Did he throw the first punch?"

Daron looked ill; he lowered his gaze to his boots.

"Yeah, I did," I said.

Daron's head jerked up, his eyes widening.

The Falcon Lord's gaze narrowed, going back and forth between us. "I will take your word for it, Captain, but just so you know that I'm not a fool; I don't believe you for one second."

I grinned at him, blood trickling from my split lip. "You mind if I go and shower now, my lord?"

The Falcon Lord snorted. "Go. But later tonight, you will join me for dinner."

I started to open my mouth to refuse.

"That is no longer an invitation, it's an *order*, Captain," he added.

"Fine," I huffed and went to collect my bathing kit.

I expected Daron to smirk at me as I passed him. Instead, he gave me a grateful nod. Huh, maybe he wasn't entirely a prick.

Chapter Six

"What are you doing here?" the Falcon Lord asked as I strode into his tent later that night. He was sitting at his war table, his gold hair swept back and his belt off, leaving his tunic to gap at the neckline. A nice amount of sculpted chest showed through that V.

"You invited me to dinner," I reminded him.

"Yes, but it's barely seven."

"Which means that I've been waiting nearly an hour to eat with you," I shot back. "I eat at six."

"Why so early?" He started to scoop up the reports he was reading.

"Uh, because I have to get up at half-past four."

"Dear Goddess," he exclaimed in horror. "Why?"

"To bake your bread," I said in a duh tone.

The Falcon Lord blinked. He obviously had no idea that preparing his food took a lot of time. I shook my head at him, a lot of wealthy people were like that, but I'd thought a warlord would know his camp better.

"Right," he murmured. "I'm sorry, I don't eat until eight."

"Yeah, I know when you eat," I said pointedly. "But I couldn't wait any longer. I go to bed at nine."

"Nine?" He just couldn't get past my schedule. "Very well then." He stood up and set his reports aside, then went to the tent flap. "Have a seat." He waved at the table, then leaned out the opening to tell one of his knights to summon dinner.

I wondered if Tod, who was in charge of the Falcon Lord's kitchen, would be annoyed or relieved to serve dinner sooner. Probably the former. His team—including Vanessa—would have to scramble to get everything prepared, which was the only reason I'd tried to wait. But I was starving, and I knew the quality of food I'd be served with the Falcon Lord would be ten times better than what I got normally, so I didn't want to ruin my appetite by snacking.

I went to his war table as I glanced around the room. It wasn't much different in the bright fae lights, just a large room with a heavy table and lots of chairs in the center. Lanterns hung from the ceiling, holding those fae lights I'd mentioned. They glowed without burning; just a small magic but it never failed to impress me. I glanced at the bedroom—that was much more interesting. I recalled it vividly, but along with the image of the Falcon Lord's beautiful furniture came the memory of his dead lovers lying around his naked body. I rubbed a hand over my face, disturbed on several levels. Shit, I had tossed that soldier's body aside as if she were nothing. She hadn't deserved that.

"It should be here soon," the Falcon Lord said as he resumed his seat at the head of the table. Then he frowned at me. "Why are you sitting there?"

I'd taken a seat one down from his.

"To give us some space to stretch out."

"Not because you're afraid to sit beside me?" He lifted a brow.

"What is it with people calling me a coward today?" I

huffed and leaned back in my seat.

"Is that what started the fight with Daron?"

I grimaced and sighed. "That and other things."

"And why did you lie for him?" He cocked his head at me, his gaze going sharp.

"I don't know what you're talking about, my lord." I grinned.

The Falcon Lord snorted and leaned back to mimic my pose. "So unaffected. So *slick*." He looked me over. "I've heard you're a singer, Shane. Quite the bard."

I blinked. "Yeah? Who told you that?"

"A little birdie." He grinned broadly at his own joke, then removed something from beneath the table—my guitar.

"That's my guitar!" I sat up straight. "You stole my guitar?"

He tsked me. "I don't steal. I *borrowed* your guitar so that I could have it here when you arrived." He handed it over to me. "Show me how you seduce your lovers."

"What?" my voice came out in a higher pitch than I'd intended. I admit that the thought that he might try to seduce me had crossed my mind, but I never thought for one second that he might turn things around and make me seduce him. *Fuck, that was brilliant. I'd have to remember that trick.*

"You heard me," the Falcon Lord drawled, his voice like warm cider—sweet and sharp but with a depth of rich spices. "Sing for me. Play your . . . instrument. I've heard you're a talented seducer."

"Me?" I chuckled. "I think you've confused me with yourself, my lord."

The Falcon Lord's eyes went half-lidded. "I don't seduce, Shane. I don't have to."

Fucking arrogant ass. The worst part was that he was right; they lined up for him. Me, on the other hand, I had to work with what nature had given me and add some music to it. That contrast, of his effortless appeal against my practiced moves, made me want to show him exactly what I could do. It made me want to see the Falcon Lord's jaw drop onto his war table.

I pushed my chair back, got settled, and started to play. I chose a tried-and-true ballad, slow and romantic. Guaranteed to make people sigh. I have a good singing voice, thanks to my father, and I worked it, dropping into a baritone to send those deep vibrations shooting toward my target. Around us, the air filled with soothing music, the notes rolling upward and down in an audio undulation that, instead of inspiring swaying, melted the muscles and lured the mind into another world. I sang about two lovers, separated by distance and circumstance. How they longed for each other, ached to hold each other. At first, I kept my stare on my guitar but when I felt his interest spike, I lifted my gaze and hit him with my *look*—the one I gave the men I wanted to fuck. The heavy, sensual stare that said, *I see you, all of you, and I want you badly.*

The Falcon Lord flinched, his eyes twitching as if I'd physically assaulted him. I nearly smiled, would have if he hadn't affected me in nearly the same way. Instead, I fell into the music, the soft chords seducing me as I seduced him. Those eyes, wide and full with surprised wonder, were so fucking beautiful. His lips parted, the fuller lower one begging to be bit, and his chest rose and fell with his rapid breaths. I wanted to chuck the guitar aside and jump across the table.

Instead, I kept singing. I kept urging the tender tones from the guitar and wrapping us in the mystery only music could evoke. I looked down a few times, just to play it cool, but kept returning to his glittering gaze. It heated as I sang, then scoured me as if searching for a weakness, making me shift my hair so my long bangs partially hid me. I could see the falcon in him—its cunning, predator plans forming—and part of me felt a dangerous triumph for making this man resort to seduction, something he'd proclaimed to never do. That was the calculation I was witnessing; the plotting of a man in lust. A man intent on having someone in the most carnal way.

My song stopped, the last chord hanging in the air between us, and we just stared at each other. The Falcon Lord's hand clenched on his armrest and his body tensed as if in preparation for a leap.

"My lord, dinner is here," one of his guards walked in and broke the tension.

The Falcon Lord took a gasping breath as if surfacing from a deep pool and looked over at his knight. "Very good," he said breathlessly and waved in the soldiers who were waiting with platters of food.

One of the soldiers who walked in was Vanessa, and she widened her eyes at me as she laid a platter of sauteed vegetables before me. I winked back at her. Vanessa pressed her lips together to hold in her laughter and hurried out. After the servers had departed, I looked back at the Falcon Lord to find him scowling.

"What?" I asked.

"I thought you were gay?"

"I am."

"Then why did you wink at that woman?"

Oh, wow; this guy was on another level. We were only flirting, and he was already getting possessive. I didn't even know how to deal with men like him. "She's a friend of mine," I said pointedly. "We work in the same area. You know, *behind your tent.*"

The Falcon Lord cleared his throat and set himself to the task of filling his plate. "I see. My apologies for assuming."

"It's all good." I started filling my plate too, eager to eat Tod's food. Every once in a while, he'd sneak us some leftovers, and they were always amazing.

"So, this is the bread you were making when we spoke earlier?" He tore off a piece of the loaf I'd baked and slathered it in butter.

It was warm but not fresh from the ovens, as he'd probably thought. I got off too early for that. Instead, I baked the bread, then the chefs reheated it just before it was served. It was much easier than trying to time a bake to go with the rest of his meals.

"That would be my sourdough with dill, yes."

He lifted a brow at me. "You like what you do." It wasn't a question, but there was some surprise in it.

"Of course. It's the whole reason I joined the army."

"You joined the army to bake bread?" He took a bite and my stare went straight to his lips, watching them move as he chewed, glistening with butter. He made a pleased sound. "It's delicious."

"Thanks. And, uh, yeah." I focused on my plate, reminding myself that this wasn't a date, and I couldn't have this man. "I want to open a bakery when I get out. This was a way to serve my country and earn the money I needed."

"A man with a dream," the Falcon Lord whispered.

I looked up and met his gaze again; it was soft, tender

even.

"Well, I don't want to be a soldier forever."

The Falcon Lord blinked, as if he'd been jolted out of a reverie, and nodded. "No one wants to be a soldier forever, Shane. We can only serve, knowing that there is an end."

"Hopefully, it's not the grave," I muttered.

"Tell me why you fear immortality," he said suddenly.

"I don't fear it. In fact, the point is that I don't fear death," I protested. *Why did he keep calling me a coward?!* "I just don't think living forever is a good idea. How can you appreciate every day when you have so many of them?"

"You can't if you have nothing to live for," the Falcon Lord agreed. Then he went on, "But when you have a purpose —a dream—immortality can be a gift. Add love to that, and life can be blissful, or so I'm told."

"You've, uh, never been in love?" I asked hesitantly, unsure how personal I could get with the warlord.

"Not yet," he said wistfully. "But I have dreams too, Shane."

That was unexpected. Not that he had dreams, but that those dreams included romance. I never would have guessed that the Falcon Lord longed for such things. I guess everyone wants to be loved, even powerful, magical warlords.

"Hey, uh, I'm sorry about your, uh, bed partners," I offered. "And your knights. How many died?"

The Falcon Lord's expression instantly went sorrowful. "In addition to the two soldiers who I was with, three of my knights were killed. Men who were like brothers to me."

"I'm so sorry."

"Thank you, but they weren't the only casualties. We found six more dead on the beach. It appears that before the Farungal came ashore, he drained the lives of those on watchtower duty, then he crept through the camp and killed my knights. They didn't even have a chance to cry out a warning. I know this since I nearly succumbed myself." He gave me a heavy look. "I'm alive because of you, Shane."

"You said thank you, that's enough for me," I murmured and started eating.

"I've countered your first argument about immortality, what else have you got?" he shifted the conversation expertly.

"That's it, I suppose," I admitted. "But accepting your offer isn't just about immortality."

"Yes, you don't want to be a valorian," the warlord murmured pensively. "You don't want the *responsibility*."

"Well, when you say it like that, it makes me sound like a prick."

"You are a bit of a prick."

I burst into shocked laughter. "Fair enough, Falcon Lord."

"Call me Taeven," he said softly.

"What?" I whispered, my humor shifting instantly to shock.

"That's my name." The Falcon Lord, Taeven, said with a smirk. "I'd like you to use it, at least when we're alone."

When we're alone; the words shivered through me.

"All right."

"You still haven't said it." He lifted an imperious brow.

"Taeven," I said, and just speaking it was a sexual thrill. My hand clenched around my fork and it took every ounce of willpower I had to look away from the Falcon Lord.

"There, that wasn't so bad, was it?" Taeven's smile turned sensual.

Oh, fuck, this was not good.

"Sure. It's a nice name."

"My family name is Rumerra. I find it interesting that it's so close to yours."

"It's . . . how so?"

"Ruhara, Rumerra," he spoke our names. "Don't you think they sound similar? Their beginnings and endings are the same. Like a good love affair, how you start and how you end are equally vital."

"I suppose." I thought about it. "But isn't the middle the best bit? Not how you begin or end, but how you get from one to the other. The meat of a relationship."

Taeven's lips parted, his expression going surprisingly pleased. "Yes, I think you're right. In fact, the best romances don't have an ending."

Immortality, I could hear the word lying beneath the others. Immortal lovers didn't have to lose each other. One wouldn't have to bury the other. Suddenly, I could see it; having him in my life forever, and a thrill of longing surged through me. All I'd have to do was say yes, and I'd have a chance at it. But those fuckers were right; I was afraid. A slice of fear cut off my voice and stopped me from accepting what the warlord offered. It was just too good to be true, and my father had warned me about offers like that.

"I'm giving you the day off tomorrow, Shane," the Falcon

Lord went on. "You'll spend it with me."

"What?" I squeaked.

Taeven grinned. "I want you to see what you're giving up before the offer is gone completely.

Gone completely? Why did that make a greater flash of fear lance through me? It prompted me to say, "As you like, Falcon Lord."

"Taeven," he reminded me gleefully.

"Taeven," I repeated morosely.

Chapter Seven

The Falcon Lord kept me up late that night, drinking. He said it didn't matter since I didn't have to wake up early, and, in fact, he wanted to prevent that so I wasn't left to twiddle my thumbs until he woke up. I didn't argue, but the man was exhausting. He didn't want to merely sit in his tent and drink. Oh no, he wanted to walk around the camp with me—and his escort of knights—while we talked and drank. That would have been fine if I wasn't full of amazing food and it wasn't my bedtime. I also didn't appreciate the overwhelming amount of soldiers who approached Taeven to proposition him. As in blatantly proposition. As in walk up and say, "How about some hot sex with me tonight, Falcon Lord?" The ease with which he brushed them off, and the way he did it kindly, made it even more annoying. I didn't want to like this guy, but with a belly full of food and wine, my inhibitions were lowered, and I wasn't able to deny that I liked him a lot. Maybe more than a lot.

"He's taken for the night," I growled at the sixteenth man to sidle up to Taeven. I wove my fingers with the Falcon Lord's and gave the guy a fuck-off look.

"Then I'll look for you tomorrow, warlord," the man promised with a grin and sauntered off, not at all disheartened.

I stuck out my tongue at his departing back.

Taeven snickered as he squeezed my hand. "I'm taken, eh?"

"I was just trying to do you a favor." I attempted to let go of his hand, but he tightened his grip. "They just kept coming." I winced. "That may have been a poor choice of words."

He chuckled, then lamented dramatically, "And yet the man I'd like to take to bed has no interest in me. Alas, that is how life goes."

"Shut up," I said in a teasing tone and knocked his shoulder with mine. "We both know you don't actually want me, not that bad, at least. You're just trying to convince me to be your valorian."

"Is that what I'm doing?" Taeven slid me a side-look.

"Isn't it?"

The Falcon Lord stopped suddenly and used his grip on my hand to pull me against his chest. I gasped, sloshing wine out of my mug, and while my mouth was open, he covered it with his. Instantly, my body surged with vibrant energy. I dropped my mug and grabbed the back of his head, groaning as his lips took possession of mine. The kiss was passionate but also teasing, his tongue flicking and twisting, and a shocking thrill ran down my chest, on a direct course for my cock. His hair was silk between my fingers and his body like a statue come to life, he was so fucking solid. Strong hands gripped my back, then moved confidently, one arm settling across me to hold me close while the other hand lowered to my ass. And squeezed. Between us rose the evidence of our mutual desire. There was no denying it now; he wanted me, and I wanted him.

Taeven eased out of our kiss just far enough to speak, "Now what do you think, Captain?"

"I think that even though you don't have to resort to

it, you're very good at seduction, my lord." I let him go and stepped back.

Taeven's eyes widened, and a couple of his guards, who were standing at a respectable distance away, made choking sounds of disbelief.

"Then why are you pulling away?" he whispered.

"Because, to be absolutely honest—and I don't think I could be anything else right now—I wouldn't survive you. If I fuck you, I'll be instantly addicted, I know I will, and when you decide you're over the newness of me, I will be absolutely shattered. No, thank you. I'll stay sane—sane Shane."

The Falcon Lord stared at me for several heartbeats, then picked up my nearly empty mug and handed it to me before he reclaimed my hand and started off again.

"You're not going to say anything?" I asked after a few steps.

"What can I say to that?" Taeven glanced at me. "It would do no good to dispute it, you wouldn't believe me, and I shouldn't expect you to."

"No?" I eyed him warily.

"No, you barely know me, and what you do know does not seem to be working in my favor."

Fuck, he was being damn reasonable and just plain nice about it. That made me want to kiss him again.

"So, I'll just be happy with knowing how highly you think of me and endeavor to get to know you better."

"What?" I whispered, looking at him in horror.

"I'm going to prove to you that I'm worth the risk, Shane." Taeven winked at me, and I swear my heart stopped beating for three whole seconds.

The Falcon Lord was going to prove himself to me. Great balls of fuck.

Chapter Eight

I almost didn't leave the Falcon Lord's tent that night, but I reminded myself that this was all a ploy to get me to be valorian—something that might not happen even if I were to consent to accept a piece of his soul. Taeven could be going through all this effort and wind up creating a dud. What then? Would he stay with me until he found his valorian and then leave me for him or her? Or would he kick me out of his bed immediately? Those were the thoughts that sent me running back to my tent.

In the morning, I woke much later than usual and it left me feeling fuzzy. I stumbled to the bathhouse, past soldiers going idly about their day, and squinted in the bright light like a mole popping his head up from underground. It had been years since I'd awoke to a risen sun, and I didn't like it. I'm a baker; I dwell in darkness. At least when I first wake up.

The hot water helped. I sighed under the spray and stretched my tight shoulders. My evening with the Falcon Lord had been surprisingly enjoyable, but it had also taken its toll—especially with the stress of what he wanted hanging over me. I scrubbed up and rinsed off, feeling much more awake by the end of the shower, then stepped out of the stall, into the narrow section between the rows. Benches ran in a line between the showers, and I'd left my stuff on the one right outside the stall I used. I reached for my towel just as I heard the soft sound of a sharply inhaled breath.

I'd been alone in the bathhouse, most of the soldiers were off eating breakfast at that hour or getting geared up to train. The showers would be busy that afternoon, post training, but not in the morning. So, I hadn't expected to see anyone when I stepped out, much less the person who was there.

I turned to face the Falcon Lord. Who was staring. At my body. At my cock, in particular.

Taeven's face was flushed and his stare molten, the gold bright against the purple. It sent a thrill through me that started a physical reaction. His eyes widened as my impressive —if I do say so myself—dick became even more so. I should have covered up, but instead, I turned to face him fully, giving him the complete Shane experience. Hey, if he was going to look, he might as well get the best view possible.

"I like yours too," I whispered, drawing his stare up to mine.

The Falcon Lord cleared his throat. "You're the first man I've met who has . . . exceeded me in that department."

I chuckled. "It's my Lekian blood. Men from Lek are known for their big dicks. Or so my father says."

"I have never been more relieved to be a top." He grinned and stepped closer. "Thank you for the show."

"Well, I've already seen all of you." I shrugged. "I figured fair is fair. You want a back view too?" I turned and presented my rear.

Taeven made a small whimper, his stare going straight to my ass, then his fascination faded as he processed what I'd said. "When did you . . .?" His eyes lit with understanding. "Oh, I see. That night." He gave me a horrified look. "You were admiring my body while I was *dying*?"

"No!" I gaped at him as I turned back around. "Not like

that. I didn't look at your nudity, not really, until you were safe. Then I couldn't help but notice, and after I left, well, I had the memory to appreciate."

Taeven smirked and stepped even closer. "Appreciate?" He drew a fingertip down the center of my chest, dragging it through a bead of water, then lowered his gaze to my achingly hard dick.

"Yeah, as I said, I like yours too," I whispered.

"Good." He lifted his gaze to mine; his eyes were full of determination. "Because you'll be experiencing it far more intimately soon."

His finger had nearly reached my cock; it paused on the tender skin just above my dark curls. I thought he was going to grab me and that erotic anticipation was the only thing that kept me from rebuking his arrogant statement. Because I wanted him to touch me there. My entire body was tense with need for it. Just a little further. But the Falcon Lord changed direction and drew his finger up to circle my bellybutton.

"Shouldn't you be drying off?" Taeven asked in a low, sensual tone. "You're so wet."

I looked him over from head to toe as if he were as naked as I, remembering him in vivid detail. The glimpse of powerful chest I got from the V of his neckline helped; it gave me a starting point. I recalled the rippling muscles of his abs, that tight little bellybutton that I wanted to dip my tongue into, the indents at the sides of his hips, the thick slabs of muscles on his thighs, and that beautiful piece of flesh that lay between. I didn't know what he looked like hard, and I was tempted to reach beneath his tunic and untie his pants so I could find out. From the bulge there, I expected it to be magnificent.

"No," I finally answered him and turned back toward the shower. "I need another rinse; this time with *cold* water."

The Falcon Lord laughed his fine ass off as I turned on the cold water and hissed. There went all that relaxation, but at least it took my erection with it.

Chapter Nine

"Where are we going?" I asked for the third time.

After my second shower, Taeven had taken me back to his tent—stopping at mine along the way to stow my bath kit —to have breakfast. As soon as we were settled at the table, I'd asked how he'd known to look for me in the bathhouse. Evidently, locating me hadn't been that hard. All he'd done was send one of his knights to find me, and he had asked around. It's difficult to hide in an army camp; soldiers are trained to notice things. After that, the breakfast conversation had been easy and casual, but then Taeven had stood up and announced that we were going for a ride. That led me to where I was now, seated across from him in a carriage nicer than any I'd ever ridden in before.

And he wouldn't tell me where the fuck we were going.

"Are you always so rigid?" Taeven asked me.

"Rigid?" I stopped inspecting the view outside my window to look at him. "I'm not rigid."

"Then why can't you just relax and enjoy the outing?"

"The outing?" I chuckled. "You sound like one of those rich people from the cities."

He lifted a brow. "I am one of those rich people from the cities, except that my city is in Varalorre."

"Why did you leave?"

"Excuse me?" Taeven blinked in surprise.

"Why did you leave Varalorre?" I clarified. "You were safe there, but you came here to lead an army. Why? And don't give me that line about honor and duty. I get it; you're all honorable for coming here to help us. But what's the other reason?"

"Does there have to be another one?" he whispered, looking distant suddenly.

"To inspire you to take the position of warlord?" I countered. "Yeah, you must be after something more than glory on the battlefield. You wanted to open up to me. So, do it. Tell me why you accepted the position."

"It *was* for glory, but not on the battlefield," he admitted. "I . . . oh, fuck, I've never told anyone this."

I leaned back to give him some space. "You don't have to do it now. You hardly know me. I'd understand if you don't want to bare your secrets."

"Tell me one of yours first." Taeven got that cunning look again.

"I don't have any juicy secrets." I shrugged. "I'll tell you anything you want to know."

"I want to know a *secret*," he insisted. "Something you haven't told anyone."

I gave it some thought. I didn't want to make it sexual, but those were the only secrets I had; everything else wasn't personal enough to hide. And, frankly, the only reason I hid the sexual things was that Stalanians were so repressed when it came to homosexuals. As in, they didn't tolerate us. At all. Fucking prudes.

"All right. I lost my virginity to my older brother's friend.

We had this secret affair for almost a year and then he got married to a woman. I was devastated."

Taeven considered this. "He was bisexual?"

"No, I don't think so. He got married because it was expected of him."

"Then why didn't he marry you?"

I blinked. Holy shit, he didn't understand. I knew the Fae were accepting of both gays and lesbians, that even some of their monarchs were, but I didn't think they were ignorant of how things were in Stalana. Especially since this particular faerie had been living in Stalana for a long time.

"Only straight people are accepted here," I said. "Any other choice is scorned and will get you ostracized. Or worse. That's why our affair was secret."

"What?" Taeven looked horrified. "I assumed it was secret because he was your brother's friend. But you're saying that you would have been ridiculed for being with another man?"

"Ridiculed is the least of what would have happened to us."

"And the worst?"

"We would have been murdered, possibly by a mob. Likely in a very grisly way."

Taeven straightened, his expression going from horror to fury. "What?!"

"Yeah, I know. It's bullshit. And it's why I've been planning on moving to Lek after I get out of the army."

"Moving?"

"Yeah, Lekians don't give a shit about who you want to

fuck. They're cool like that." I grinned. "Hell, they're cool in a lot of ways."

"I've never been to Lek," he murmured, still trying to process what I'd told him. "Have you?"

"Yeah, my parents took me and my brother when we were younger. It's amazing. Always warm and sunny without being humid, and the grasslands are the color of honey. It's like an ocean of gold stretching beneath a brilliant blue sky."

Taeven smiled wistfully. "Tell me more."

"There are all sorts of unusual animals that you don't find here," I gladly went on. "Horses with black and white stripes and some with necks so long that they can eat the leaves off the trees."

"You're having me on." He shook his head.

"No, I swear!" I leaned forward in my excitement. "There are lions there, just like the Lion Faeries but smaller."

"Now, lions, I've seen before. They have them in the Feline Kingdoms," he said.

"Oh," I murmured, then brightened. "Have you seen elephants?"

"Elephants? No."

"They are giant beasts, the size of Trolls. They're covered in thick, gray skin and they have long noses like big hoses that they use to pick up things. They sniff up water, then bend their long noses to shoot it into their mouths."

"From their noses?" Taeven made a disgusted face.

I laughed. "It isn't as gross as it sounds. They have these big, floppy ears, tiny little tails, and the males have enormous tusks that curve down from their mouths. They're really slow and generally tame. The males will defend their families if necessary, but otherwise, people can walk right up to them. Some people even ride them like horses. Oh, and they bury their dead."

"You had me going until that bit." He shook his head at me chidingly.

"No, I'm telling the truth!" I protested. "They bury their dead under branches and will stay beside the body to mourn. I swear."

"I suppose that isn't so startling," he mused. "We faeries have an obvious connection to animals, and we know for a fact that they feel emotions as we do. I just didn't think an animal would have the dexterity required to bury a body, but if they're simply covering it with branches, that's more believable."

"Sometimes I think that animals must feel emotions more purely than we do. They don't have all the issues that complicate things."

"That's very perceptive of you," he murmured. Then he declared, "I think I shall visit Lek someday. It sounds nearly as magical as Varalorre."

I grinned. Most of the people I'd told about Lek were shocked but in a fearful way. None of them ever expressed a desire to visit the continent. It made me feel closer to Taeven that he found my descriptions fascinating enough to want to see it all for himself. In a way, Lek was a second home to me, and although I'd been raised on Stalana, I felt deeply connected to the continent of my ancestors.

"The people there are as warm as the weather," I went on. "They're so welcoming, and they don't judge you on things that don't matter."

"Things like sexuality?"

"Exactly. They care more about the kind of person you are; the way you treat others. I like that."

"But you'd have to leave your family behind," he said softly.

"My brother got married and started a family of his own." I shrugged. "My grandparents are dead, and my parents visit Lek often. I wouldn't be entirely cut off. Plus, I have distant relatives there." Then I narrowed my eyes at him. "But you've distracted me. It's your turn to tell me your secret."

Taeven sighed deeply. "I'm afraid I've built it up to sound more interesting than it is. It's actually kind of common and boring. I joined the Royal Army to make my father proud. He was a general for many years before he decided to retire. I'm an only child—we fae aren't as fertile as you humans—and my father hoped that I would follow in his footsteps."

"That's kind of nice," I offered.

"Yes, it would be, if this is what I wanted to do, and I had come here with those honorable intentions you mentioned."

"Your intentions aren't honorable?" I lifted a brow.

"No, that's not what I mean." He looked uncomfortable again. "Of course, I want to win the war and protect our homelands. But I didn't take the position for those reasons; I took it purely to impress my father." His jaw clenched. "And I've missed my home every day since. To tell the absolute truth, I want nothing more than to return. So, you see, I'm not that honorable. I just want to live through this so I can go home."

"Just like me," I whispered.

Taeven blinked in surprise. "Yes, I suppose so."

"So, you understand why I don't want to be a valorian."

"No, I'm afraid I don't, Shane," Taeven said gently. "I

want to win this war so I can leave without looking back. To do that, I need to find my valorian. You want to survive and move somewhere that you'll be accepted for all that you are. The best way for you to do that is to become immortal. As a valorian, you can end this war with me, then, instead of moving to Lek, you could come with me to Varalorre. In my kingdom, you will be more than accepted, you will be respected. And you'll be close enough to your family that you could visit them often. You could fly back anytime you wished."

Fly. I'd flown before and had loved every minute of it. Unlike some of the other Avian armies, the Falcon Army hadn't paired humans with faeries to fly into battle together, so I haven't flown as much as I would have liked. Not that I'd want to ruin the experience by combining it with battle, but still. . . to fly. On my own. As a giant falcon. The thought was nearly as tempting as the Falcon Lord himself. And to live with him in Varalorre? Yeah, that might be better than opening a bakery in Lek.

"Have you considered the fact that you might be wrong?" I asked him softly.

"About you being my valorian?" Taeven asked with a lifted brow.

I nodded.

"No, I don't have to consider it. I know I'm right."

"What if you aren't?"

"What do you mean?"

"What if, after all this work you're putting into convincing me, I'm not your valorian? Then you would have extended my life—something I don't want—and you'd be short a piece of your soul for nothing."

"Not for nothing," he protested. "I would never regret

sharing my soul with you."

"You aren't listening, Taeven," I said sharply. "*I* would regret it."

He flinched as if I'd struck him. "I see."

"Not because of you," I hurried to explain. "Because I don't want to live hundreds of years, watching the people I love grow old and die while I stay young."

Taeven blinked. "I hadn't considered that."

I let out a relieved breath. "Finally, you understand."

"But that won't happen to you, Shane. You are meant to be my valorian. And in Varalorre, you wouldn't be watching everyone grow old and die."

I growled in frustration and was about to say more when he spoke again.

"Look, we've arrived."

I looked out the window at the soaring buildings of Fellbrook. Taeven had brought me to the nearest city for our outing. My stomach zinged with excitement. It had been a long time since I'd been to Fellbrook, since before I'd joined the army, but I fondly remembered the days I'd spent there. And especially the nights.

"Well done, Falcon Lord," I said as if he'd just set a chess piece down and called, checkmate.

Taeven grinned smugly.

Chapter Ten

Despite the protests of his knights (he'd brought two with us, one of whom drove the carriage and both of whom rode on the driver's perch outside), Taeven and I left them at the carriage and strolled through Fellbrook alone. As soon as we started walking, he reached for my hand.

"Are you insane?!" I hissed and jerked my hand away from him. "I just told you how Stalanians are."

"No human would dare accost me," he said scathingly.

"Maybe not, but they'd remember me and come at me when you weren't around. In case you forgot, I kinda stand out."

Taeven blinked, frowned, and grumbled, "I don't like this. We should be free to behave as we wish as long as it's not hurting anyone else."

"An enlightened view, my lord," I huffed. "Too bad most of the *good* people of Fellbrook don't share your opinion."

"Ridiculous," he muttered.

"One of the hardest things to accept is that some people are ignorant or just plain mean and there's nothing you can do to change them," I said with a shrug. "All you can do is choose your battles wisely and decide how you want to live. Is it worth it to hold your hand if I'm hunted down and murdered later? Sorry, you're hot and all, but no, not by a long shot. So, I'll be content with walking beside you, knowing that you want to hold my hand."

Taeven smiled softly. "Then I'll be content with that too. For now."

"I can't believe you've left your camp to go walking through Fellbrook with me," I said to get us off the subject.

"I can take a day off," he said defensively. "When we go to Varalorre, I'll have to take weeks off. General Gravenne will watch over things for me."

"I'm just a foregone conclusion to you, aren't I?" I narrowed my eyes at him.

Taeven snorted. "Do you think I'd bring you out here on this elaborate date if I thought you were a foregone conclusion? I've never worked so hard to get a lover in my entire life, and it's only been a day."

Slightly mollified, my glare softened. "And yet you talk as if I'm already your valorian."

"My father taught me to focus on the result I want and act as if it has already occurred." He slid me a lusty look. "But you won't let me hold your hand so I have to resort to words."

"Act as if it has already occurred," I murmured. "That works?"

"You'd be surprised." Taeven grinned broadly, and it was so damn beautiful that I stumbled.

The Falcon Lord steadied me, his hand lingering on my back. "Are you all right?"

"Yeah, just warn me next time," I grumbled.

"Warn you about what?"

"About all that." I waved at his face. "You can't just drop a smile like that on people like that. You gotta prepare them."

"Prepare them?" Taeven asked, amusement tinging his tone. "How so?"

"You know, be like, 'Hey, Shane, I'm about to smile and it will make me so fucking handsome that you're going to lose your shit. So, prepare yourself to be amazed.'"

Taeven laughed so loud that people passing by stopped to stare. It could have been because he's just as breathtaking when he laughs, but I was guessing it was more about the volume and abruptness.

"Shh," I hushed him as I smiled politely at the gawking people. "Tone it down, Tae, everyone's looking."

Taeven stopped laughing to smile at me affectionately. "What did you call me?"

"I . . . uh," I stammered.

"Only my family and closest friends call me Tae."

"I'm sorry, I won't—"

"I like hearing you say it," his voice dropped to a low rumble. "Feel free to keep doing so. Especially in bed."

"Oh. Uh." I swallowed past the dryness in my throat. "All right."

"Ah, here we are!" Tae exclaimed and turned toward a bright red door.

We were in the shopping district, where the buildings were only one to two stories tall, as opposed to those in the residential areas that went all the way up to six or even a phenomenal seven stories. I would never want to live in one of those tiny boxes they call apartments, but I could appreciate the innovation of their construction. Anyway, the shop we stepped into sold food. Not just any food, but desserts. I stopped just inside the door and gaped at the glass displays of delicate pastries decorated so beautifully that they'd be a shame to eat.

"Great balls of fuck," I whispered.

"This is the best pastry shop in the city." Taeven grinned. "What would you like?"

"Uh." I stepped closer to a glass display and peered at the rows of desserts. "I can have one?"

"You can have as many as you want," he whispered in my ear. "Take your time. I want you to be sure you get the ones you *truly hunger for.*"

I shivered and would have given him an annoyed look if my eyes hadn't been glued to the pastries.

"My lord! How may I assist you?" A large man in a white uniform hurried over to us, breaking away from a team of salespeople even though the shop was busy and there were lots of people who hadn't been helped yet.

It's good to be fae. Or, in my case, with one.

"Oh, I think we'll need a bit more time to decide," Taeven said. "My friend is a baker, and he's very impressed by your desserts."

"You're a baker?" The man grinned at me broadly. "It's always nice to meet a culinary brother."

"Oh, I'm not in your league, Sir," I protested. "I mainly bake bread. The closest I've come to these beauties is probably my cream puffs."

"Ah, but the pastry dough for puffs is difficult to do," he protested. "Once you've mastered that, you are just a few steps away from grander delights." He stepped out from behind the counter and pointed out several items. "All of these use that very same dough."

"Really?" I bent to gape at some of the amazing desserts.

"All you need is a steady hand, a good recipe, and patience," the baker said. He looked from me to the Falcon Lord. "Come in back, and I will show you."

"What?" I squeaked.

The man laughed. "I have some shells prepared; it will only take a few minutes to show you how to assemble them."

"I would be most honored to watch." I held my hand out to him. "Shane Ruhara."

"Samuel Ricard," he replied.

"And this is Taeven Rumerra, the Falcon Lord," I introduced them.

"I didn't realize you were a warlord." Samuel bowed deeply to Taeven. "I'm honored to have you in my shop. Please, come on back."

Samuel led us behind the counter and around the busy staff, who gave us shocked looks. We went back into a workroom crowded with massive steel mixing bowls so large that they sat on the floor, and a huge table covered in flour. Ingredients lined the shelves and tools hung on the walls. I felt instantly at home.

"Here we are." Samuel waved at the table, in particular at the glass bowls heaped with crispy, puffy pastry shells. "You'll recognize these, I'm sure." He grabbed a paper doily, then set a shell down on it. "One moment."

I gave Taeven an excited grin as the baker went to an enormous icebox and took out a cone-shaped piping bag full of cream. He brought that, along with some bags of chocolate and frosting to the table, then proceeded to construct a beautiful eclair-like dessert, going slowly enough that I could follow the process. When he was done, I just gaped at it.

"Would you like to try your hand at one?" Samuel offered me the bag of cream.

"I'm afraid to waste your supplies."

"Nonsense, you'll be eating it when you're done." He grinned. "No waste."

"Then I'd be delighted." I took the bag of cream and proceeded to mimic what he'd done.

Samuel watched carefully, giving me tips on how to angle the bag for decorating and such. When I was done, I was shocked by what I had made.

"Well done, Shane." Samuel waved a hand at the dessert. "Now, you reap the rewards."

"It's too beautiful," I protested.

"Yes, but its purpose is not just to be admired, but to also be eaten," he shot back. "First you consume with your eyes, then with your mouth."

I cleared my throat, taking his words in a way that I was certain he hadn't intended.

"Yes, it sounds erotic," he shocked me by saying. "But great food, especially a great dessert, has an element of eroticism to it, don't you think? There is nothing as sexy as pastry." He waved his hands outward toward my creation.

"If you don't eat that erotic pastry, I will," Taeven declared. "And I'll probably come in my pants as I do."

"Now that, I must see!" The baker quickly scooped up the dessert he'd made and offered it to the Falcon Lord. "Have all the pastries you want, my lord."

The three of us burst into laughter, but then Tae took a bite and started groaning. Samuel was nearly right; there's nothing as sexy as pastry *when the Falcon Lord is eating it.*

Chapter Eleven

We left Samuel's shop half an hour later with several boxes of desserts tied together with string, and one of Sam's precious recipes. Yes, he was Sam by the time we left. When he heard that not only was Taeven the Falcon Lord but that I was also a soldier in his army—his personal baker—Samuel had copied a recipe from its worn and stained card onto a bright new card and presented it to me as if it were a coffer of gold. It was the recipe for the pastry he'd shown me how to assemble. When I tried to protest, he declared that it was the least he could do to support the troops and that it would delight him to no end to know that I was serving his pastries to the Falcon Lord.

Happily holding the stack of pastry boxes by their string handle, I strolled down the street with Taeven, grinning ear to ear. We were going to find a nice park bench where we could sit down and eat a few of them, then take the rest back to his knights. But on the way to the park, we passed an alley, just a narrow space between apartment buildings, and noticed a fight occurring within. No, not a fight, but an assault.

"Fucking faggot!" one of the men growled as he kicked a fallen man in his belly.

I flinched, and Taeven's face settled into a cold rage. Six men were beating on one, all of them saying things even nastier than the phrase that had stopped us. I set the boxes down and started forward, stretching my shoulders and cracking my knuckles. I may not want to attract that kind of attention for myself, but that didn't mean I was going to allow it to happen to someone else. Before I could take two steps, Taeven shot past me with a shriek that echoed off the walls. A fucking war shriek, the kind only heard on the battlefield. You may think that a man shrieking like a bird would be amusing. Let me assure you, it is not. A falcon war shriek is chilling. It's an eerie, primal sound that claws through your body and sets your bowels to clenching. A warning that death was coming, probably from above, and probably faster than you expected. Too fast to stop. And it didn't lie.

Taeven's fist hit a man's jaw as his shoulder simultaneously bashed another in the sternum, sending both men flying—one into a wall and one onto the ground. The one who hit the wall crumpled to the ground unconscious while the other gasped for breath and clutched his chest. The rest of the bastards jerked away, staring at the faerie warlord with horrified expressions.

"Where are your slurs now?" Taeven snarled. "Why don't you call me a faggot? I'm a lover of men. Say those things to me. Go on. Or do you only say them to men you know you can overpower?"

One of them tried to run, but Taeven reached out almost casually, grabbed the man by the front of his shirt, and flipped him overhead to crash into the wall behind him. All without looking.

Eyes wide, I shot forward and helped the fallen man to his feet—the one they'd been beating on, not the assholes— then pulled him quickly out of the danger zone. He moaned, his face a fucking mess, all swollen and bloody.

"I've got you," I said. "It's going to be all right."

"Nothing to say now?" Taeven continued to rage at the

other men. "You fucking cowards! Beating on one unarmed man. Not so brave when the odds are evened." He narrowed his eyes at them. "Let me tell you something that you cretins have failed to comprehend. Homosexuality is as natural as heterosexuality. It is simply a way to keep us from overpopulating the planet. The Fae Goddess herself has blessed it. So who the fuck are you to say that it's wrong? Are you gods?!"

The men whimpered.

"No, you're barely men. Ganging up on another man for something that is beyond his control. Persecuting people who have done nothing to you. That is the height of dishonor. You are an embarrassment to your race. Go home and pray. Beg your god to forgive you because I will not."

One of them had enough nerve to say, "Our God says it's a sin."

"Does he now?" Taeven cocked his head at the man. "He has said this directly to you?"

The man snorted. "No, of course not."

"Of course not? My Goddess speaks to her people. We have no miscommunication, as there seems to be between you and your God. Ask yourself what kind of god would condone this." He waved a hand toward the man that huddled against me. "Do you truly think any divine being would approve of your violence? That this ethereal entity you worship is looking down now, proud of his children for beating on another child of his. For using him as an excuse to vent your impotence and insecurities upon another human being. Do you think he will welcome you into his heaven for this?!"

The men flinched back.

"Enough, Tae," I said with a dark look at the men. "They will never change. Frankly, I hope they don't. Let the motherfuckers burn in Hell."

"Is he right?" Taeven peered at the men as their friends groaned and tried to get to their feet. "Is there no hope for you? Will you go forth and continue to hurt people despite my words?"

"As if they're going to answer that honestly," I huffed. "Come on, forget them. We've got to get this guy some help."

"I have eyes and ears all over this city," Taeven leaned forward to say menacingly. "And now, they will be watching and listening for you. If I hear that you've hurt someone else, I will find you, and I will send you to your God for him to pass his judgment upon you. And I will sleep well that night, knowing that my Goddess approves."

One of the men pissed his pants.

Taeven turned on his heels, picked up the beaten man like a child, and carried him out of the alley.

I was fucking smitten.

Chapter Twelve

We carried our pastries and new friend back to our carriage. Well, Tae carried the guy while I ran ahead and got the knights to bring the carriage back to Taeven.

"Thank you," the man said again as Taeven helped him into the carriage.

"I'm just glad we reached you before it was too late," Taeven said.

"Do you know where the closest medical clinic is?" I asked him.

The man directed us to his doctor's clinic and, luckily, his doctor was able to see him immediately. We left him in the doctor's care and headed out, but Taeven stopped to speak with a nurse.

"That man we just brought in was attacked," Taeven said to her. "I can describe his assailants."

The nurse looked from him to me.

"Well? Aren't you going to summon the authorities?" Taeven demanded. "Humans have a justice system, do they not?"

"Uh, yes, my lord," the woman stammered. "But in the cities, attacks are hard to . . . well, you see, unless you know who his attackers were, have names, it's difficult for the Police to locate them. There are, uh, a lot of ruffians living here and, unfortunately, it's easy for them to hide."

"But he could have been murdered!" Taeven growled.

"Tae." I grabbed his arm. "It's not her fault."

"Whose is it?" he demanded.

"No one's," I said sadly. "A city this size is difficult to monitor. They'd have to send policemen out to search the streets based on what descriptions we give them and then it would be our word against theirs. Not to mention the fact that we don't live here."

"What has that got to do with it?"

"We won't be here to verify if they catch the right men."

"But Harrison will be." He waved his hand back to the exam room and the man we'd saved.

Tae must have gotten the guy's name while I had run off for the carriage. I don't know why, but that made me like him even more.

"Thank you for your help," I said to the nurse as I pulled Tae to the side of the waiting room. To him, I whispered, "I don't think Harrison is going to want to report the attack."

"Why not?"

"Think about it, Tae. The Police are going to want to know why he was attacked. Even if he tells them it was just a robbery gone wrong, those men might blab to the Police that Harrison is gay. Then he might get into even more trouble."

"How so?"

"With the Police. There will be at least a few gay-haters on the police force. They won't do anything in public, but they could make life miserable for him on the sly."

"I'm really starting to dislike humans, Shane," Taeven growled.

"We aren't all bad. I've never met a human soldier who cared about my sexuality. At least, not in a bad way. I'm sure there are more people like them here, they just don't have the freedom to speak out about it as soldiers do. Then there are the other continents, full of people who live differently. You can't judge an entire race by the actions of a few."

Taeven sighed. "Fair enough. I just hate to walk out of here without getting Harrison some justice or at least some assurance that this will not happen to him again."

"You saved his life and put the fear of death in his attackers. I'll bet that's more than anyone has ever done for him. Take the win, Tae."

He ran a hand over his hair and grimaced. "It doesn't feel like a win."

"You can't start a revolution." I smiled softly and squeezed his shoulder. "You don't have enough free time."

Taeven chuckled, then nodded. "Very well. Let's get back to the carriage before Tasathor and Altarion eat all the pastries."

"Damn it, I will knock them on their asses if they have!" I stormed out of the clinic with a laughing warlord on my heels.

Chapter Thirteen

Tasathor and Altarion had eaten one pastry apiece. For their restraint, we rewarded them with one more each after we arrived at the park. As Taeven and I headed to a bench, the knights climbed inside the carriage to relax and enjoy their treats.

The winding park paths took us through patches of trees and along flowerbeds blooming in pastel colors. Birds chirped softly above us and the scent of lilacs scented the air. We found a bench in a spot of sun and after slowly savoring our desserts, we sat back and watched the people wander by. Some of them walked through the park alone, munching on a snack or their lunch, but most were mothers with children, out for some exercise and play. Their laughter became a pleasant backdrop to our conversation.

"Do you really have spies in this city?" I lifted a brow at Taeven.

Tae snorted. "Of course not. I said that to intimidate them. But I'm seriously considering placing a patrol here."

I chuckled, then my gaze dropped to the falcon feather at the end of his braid.

"Why the feather?" I waved a hand at it. "I mean, I get the obvious reason, but that's too small to be a Falcon Faerie's feather. Is there a story behind it?"

Taeven went quiet and pensive a moment before responding to my question with one of his own, "Have you heard of messengers?"

"People who take letters to other people?" I grinned, knowing that couldn't be the answer.

"Yes, but I'm referring to the Goddess's messengers."

"You said she speaks to your people, is that how she does it, through messages?"

"It's one of the ways." He did a sort of side-nod. "She also speaks directly to faeries on occasion. I'm told that valorians hear her voice when they're transformed."

A shiver ran through me. I wasn't a religious man, but I might become one if a god spoke directly to me and proved his or her existence. Taeven was so certain of his Goddess, but it wasn't a fanatical certainty, just that of a man who knew what he believed was fact.

"Sometimes, when a faerie is deeply troubled, the Goddess will send a messenger to comfort and guide them. It's seen as a sign of her affection for that faerie." Tae's expression went grim as he continued, "Just before I left Varalorre, I was in a dark place. I didn't want to leave. Although I'd excelled at warfare, it wasn't what I wanted to do."

"No one wants to do this. I mean, yeah, a few do, but they're psychos, you know? Normal people don't like killing, not even when it's Farungals. We do it because someone has to."

Taeven's expression softened. "Yes, you're right. But I, as I told you earlier, didn't want to go to war for any reason of my own; it was all for my father. That made me feel cowardly and then it just got worse from there. I started to question my worth and my honor. I began to have nightmares about leading my army to ruin—destroying it completely because I was the wrong man to be its warlord. I didn't have the passion for the fight that other soldiers seemed to have. I felt . . . out of place. As if I had let my desire to please my father sway me into making a horrible mistake."

"You were having doubts." I nodded. "I freaked out too, the night before I got transferred from boot camp to your army."

"You did?" he asked as if surprised.

"Tae, we all do. It's normal. We're taking a job to kill and possibly be killed. It's fucking scary. I'll bet you anything that every warlord has had those doubts."

He looked dubious. "I don't know, I'll concede that maybe most of them have, but there are a few who I believe are beyond such worries."

"Then they've got other issues," I huffed.

Taeven laughed brightly, then he simmered down to a smile and said, "You just eased an ache inside me that I didn't realize I still carried." He shook his head in amazement. "And you did it so casually. So quickly. Thank you for that, Shane."

I grinned at him. "Aw, you just needed someone to point out the truth to you."

"The truth?"

"That you're not alone. That every soldier, from a private to warlord, has felt what you have."

"That's important, isn't it?" He asked wistfully, his gaze going tender as he stared at me. "Knowing that you're not alone."

"Yeah, it's important," I whispered, seeing a kinship in his stare that made me feel less alone too. Then I cleared my throat. "You didn't finish telling me about the feather."

"Oh!" Taeven blinked, coming out of the daze we'd been in together. "I was thinking about turning down the post as warlord." He looked away from me, his stare going distant. "I remember staring at the sky, thinking that I'd like to start flying and never stop. Just go somewhere far away where no one knew me and start fresh. Maybe get it right."

My chest and throat tightened. I knew that feeling—even the flying part. I'd often watched the birds, thinking to myself that very same thing; that I'd like to fly away and start over. Go somewhere no one knew me, where they wouldn't judge me. That this man, so powerful and divinely handsome, would feel the same way, rocked me to my very core. He had said that it was important to not feel alone, but there was more to it than that. There had been a wall between us, one that I'd put there. I had seen him as beyond me; someone so incredible that I could never cross over to his side of the wall. Forever out of my reach, despite everything he said. Now, suddenly, he was standing right before me, extending his hand. Nothing standing between us. Tae was just a man with fears and dreams like any other. A man like me.

"It was cold that day," Taeven went on, ignorant of my epiphany. "Winter is harsher in the mountain cities because they're so high up. I stood at the edge of a cliff," his voice fell into a whisper. "Rocks skittered over the side, down the sheer drop. I was mere seconds away from shifting, from just . . . fleeing."

I didn't care if anyone saw us. I reached over and took his hand. Taeven looked down at our joined hands in shock, then up at me. His bleak expression shifted to joy—pure joy—and the tightness in my chest transformed with it, becoming something light and bubbly.

He wove his fingers with mine and continued, "Then the

Goddess sent me a messenger—a falcon."

"A falcon?"

"She sends the beasts as her messengers," he explained. "It's her way of showing us that she is a part of us. That although she is not a shapeshifter, her magic flows through the animals as it flows through us. She is a goddess of nature, which is why we can control the elements."

"What did the falcon say?" I whispered.

Taeven chuckled. "The bird was only a bird, it didn't speak, not with words. It gave a cry and landed on my shoulder."

"It landed on your shoulder?" I gaped at him.

Taeven nodded. "And when it touched me, I felt her touch. I knew that I was meant to go to Stalana. The Goddess wanted me to become the Falcon Lord. This amazing peace filled me. I knew it would be difficult but worth the hardship. If the Goddess herself wanted me to fight, I would fly into battle instead of away from it. I would fight until she bid me stop."

"And you think you're not brave or honorable," I whispered in wonder.

He shrugged. "It's easy to be those things with the support of a goddess. The bravery and honor are hers, not mine. I merely obey."

"Oh, now that's bullshit." I grimaced at him.

"What?" Tae asked with a chuckle.

"She may have comforted you and conveyed her wishes, but the determination to fight for her is all yours, Tae. Don't give that away. You *chose* to listen."

"Thank you." He let go of my hand to stroke my cheek.

My cheeks warmed at his touch, and I looked away. Now that he was someone I could have, every touch felt more important. More real.

Taeven dropped his hand and finished his story, "After the falcon delivered the Goddess's message, he flew away, but a feather fell from his wing. This feather." He touched the feather at the end of his braid. "It's become a sort of talisman for me."

"That was a far better story than the one I was expecting," I declared with a wry grin.

The Falcon Lord burst into laughter again, and I smiled at him foolishly, utterly besotted.

Chapter Fourteen

Taeven sent his knights off with the carriage while we strolled through the city once more. The longer I was with him, the more comfortable I became until it felt as if we'd been friends forever. Gone was that nervousness and fear. Being with Taeven was as easy as being with any of my soldier buddies, easier even. I felt closer to him than I did to them, which was ridiculous since I'd known them for years, but that's the truth of it. He kept revealing more and more of himself to me, and I kept recognizing those parts of him as brothers to parts of myself. By the time we sat down to dinner in an open-air cafe, I was happier than I'd been in years. The kind of happiness that makes you realize that you've never been truly happy before.

That should have scared the shit out of me, but it didn't. I knew I could trust Taeven, and I knew he was right there with me, feeling what I felt. He had intended to prove himself to me, and he had, but he'd gotten a little more than he'd expected. In revealing himself, he'd seen parts of me in return. And it was obvious that he liked what he saw.

This growing bond between us turned dinner into an exciting event. Every glance and brush of his hand became foreplay. I knew it was over; Tae had won. At least, this round. I wasn't ready to become his valorian, but I was ready to be his. It had taken the Falcon Lord a day to seduce me, that was it. I should have been upset by that, but I wasn't. I was impressed in so many ways. He wasn't the arrogant, entitled warlord I'd thought him to be. No, Taeven Rumerra was nothing like the image I had of him in my mind. I wouldn't have succumbed to the wiles of that warlord, but this man—this vulnerable, brilliant, brave man—already had me. Sex would simply be icing on the cake.

I studied the angles of Taeven's face and the way they shifted when he spoke. I listened to the nuances of his voice as if memorizing them and found art in the curve of his hand resting on the table. I sank into the stories he told me about his childhood in Varalorre and told him far more about my life than I'd told anyone else. I was so smitten that I got sloppy. I let Tae hold my hand as we walked away from the restaurant later that evening. Although, I don't think it would have made a difference if I had stood two feet away from him; the men were after us regardless.

Black bags were thrown over our heads seconds before they started punching us. We were shoved into an alley, and I fell on the filthy ground, scrambling to get the fabric off my face. I heard Tae's soft grunts as he was hit, and something broke inside me. I roared in fury and lashed out wildly.

Someone laughed. "We've got a wild one, boys."

"A rabid dog," said another. "Best to put him down."

"Fucking faerie faggots," another spat. "Abominations!"

A kick landed in my ribs, and I crumpled into a ball, but finally managed to get the hood off. It was the same men from earlier, the ones who'd been beating on Harrison. Except they'd got some friends to bolster their ranks.

"That's why you helped that freak," one of them said. "Because you're just like him."

"Not so brave now, are you?" The one who'd pissed himself sneered at me. "Not now that things are even."

"You mean, now that things are in your favor?" I snarled as I got to my feet. I was about to launch myself at him, but a blur came from my right and barreled into the man first.

Taeven.

I've never seen anything like Taeven Rumerra mad. No, not mad; he'd been mad earlier, now he was furious. Livid. *Enraged*. No word was large enough to encompass the pure, primal anger that rolled off him. I scrambled backward until I hit a wall, just trying to get out of his way, then watched with wide eyes as the Falcon Lord pummeled the men—all ten of them— into bloody meat. And he didn't even shift to do it. He was like one of those ancient warriors from the North, the ones who used to sail on great dragon ships and invade other lands. They had warriors who would go into a crazed bloodlust during battle—a temporary insanity that would drive them to mindlessly kill. That was what I witnessed in Taeven.

Golden hair wild, amethyst eyes glittering with venom, and muscles clenching into merciless weapons. Taeven spun and punched, kicked and clawed, even bit and spat blood into the faces of the men he savaged. Hands scrabbling at the wall behind me, I got to my feet unsteadily and watched Taeven wrench a man's neck, snapping it effortlessly after tearing strips of flesh from his face. And the shrieks, fuck they were haunting—hollow, predator sounds full of vengeance. The Falcon Lord hadn't shifted and yet he had transformed from a man into a creature. A sort of in-between monster, neither man nor beast. One without mercy or sympathy. A cold killer.

In mere seconds, four lay dead on the alley floor in puddles of blood and gore, and the survivors went into a fearful frenzy, jumping at Taeven all at once. I would have tried to help him if I hadn't thought he'd accidentally hurt me too. And Tae didn't need my help. In fact, it was the opposite. He was going to kill them all if I didn't stop him.

"Taeven!" I shouted. "Tae, stop. You're killing them!"

"I know, and I'm enjoying every fucking second," Taeven growled into the face of a man he was beating.

Another man, bleeding from savage wounds and both legs broken, started crawling pathetically for the alley's mouth. Taeven casually kicked backward, hitting the man in the head and knocking him out.

"Don't do this," I said gently as Tae began to strangle the man he held.

In addition to the four that I was pretty certain were dead, the other five men were lying in broken, groaning, bloody piles around the alley, several of them crying pathetically. He'd disabled them so he could kill them at his leisure. So that they couldn't run away. It would have been fucking diabolical if I'd thought for one second that he was in control of all his faculties. But he wasn't, and I knew he'd regret this later. Did these men deserve to die? Maybe, but I wasn't God, and this wasn't a war. Tae had won the fight; he didn't need to go further. Which meant that if he killed them now, it would be murder.

"Tae, they're down. You've won. We can summon the Police, and they will see to it that these men are punished properly," I tried again.

"*I* will punish them properly," Taeven snarled and smacked the man's head against a wall. "I don't trust your police."

"Tae." I laid a hand on his shoulder, and he shuddered. "Please, stop. You're not a murderer, you're a warlord. You lead, remember? And this isn't the actions of a leader."

Tae flinched, his grip lightening enough for the man to

gasp a breath. "They hurt you," he whispered. "I failed to protect you."

"You don't have to protect me, big guy," I said gently. "I would have been fine; I was just taken by surprise."

Taeven dropped the choking man casually and turned to lay a bloody hand on my cheek, right over a sore spot where I'd been hit. I winced, and his eyes filled with fury again. *Holy shit, was this all for me?* Tae started to turn back to the man who lay crumpled at his feet.

"Tae, no!" I grabbed his arm. "I'm all right. You did protect me." I switched tactics. "I'm safe because of you. You can stop now."

Taeven blinked and looked back at me. I must have looked awful because his jaw clenched.

"I'm all right," I said again. "I'm a soldier too; I can take a few hits. This is nothing." I waved at my face. "Just a bruise. Nothing's broken. But damn, Tae, I think you broke like fifty bones tonight." I looked around at the slaughter. "Fucking impressive for a man who doesn't like to fight."

Taeven suddenly pulled me into his arms, tucking my head in against his chest, and I tried not to wince when my ribs protested.

His body trembled around mine as he stroked my hair. "I heard you. Heard what they said to you. I saw Harrison again in my mind, and I couldn't let that happen to you. Not to you. I just . . ."

"You fucking snapped." I pushed back enough that I could see his face. "You were brutal. I've never seen anything like that. Was it really because of me?"

Taeven leaned down to press his forehead against mine, as if only I could bring him calm. He exhaled raggedly and whispered, "Yes."

Great balls of faerie fuck. That cinched it; I was in love.

Chapter Fifteen

I ran back to the restaurant, and they sent someone to fetch the Police. It would have been a different story if Taeven had been human, but because of his race and rank, we were both treated with great respect. The surviving men were transported to a clinic to be patched up under guard, after which, they'd be taken to jail for assaulting a faerie. Faerie assault wasn't just stupid in Stalana, it was also a serious crime. Because the Fae had come to our defense against the Farungal, any attack on one of them was seen as a terrible betrayal. So, we were barely questioned, only enough to assure the officers that we'd been attacked first and had defended ourselves. The dead men were written off as suicides. In other words, the officers determined that they were idiots who had gotten exactly what they deserved for having the gall to attack a fae warlord. Then we were released with the apologies of the city of Fellbrook.

The Police gave us a ride to our carriage, which, oddly enough, was parked in front of a fancy hotel. After they rode away, I headed toward the carriage, but Tae grabbed my hand and angled me toward the hotel instead.

"We're staying the night," Tae said softly. "I sent Tasothor and Altarion to procure us accommodations here. They're already in their own rooms, for which I'm extremely grateful. I do not wish to hear a lecture over going out unescorted."

"We're spending the night?" I whispered, a nervous thrill

shooting through me.

Taeven grinned wickedly as he escorted me into the opulent lobby of the Wolford Hotel. I'd never been inside the prestigious hotel, it was way out of my price range. So I ended up gawking at the vaulted ceiling draped with crystal chandeliers and the paneled walls with their gilded moldings. The floor was polished marble and the whole place smelled like lemons.

The other guests gaped at us, some of the women bringing their hands to their lips in horror, and a glimpse in a wall mirror told me why. I was a hot mess. A bruise was forming around my left eye, I had a swollen cut on my cheekbone just below it, and blood from Taeven's touch was smeared there. My soldier's uniform was also filthy, and I don't think I would have been allowed through the doors of the hotel without Taeven beside me.

Tae, by contrast, looked amazing. Somehow, even with the bloodstains on his clothing and his hair wild, he managed to look exciting instead of horrifying. Like a conqueror, fresh off a battlefield. I just looked like one of his victims.

"My lord!" A little man in a suit hurried over to us. "What has happened? Shall I summon the Police?"

"We were assaulted," Taeven said stiffly. "But it has been handled. The Police are dealing with the perpetrators."

"Oh, dear. Oh, my! I'm so sorry! What horrid people!"

"If you could just show us to our room?" Taeven asked. "I believe my knights have reserved one for us; I'm Taeven Rumerra."

"Yes, of course. Yes, they said you'd be arriving tonight," he stammered. "I have the key right here." He pulled out a keyring. "If you would just follow me."

The clerk led us through the lobby to a spiraling staircase that went up to a landing. There, we had to climb another set of stairs, several flights, the first of which had me huffing in pain. That kick to the ribs had been rough.

"Do you need me to carry you?" Taeven asked.

"No, thanks." I grimaced. "That will only hurt me more."

"I'll be careful."

"I meant my pride."

Taeven snorted and scooped me up.

"Tae!" I protested, then groaned and clutched my ribs.

"I knew I should have insisted on you seeing a doctor!" Taeven growled.

"I can have one sent up to your suite, my lord," the clerk said immediately.

"Thank you. That would be appreciated." Tae nodded.

I gave up and leaned my head on his shoulder, sighing in relief. The adrenaline was leaving, which meant that the pain was settling in. We finally made it to the third floor, and the man took us to a door at the end of the corridor. He unlocked it and hurried inside to start lighting the lanterns.

"The bed?" Taeven asked.

"The bedroom is to your left, my lord."

Tae hurried into a dark room, the clerk trailing him with a box of matches. As he laid me down on a massive bed, the clerk lit the bedside lantern for us, then discreetly left to finish lighting the other rooms. I started to get up.

"What are you doing?" Tae asked anxiously.

"I want to shower; I'm a mess."

"Oh. Do you need help?" Tae blinked, realizing after the fact what he'd offered.

I chuckled. "I don't think that would be a good idea. I'll be fine."

I headed into the attached bathroom and after I'd shut the door and got undressed—gawking at the marble counters and gold fixtures—I heard the murmur of Tae talking to the clerk. I shook my head, hardly believing where I was and what had happened. Whose life was I living? Yeah, I'd gotten injured, but I'd also been defended by the fucking Falcon Lord, who had gone ballistic at the thought of me being hurt. Then he'd brought me to the most expensive hotel in Fellbrook. This place had little soaps in the shape of flowers set out in dishes beside the sinks. Fucking flowers!

The shower was as luxurious as the rest of the room —a large stall set beside an enormous tub. Glossy blue tiles lined the stall with golden fixtures shining against them, and a porcelain niche held complimentary soap as well as bottles of shampoo and conditioner. I, unlike most soldiers, use shampoo instead of soap on my hair—something taught to me by my mother, but I didn't often splurge on conditioner. It helped with the tangles but was an extra expense I couldn't afford. Yet here, it was offered for free. I slathered it on; it smelled like mint and apples.

After a hot shower, I felt much better, though the injury to my face looked worse. I winced at my reflection in the small patch of mirror that I'd wiped clean of fog. Tae had probably hoped this would be romantic, yet another part of his seduction, but there I was, looking like a boxer who'd lost his fight. Still, even with my tender ribs, I wanted to make use of that bed. This would be our first time together, and I wanted it to be somewhere special instead of in camp. Plus, I didn't want to wait. It had been all I could do to stop myself from jumping his bones as soon as we were in the bedroom.

With that thought in mind, I stepped out of the bathroom in only a towel.

"The doctor is on . . . his way," Taeven trailed off as he stared at me.

"My clothes are dirty. I'll just slide under the blankets for my examination." I shrugged as if I wasn't trying to be sexy. Nope, not trying, just happen to be wet and wearing a towel.

"Your examination?" Tae's eyes widened.

"By the doctor," I said with a smirk.

"Oh, yes, of course. Uh, I'm going to wash my hands and face. If you hear a knock, give a shout."

"All right." I casually pulled my towel off and tossed it onto a chair, then took my time drawing back the blankets.

A soft whimper came from behind me when I bent over.

Smirking, I slid onto the bed, and when I glanced over my shoulder, Taeven was gone. I chuckled, feeling attractive despite my bruised face, and settled back against the pile of pillows. It was the most comfortable bed I'd ever been in, and I sighed in delight, my pain lessening with my relaxation. Smoothing the velvet coverlet, I looked around the room while I waited for Tae. There wasn't a single piece of furniture that wasn't adorned with carving or gilding. The bedside table alone probably cost more than I made in a year. Above my head, indigo silk turned the bed into a pavilion, draping the bed posters to flow down each one to the floor. There was even a crystal bowl of mints set beside the gold oil lamp.

"So this is how rich people live," I murmured and popped a mint in my mouth.

"This is how rich *humans* live," Taeven corrected me as

he came back into the bedroom, his face freshly washed and his chest bare.

I gulped, my gaze going instantly to that mouthwatering chest as thoughts of licking it flared to life. I'd been trying to suppress my attraction to Taeven, but now, I embraced it, and my naughty thoughts flowed straight into my dick. I subtly moved my hand to press down the rising bulge of the blanket.

"Oh?" I sounded breathless.

"Rich faeries live far better." He grinned, once more the arrogant warlord. "You'll see soon enough."

"Tae, I—" I started to tell him that I still didn't want to be his valorian but a knock cut me off.

"Later," he said gently, his expression softening into one more appropriate for the man I'd come to know. He hurried to the door and returned in seconds with a portly man toting a black, leather bag. "Shane, this is Dr. Murdock."

"Hello, son," the doctor came up to the bed and set his bag on the foot. "Had a bit of a run-in with our local hooligans, eh?"

I grinned. "You should see them."

Dr. Murdock glanced at Taeven. "I can imagine." He cleared his throat. "Now, is the injury to your face the worst of it?"

"I was kicked in the ribs too." I waved my hand over my side. "It hurts, but I don't think anything is broken."

"I have a salve that will help with bruising and pain," he said as he pulled a jar out of his bag. "I'll leave it with you to apply as necessary." He set the jar on the bedside table. "That cut needs stitches though."

"Stitches?" I made a face at him.

"Unless you want an open wound dripping puss down your cheek." He lifted a brow at me.

I cringed. "That was graphic."

Dr. Murdock chuckled as he removed a bottle of liquid and poured some of it onto a cloth. He cleaned the wound first, then his needle, but when he came at my face with it, I flinched back.

"That antiseptic has a numbing agent in it," the doctor said. "It won't be as painful as you imagine."

"I don't like needles," I muttered.

Taeven climbed on the other side of the bed and settled beside me to hold my hand. The doctor didn't even blink—impressive. I squeezed Tae's hand and nodded to the man.

Four stitches later, my fingers were aching, and Tae was wincing.

"There, all done," Dr. Murdock declared.

"Thank God," I muttered. "That was *not* numb."

"I said it wouldn't be as bad, not that it would be painless," the doctor reminded me as he taped a bandage over the wound. "Now, try to keep it dry, except for the salve. But use the salve only the first three days. Then the wound needs to be completely dry to close. The stitches will need to come out once the wound closes. Just snip the loops and pull gently. You can continue to use the salve on your ribs until the soreness goes away." He prodded my ribs as he spoke. "Is any of this excruciating?"

"Nah, it's seriously tender, though."

"Very well. I will leave you some pain medication to take twice a day as needed." He pulled a bottle of pills out of his bag and set them on the bedside table beside the salve. "You will likely bruise, but if you see redness spreading over your stomach or have any excessive swelling, you need to see another doctor immediately. And if the tenderness gets worse instead of better, you may have a broken rib and that would need to be bound. No strenuous activity for at least a day—until you know for certain that those ribs aren't broken."

"Yes, Sir," I said obediently.

"All right. I'll leave you to it." He snapped his bag shut. "Take one pill now and another in twelve hours."

"Thank you, Dr. Murdock."

"You're welcome." He gave me a pat. "And thank you for your service to Stalana."

"I'll walk you out," Taeven offered as he stood.

When he returned, I had the blankets shoved down and my arms crossed behind my head.

Chapter Sixteen

Taeven stopped short and gaped at me. I lifted a brow at him.

"Are you sure?" he whispered.

"Don't I look sure?" I grinned.

"What about your ribs?"

"I'll deal."

"Dr. Murdock said no strenuous activity for a day."

"Then I'll be careful to not strain myself."

"I should shower."

I flopped my arms down and growled, "Taeven get your fine faerie ass over here right now!"

Tae chuckled and kicked off his boots. Seconds later, his pants and socks were gone, and he was striding toward me with a wicked smile and a burgeoning erection.

"That's more like the reaction I was hoping for," I muttered, but I did so breathlessly.

Because he was naked. And glorious. And oh, fuck, I was about to have him.

But then Tae stopped and looked at the bottle of pills. "I want you to take a pain pill first."

"Ugh!"

Tae ignored me and went to the bathroom. He returned with a glass of water and handed it to me before opening the bottle and tapping out a pill. I obediently took the medication and as I set the glass down, I felt the bed shift. When I turned back toward Tae, I found him crawling over to me. I made a soft sound, somewhere between pleasure and anxiety, as he straddled me. His body became a cage, his hands and knees bracketing me, but I had never been so happy to be confined in all my life. Hesitantly, I reached for him. Made contact with that smooth, warm skin. Drew my palm along the curves of his chest. *Holy shit, he felt amazing!* Like silk over steel. With a deep moan, Taeven lowered his mouth to mine.

It was even better than our first kiss, full of a tenderness that Tae had lacked before, one born of knowing someone and, most importantly, liking them. His mouth was less demanding, more languorous, taking the time to learn the curves of mine and delve deep. Wine and cream lingered on his tongue, sweet and sharp, enhancing his flavor. I grabbed his long hair and pulled him closer.

Slowly, agonizingly, he laid his powerful body over mine, careful not to crush my ribs. His cock teased mine at first, then settled beside it. The feel of it there—warm and velvety and heavy—made my shaft harden to an aching degree.

Then he began to grind.

Oh, fuck, I've never had a man do that to me. Taeven pressed down until our cocks were held tightly between us, and that's where the grinding came in. Once he had us pinned together, he began to undulate his hips, moving them not only up and down but also in circular, swirling motions. It was similar to being stroked by a fist but more teasing, and the sensation of his cock against mine sent it over into blissful eroticism.

"Oh, fuck!" I pulled away from his kiss to exclaim.

"Did I hurt your ribs?" He immediately withdrew.

"Yes, but I don't fucking care." I grabbed his ass—his firm, pert ass—and pulled him back to grind me more as I lifted to push against him.

Tae grinned and bent down to start kissing my jaw, making his way up to my ear. "You have the most beautiful cock I've ever seen."

"Beautiful or big?" I shot back.

"Both." He laughed.

I used his distraction to roll him onto his back. Taeven lifted a brow as I straddled him.

"This way, you won't have to worry about hurting me," I said with a wicked grin. I had intended to climb right onto that dick, but, looking down at it, I couldn't resist tasting it first. "You have a beautiful cock too. Beautiful and big. I'm dying to know what it tastes like." I shimmied down until my mouth hovered over the weeping, flushed tip and felt the muscles in his legs tense. "Do you mind if I suck it awhile?"

"Do I *mind*?" He laughed again. "Have at it, Captain. Suck my cock as long as you wish. I am at your disposal."

I licked my lips and held his gaze as I lowered my head. Tae's smile froze, his stare going hot, and when I slipped him into my mouth, the Falcon Lord gave a shout of bliss. As I moved down that impressive length, his hand went to my head, not pushing, just holding. Stroking. He slid his fingers through the length of my hair, pushing the bangs back from my face, then trailed his touch down to rub his thumbs over my cheekbones as he watched me move up and down him, lips drawn in to keep from scraping him with my teeth. I took him as deep as I could go, then worked that liquid down the base with my hand. Once he was slick, I sped up, and Taeven's eyes rolled back into his head.

"Oh, that's so fucking good," he panted.

The wet sounds of my rapid sucking brought moisture to the tip of my dick, and I rubbed it against him as I pumped my cock into the crevice his shins made. Tae writhed below me, his body becoming a beautiful, gleaming thing in the soft lights. While he tossed his head, I lowered my hand to play with his balls.

"Shane!" Taeven shouted.

I jerked back. "Don't you dare come before you get inside me."

Taeven trembled but grinned, setting his gaze back on me at last. "Wouldn't dream of it."

He set his hand on his cock and pumped himself a few times. My eyes widened at the thick sheen he left behind.

"Nectar," he explained. "It will help things go more smoothly."

"You can fucking summon lube to your palm?" I gaped at him.

Tae grinned back. "Are you going to ride my cock now or do I have to flip you on your belly and hold you down?"

Oh, that did something to me. My body clenched as a shiver ran through it and my dick twitched.

"I don't think my ribs can handle that tonight, but believe me when I say that I'm looking forward to you holding me down and shoving that monster inside me as soon as I'm healed."

"Good, but if I don't start fucking you this instant, I'm

going to go feral." He grabbed my cock and rubbed nectar over it, making me jerk in shocked pleasure.

"Oh, fuck," I whispered as I rose onto my knees to pump into his grip.

"That's it, fuck my fist. Let me see you writhe. I want you as eager as I am when I enter you."

"Oh, I'm eager," I panted, my balls dragging along his wet cock.

I held Tae's gaze as I reached below me to angle him at my entrance. I moved over the slick tip, working him in slowly, and we both started breathing heavily. Taeven kept pumping me, and I couldn't stop my hips from undulating. All I could do was ensure that they moved up and down as well as forward and back, taking him deeper and deeper into me.

"You're so thick," I gasped. "Oh, God, that's good."

I finally sank down to the base, and we both groaned in delight. One of Tae's hands went to my hip as he continued to work me. His fingers clenched into my flesh as he began to pump up, into me. In response, I leaned forward and set my hands on his chest, bracing myself against the Falcon Lord's lust. It became savage quickly, his face shifting from sweet tenderness to primal arousal in seconds—lips parted and eyes hotter than my baking pavilion at midday. Tae stopped stroking me to grab my other hip too, then went fucking wild—teeth bared, muscles pulsing, and stare molten. I loved it, but I wanted some of that tenderness back. I wanted to see the man who I'd connected with. So, I slid my hands up to hold his face.

Tae blinked, his stare softening to roam my face as if he was seeing me for the first time. "Shane," he whispered and his hips went still.

"There you are." I lowered my palms back to his chest

and started to ride him as I'd wanted to—a steady but slow rhythm. "I was hoping to have a little more time to enjoy you before we got carried away."

Taeven grinned, then let out a sharp bark of laughter. "No one has ever brought me back like that. When I hit that point, I'm lost to lust."

"I figured." I ground down on him. "And there's nothing wrong with that. I look forward to getting lost with you . . . later. Let's enjoy this for a while."

Tae's hand went to my cheek to stroke me gently. "Ride me as slow as you like, but when you're done, I'm putting you on your hands and knees and fucking you like a beast," he said so sweetly that the words almost didn't register.

Then I burst out laughing, and he groaned.

"What?" I looked down at him in surprise.

"When you laugh, you clench around me."

"Is it too tight?" I went still.

"No, it's wonderful." He grinned wickedly before he reached up and tickled me.

"Stop!" I shouted and laughed at the same time. "You evil bastard!"

Taeven laughed with me, but finally let up so I could collapse across his chest. Inside me, his cock pulsed, as mine did between us. I lifted my head to look up at him and brushed the hair back from his face. Our laughter faded and the heat returned rapidly.

"I'm so sorry, Shane," Taeven whispered.

"What? Why?"

"I said you could ride me as long as you wished, but I

can't wait any longer."

Taeven rolled me and slid his arms beneath my knees to lift my legs up and out to the sides. The position left him above me without pressing on my ribs. The Falcon Lord bent his body over mine, his golden hair falling around us, and began to thrust deeply into me, stretching me open and hitting all the right spots. It still hurt my side, what with his slamming and my bent position, but the pain faded into pleasure until I barely felt it at all.

"I forgive you," I panted and clutched at his shoulders.

"Does that mean I can go wild now?" He grinned.

I took my legs from him and spread them further apart. "Have at it, babe. Fuck me like a beast."

With a sharp shriek, surprising in its sexy tone, Taeven started slamming into me, but this time, he was still with me, his stare focused on my face. "Shane," he panted. "Stroke yourself for me. I'm going to come soon, and I want you to come with me."

I started rubbing myself, watching his powerful body move over me, the muscles clenching and releasing as he drove his cock into my channel. I'd never felt so full, filled to my limit. Pleasure zinged from front to back, nerves that had never been touched by a man getting rammed to life. Screaming life.

"Shane!" Taeven shouted urgently.

"Yeah, babe, I'm coming." I groaned through my release, angling myself so I spilled across my chest, and as I did, Taeven pulled out and, with another primal shriek, added his thick streams to mine. The feel of that hot liquid on my skin sent my whole body shuddering through aftershocks, and as Tae lowered my legs to the bed, I twitched uncontrollably.

And then the motherfucker left.

I shuddered again as I gaped after him, admiring his ass regardless of my annoyance. But Tae came back seconds later with a warm, wet, cloth and gently washed the cum from my chest. Once I was clean, he tossed the cloth onto the bedside table, pulled the covers over us, and tucked me in carefully against him, sliding his arm under my pillow so I'd be comfortable.

I fell asleep with a grin on my face.

Chapter Seventeen

I woke to a freshly showered and dressed warlord.

"Good morning," I murmured and stretched.

"Good morning." Taeven beamed at me. "I ordered us breakfast. It should be here soon."

"Great. I'm starving." I sat up and winced.

"Is it worse?" Tae hurried over, his gaze going to my bruised side.

"Nah, just looks worse cause the bruise is setting in."

"It looks awful. Here, lay back." He grabbed the salve and applied some to my ribs, then lifted the bandage on my face and gingerly rubbed some there.

Through his gentle ministrations, I watched him adoringly, then I stood up and pulled his face down to mine to give him a quick kiss."This is how humans heal; I'll be fine. Now, I'm going to shower again."

"Again?"

"It's a phenomenal shower. And there won't be any soldiers showering beside me."

"But there will be a warlord waiting outside again," he teased.

"Yes, but this time, my warlord is prepared for the magnificence of my body." I grinned and posed to show off said body.

"I don't know if I can ever be prepared for that." He slid a hand over my bare ass and squeezed.

"Don't start anything you aren't willing to finish."

I had a second to see him lift his brow, then Taeven spun me around and bent me over the bed, making sure to keep me far enough away from the mattress so my ribs didn't touch it. He was inside me in less than thirty seconds, all slicked up from that amazing fae nectar, and a few minutes later, we were both groaning through our climaxes.

"Now I really need a shower," I declared as I stood, his desire dripping down my back.

"You shouldn't have taunted me like that; falcons can't resist prey." He smacked my ass, then pulled up the pants that he'd merely dropped to his ankles to fuck me.

"I'll remember that." I smiled in a way to suggest that I'd be using it to get sex in the future.

"Hurry up," Tae called after me. "Breakfast will be here any moment. I asked them to send a side of butter so I can slather it over your cock and suck it off you."

Great balls of fuck!

"You know, maybe I should wait on the shower." I turned around.

Taeven looked me up and down lasciviously. "Wait on getting dressed too."

With perfect timing, a knock came at the door. He winked at me and went to answer it, leaving me standing with a semi-hard dick and an open mouth. Who was this guy? Butter on my cock? Um, yes, please. I'll take an extra side of that. But I didn't want to sit at a table with him naked, so I used a wet washcloth to clean off my back, then slid into one of the thick, soft robes that were hung on hooks in the bathroom. I went out into the living room to find a hotel employee setting out our breakfast on a small table near the window. He glanced at me, then did a double-take before looking back at Taeven. He didn't say anything, just finished setting up breakfast, but Tae had caught the look.

"Anything else, my lord?" the man asked.

"No, just get the fuck out," Taeven growled.

The man paled and hurried toward the door.

"He might have just been surprised," I said as he fled.

"No, he wasn't." Taeven stretched his shoulders and neck. "I saw the skin around his eyes tighten. He was judging us."

"Hey, that's what people do; they make judgments. Who gives a fuck what he thinks? It's his actions that matter, and he didn't do anything horrible." I laid a hand on his arm. "Don't let your assumptions ruin our morning."

I felt the tension drain out of him as he smiled at me.

"You're right. Sit down; let's eat before it gets cold."

There were pancakes, cheese omelets, fresh fruit, juice, coffee, biscuits, and jam. Oh, and butter. I grinned broadly when I saw the bowl of whipped butter next to the jam.

Taeven caught my look and grinned back. "We'll have to be sure to save some of that."

"I'd recommend that you use the jam instead; it'll be sweeter."

"And stickier." He shook his head. "A little sugar sprinkled over the butter will do the trick."

"Yeah, it seems as if you have lots of those," I muttered, suddenly wondering who had taught him to butter a man's dick.

Taeven went silent while he poured coffee for both of us. Finally, he said, "I've had many lovers, Shane. Too many to count."

"Fantastic." I rolled my eyes. "Thanks for sharing."

"And I barely remember them," he continued, giving me a stern look for my interruption. "I can recall the names of those who died the night you saved me and a few who were my friends before we became lovers, but other than them, the people I've bedded were inconsequential. Merely a good time. A release of tension. You, however, are burned into my memories forever. You mean something to me. Yesterday, I connected with you in a way that I never have with any of my bed partners. So, forgive me if, now that you've succumbed to my seductions, I employ some tricks to keep you."

I went liquid and sort of melted into my seat. "I feel the same," I whispered. "I mean, not about the tricks and lovers thing, but yesterday. It meant a lot to me."

"I assumed it did." He grinned. "You went from pushing me away to opening your arms. Or rather, crossing them behind your head."

I laughed, then shook my head as it reminded me of our lovemaking. "That was the first time I've laughed during sex."

"Me too." He fixed his coffee with a soft smile on his face. An expression of blissful peace. Then he set the cream down and looked up at me to add, "And it made it all the more special. I will treasure that memory."

"Me too," I repeated his words. Then I smirked. "You got me good, Falcon Lord. Well done."

"Do I?" Taeven started filling his plate and motioned for me to do the same. "Then we can proceed after breakfast?"

"Proceed with what?" I went still.

His sharp gaze locked on mine. "With the soul transfer. I assumed that your acceptance of me included an acceptance of my offer."

"You assumed wrong."

Taeven dropped the serving spoon with a clatter. "Excuse me?"

"Just because I want to be with you, it doesn't mean that I want to be immortal."

"You let me . . ." He took a deep breath and let it out slowly. "Do you think that I want to form an attachment to a mortal man?"

I gaped at him. My mother had once told me that to understand someone, I had to step outside of myself and see things from their perspective—imagine myself as that person, with all their needs and desires. I had failed to do that with Taeven. I hadn't thought about what he might be going through. How my refusal would affect him. At least, not beyond the obvious ways. It hadn't occurred to me that any feelings he developed for me would become painful if I wasn't immortal. By refusing his offer, I was refusing his love. He wouldn't allow himself to feel anything more for me. He probably resented what he did feel, maybe even felt tricked into it. Shit. His assumption had been fair. From what I'd told him, he was an obstacle to my becoming his valorian, and we'd done away with that obstacle last night. So, it wasn't a stretch for him to assume that I'd want to take the plunge. Or that we would have the option of being together forever.

Forever. Fuck.

I was an utter asshole. But did that guilt warrant my acceptance? Did I take a chance on Tae and give up my mortality for a man who, even though it had only been two days, I knew I was in love with? And what if it didn't work? Would he leave me if he couldn't have me forever? Or would he stay with me knowing that we'd have more years together than we would have if I were mortal? And what would happen when he found his true valorian? Would I be cast aside? Fuck, it was a lot to risk, but he was staring at me with those amazing eyes, waiting for me to say something, and damn if I didn't want to say yes.

"Can I have a little more time to think about it?" I finally asked.

Taeven shuddered, and I wasn't sure if it was from relief or sadness; his expression held both.

"Yes, you can have a little more time," he said softly. "But you cannot have it with me."

"What?" I gaped at him. I'd assumed he'd pull out all his sexy tricks to get me to give in.

"I already care too much about you," he said crisply. "If you remain mortal, I will have to end things with you. I can't become attached to a mortal, Shane. I'm sorry, I just can't. Especially not when it would mean that I'd have to start looking for someone else to be my valorian."

The thought of him sharing his soul with someone else sliced me deeper than I'd thought it would. I took a shaky breath and stared out the window, trying to compose myself. I reminded myself that it had only been two days. I shouldn't be so devastated by the thought of losing him. Fuck, I shouldn't be in love this soon. But my mind kept pulling up images of Tae—carrying Harrison, holding my hand, eating pastries on a park bench, tearing apart men who wanted to hurt me, and then, the big one, his face above me, set in an expression of sheer joy as he came.

"All right," I whispered, my heart bleeding with the words.

Taeven nodded and set his attention on the food. We ate like strangers, the good mood gone completely, and when we were done, I went into the bedroom and pulled on my dirty clothes, not bothering to take the shower I'd been looking forward to. I did, however, take the shampoo and conditioner. And a flower soap. All right, all the flower soaps.

Chapter Eighteen

"What the fuck is wrong with you?" John snapped at me later that day.

Taeven and I had spent an uncomfortable hour together in the carriage for the ride back to camp. As soon as we arrived, he told me that I had two days to make a decision, then he'd start looking for someone to replace me. With that, the Falcon Lord strode away, his guards flanking him and giving me nasty glares as they left. Slumping under the weight of indecision and heartache, I went to find my friends. Because after a day like that, I needed to vent to a few sympathetic ears. But my venting wasn't helping, and those ears weren't turning out to be so sympathetic.

We sat around a spread of leftover food that had been made for the Falcon Lord and his Guard—who had asked for lunch after returning from Fellbrook. It all tasted delicious, but part of me resented the fact that I was eating Taeven's scraps. No, not resented. I wasn't upset with him; I was upset with myself. Eating the food that had come from his table didn't make me angry, it made me sad. Deeply sad.

"I know," I answered John. "You guys can't understand why I don't jump on this and him, but losing my mortality is a huge thing for me."

"No," John huffed. "I mean, what the fuck is wrong with you; you couldn't have waited until *after* he sucked your buttery cock to tell him that you weren't going to accept his soul? You fucking idiot."

There was a moment of horrified silence, then we all, myself included, burst into laughter.

"You're an asshole," Vanessa declared. "That's why you don't have a boyfriend, John."

"I have as many fuck-buddies as I want, Van," he shot back. "And that's how I like it." He swung his gaze back to me. "That being said, I'd give them all up to have the Falcon Lord suck my dick—buttered or not. And, by the way, I'm so buttering the next cock I suck. That's fucking brilliant. It gives some flavor while greasing it up. I think butter will be my new lubricant of choice."

"Such an asshole." Vanessa shook her head.

"Don't act as if you're not going to try it," he huffed at her.

Vanessa grinned wickedly. "With a sprinkle of sugar, baby!"

"But seriously, Shane." John set a stern gaze on me. "If you like him so much, why not take a chance on him? Do you know how rare a connection like that is? And you're gonna give it up just because it's risky? That's bullshit. All relationships are risky."

"Yes, but they don't all transform you into another race —an immortal race," I shot back.

"Yeah, but the good ones always change you," Evan said softly. "Maybe not on the outside, but inside they do. That's love, Shane. Fucking deal with it or learn to live without it."

We all went quiet. As much as Vanessa had teased John about not having a steady lover, that was not uncommon in the camps. Soldiers had to live with the fact that they could die at any moment. Instead of making them more prone to love, it made them love-shy. We were all for living in the moment and having a good time, but forming an attachment to someone who could die the next day wasn't a good idea. Almost as bad as falling in love with a mortal man when you were an immortal fae warlord.

So the question was; was loving Tae worth losing my mortality? Was it worth the risk of him leaving me in the lurch after I'd made that sacrifice?

I just wasn't sure.

Did I want to learn to live without love? No. That I *was* sure about. But it didn't mean that I had to love Taeven. Oh, who the fuck was I kidding? I already loved Taeven. The real question was, could I live without him?

I thought about being with someone else. About fucking them without laughing. Riding them without watching them go savage and without having the power to calm their rising beast. My chest ached, and I suddenly wanted to cry.

I stood up abruptly. "I gotta go," I muttered and hurried away.

No one tried to stop me. I'm sure they understood that I needed to be alone. But halfway to my tent, a strong hand grabbed my upper arm and swung me about. I expected to see one of my friends, but I ended up face to face with Doran. I stared at him, fascinated by his beauty. Not because it was so great but because it didn't affect me anymore. And it wasn't because of the fight we had. It was because he'd been replaced. Completely replaced. There was no fucking comparison.

"What did you do?" Doran growled.

I jerked my arm out of his grip and glared at him. "It's

none of your business, dickhead." I tried to walk away, but he angled himself in front of me.

"Look, I owe you for what you said to Taeven. That was decent of you," he muttered grudgingly. "But the Falcon Lord came back from Fellbrook a changed man. He's been . . . mean. And he's not cruel, not usually. So, just tell me, what did you do?"

I ran a hand over my hair and sighed. "I fell in love with him."

Doran gaped at me. It was easy to admit my feelings to him because he didn't care. He wouldn't give me sympathizing looks like my friends might. And, frankly, seeing his shock was a balm to my injured heart.

"You *what*?" Doran whispered.

"You heard me; I'm not repeating it. Fuck, it's the first time I've said it aloud, and I'm kind of regretting that I said it to you."

Doran stared at me for a few, long heartbeats, then grabbed my wrist and started pulling me away.

"What are you doing?" I tried to wrench free, but he wouldn't ease up.

"You and I are going to have a serious talk, and that talk is going to involve wine."

I relaxed. Doran wanted to talk? Now? After I'd lost interest in him? Go fucking figure.

"I've talked about it enough," I grumbled. "I just want to be alone."

"No, you don't." He dragged me up to a tent much larger than mine, though not nearly as big as Taeven's, and pulled me inside.

It was spacious enough that in addition to a sizable cot, there was also a dresser and a small dining table. The perks of being a fae knight, I suppose. Doran pushed me toward the table, then fetched a bottle and two glasses from the top of the dresser. He sat down, poured us both a glass, then set one before me.

"Drink," Doran said.

I drank. Then I had a coughing fit. "Are you crazy?" I shoved the glass away from me. "That's fae wine, and I'm mortal."

Doran grimaced. "Fuck. I forgot." He stood up. "Stay here." With that, he strode out.

I spat into my glass while he was gone, trying to get as much of that shit out of my mouth as possible. It was delicious and a few sips would have been fine—I'd tried it before, which is how I'd recognized the flavor—but a glass of the stuff could have killed me. That single sip had sent me into a relaxed pre-drunk state, and the last thing I needed was to get sloppy drunk around Doran.

"Here." Doran came back into his tent with a new bottle. He set it before me, then took my glass and tossed its contents out through the tent flap.

I poured some wine in my glass, swirled it around, and went to dump that out as well. Doran lifted a brow at me.

"Unless you want to clean puke off your floor, I have to make sure the glass is clean."

Doran grunted. "Fair enough. Sorry about that. I don't often entertain humans."

"Not even for . . ." I waved a hand at his bed.

"No. I don't think it's wise to mingle. Too complicated. I

stick to my own kind."

"Wow . . . I don't know if that's racist or just smart." I poured myself a fresh glass as he sipped his.

"I don't have anything against humans. I just don't want to take the chance of liking one, then losing him."

"Fair enough," I muttered. It seemed to be the theme of the day.

"Why did you refuse to take his soul if you love him?" Doran went straight for the jugular.

"It's not about him," I grumbled. "I mean it is, but there's more to it than him. I don't want to live forever. If I had him, sure, it would make a difference. But if I had him and then lost him, I would have to face eternity alone. Because let's face it, there could be no one else after being loved by Taeven Rumerra."

Doran's jaw clenched.

"You know what I'm talking about, don't you?" I asked softly.

Doran looked up sharply.

"How long have you been in love with him?"

Doran let out a long sigh and looked away. "Since before we came to Stalana. I took the post to be with him."

"You came here together?" I asked in surprise. I couldn't imagine Taeven bringing a boyfriend with him to the war.

"No, we were never in a relationship. We got together once." He shook his head and rubbed a hand over his face. "Just once, years ago, and I can't stop thinking about it. I've taken other lovers, many of them, and none have come close to easing the ache he left in me."

I nodded. "I get it. I'm right there with you. Now imagine having him as yours, truly having him, then something takes him away from you—either another lover, death, or Taeven himself. What would that be like? Having him hold you every night, maybe even love you back. Whispering words of forever to you and then, bam! No Taeven. Snatched away right after you thought he was yours."

"Hell," Doran said firmly. "It would be absolute hell. But those are only possibilities, and I would risk them and more to have him. You're a fool and a coward to turn down the chance of heaven because of a glimpse of hell."

That hit me like a punch in the gut. "Maybe. But a coward survives."

Doran snorted. "A coward dies a thousand times a day. He will haunt you. Believe me, he will. You'll see him in your mind—memories and possibilities—and it will kill you. Over and over again."

"Holy shit," I whispered. "You're dark, man. Dark and fucking . . . depressing. You've got it bad."

"And I know I will never have it good," he countered. "I have no chance with him. I'm in hell already. So, watching you choose this willingly when you could have him . . ." He shook his head. "I want to strangle you."

"You and me both." I sighed.

"Have you considered that this is what he's feeling too?" Doran asked softly. "That you're choosing this hell for both of you? Taking away his chance at happiness too."

"That's fucking low," I huffed.

Doran shrugged. "I've never seen him like this. He's wrecked. All from *one day* with you."

"Yeah, well that makes two of us."

"You're an idiot."

"Maybe. But I can't help wondering how many of the valorians would have refused if given the chance."

"What?" He gaped at me.

"I can't be the only one who thinks that immortality is unnatural," I said, perhaps a little petulantly. "Maybe the only reason they all became valorians is that they weren't given a choice."

"They were saved from death!"

"Yeah, as I said, they weren't given a choice." I shrugged. "I'm not saying they aren't glad to be alive and all that. But if they'd been offered this when they weren't about to die, they might not have chosen it."

"And you think I'm fucked up," he muttered.

"I'm just saying that I have the chance to choose, and I'm going to make sure I make the right decision."

"You know what else you've been given that the other valorians haven't?"

"What?"

"The chance to fall in love with your warlord before you see his soul, and for him to do the same with you." Doran set his grim stare on me. "The others were plunged into a mystical relationship with no foundation of a previous connection. But you and he have the chance to form a bond *before* you take a piece of him. Before you see his true magnificence which, I'm certain, must be staggering."

"What are you talking about?"

"Don't you know?" He frowned at me. "When a warlord

shares his soul, the magic takes you into the spiritual realm where you see each other's souls. You will see who Taeven truly is, all the bad and the good. I'm told it's that experience that leads to love between a warlord and his valorian. It's a bond very few can resist; only one man has so far. But you and Taeven already have something strong between you. Imagine what it will become after you possess a piece of his soul."

"But what if he doesn't like what he sees?" I whispered in horror.

"You mean your soul?" Daron blinked in surprise. "Why wouldn't he?"

"I don't know. My soul could be mediocre, especially compared to his. Fuck, you've just made this even more stressful."

"I . . . but if you're chosen by the Goddess and the Beasts, then your soul must be beautiful."

"*If* I'm chosen," I growled. "That's the fucking point. What if I'm not chosen? Then he'll have seen my ugly soul and be faced with my failure to be the man he needs me to be!" I stood up, downed my glass of wine, then started to turn for the door, but thought better of it and grabbed the bottle. "Fuck you, Doran! You're such an asshole!" I stormed out.

Chapter Nineteen

I slept horribly that night; I kept having nightmares of Tae seeing the true me and cringing away in horror. I'd been leaning toward accepting his offer, but after hearing that he'd have to see my soul in the process, I now leaned in the other direction. To the point of abject terror.

My father says that you never truly know yourself. That knowing who you are is a form of enlightenment. That all of us have images in our heads of who we *think* we are, but most of those are masks—false beliefs that we put in place to keep us sane. A man who believes himself to be brave could, in actuality, be a coward. One who thinks himself kind, could be secretly cruel. A wise man, actually a fool. Dad says that a lot of what a person does is about feeding their false image of themselves. And I was fucking scared out of my mind to have my false image torn away and my truth bared to Taeven.

Love flourishes in truth, yes. But it also blooms in blissful ignorance. Those lies we tell ourselves are integral to our happiness. If Taeven saw my truths, he might share them with me, especially if those truths drive him away. He'd have to give me a reason for leaving, right? Could I survive hearing Taeven confess that my soul was so ugly that he knew he'd never be able to love me? Fuck, being with the Falcon Lord was becoming more and more difficult. Losing my mortality was bad enough but literally baring my soul? That was too much to ask of anyone.

I contemplated all of this on my 5 AM walk to my baking pavilion and by the end of my stroll, I decided to tell Tae that it was over. That he should look for another valorian. Then I reached his tent. I would have stood and stared at it if there hadn't been guards standing to either side of the entrance flap —knights who glared at me. I hurried away and vowed to take a new route the next morning, maybe around the back. But seeing that red and black striped tent, with its falcon pennant drooping dismally from the central pole, had shaken me. Just knowing that Taeven was inside it was enough to set my body to shivering. I wanted to stride in there and wake him up with kisses, then laugh as I made love to him. I wanted to see him smile again and know that I had put that smile on his face.

If only I wasn't such a coward. There, I'd accepted a truth about myself. A truth that he'd see in my soul.

The sound of distant clangs brought me to a sudden stop. I glanced over at Tae's guards, but they were already inside his tent. I knew I should move, but I wasn't sure where to go. Then he was there. Taeven came barreling out of his tent in a war robe—a garment worn into battle by faeries so they could shuck it off quickly and shift. He stopped short when he saw me.

"What's happening?" I asked him.

"Those are warning bells from the Unsidhe Camp," he said crisply. "Get into your armor; we need to render aid."

Then he was naked and shifting. With a glimmering haze, a giant falcon appeared in the warlord's place. And he wasn't alone, his knights had shifted too. The Falcons took to the sky, launching themselves with powerful leaps. One of them broke from the flock and set to circling the camp, shrieking a call to arms, while the rest headed to the nearby Unsidhe Camp. The rest included the Falcon Lord.

"Fuck!" I hissed and ran back to my tent.

It took me only minutes to armor up since I was already dressed. Which meant that I was among the first humans to head for the Unsidhe Camp. Along with the soldiers who had been on guard duty, my fellow chefs and bakers were with me, all of us early risers. It would be the first time that our units reached the battle before the others. We cast grim looks at each other as we ran, and I knew that we were all thinking the same thing. But despite what people thought of us, we were soldiers and we were up to the task. In addition to their swords, the chefs had their precious knives strapped to their belts— their cooking gear. They hadn't bothered to remove them. The Farungals were about to learn just how proficient army chefs were with their knife skills.

Falcons swarmed through the air above us, diving to attack the monsters, but my group was the first to offer ground support. I went utterly calm when I saw the Farungal troops running through the Unsidhe camp, all of my aches fading under that cool focus. I pulled my sword as I ran to intercept my first target.

Shrieking the wordless battle cry of the Falcon Army, I swung, slashing through thick, scaled skin while bashing aside the stabs of a barbed tail with my shield. Beside me, chefs fought two-handed with swords in one and knives in the other, not bothering with shields. They laughed as they diced up our enemies, starting with their tails, and I couldn't help but grin to see it. Crazy fucking chefs; they'd probably outlive us all.

Around us, Leanan-Sidhe hissed and spun, sharp nails slicing and hair wild. Trolls lumbered about, kicking Farungals down for the rest of us to finish or bashing them with their giant fists to send the monsters tumbling into their own ranks. Red Caps grinned gleefully as they sliced Farungal throats, and Sylphs, those ethereal creatures of mist and air, swirled about the monsters and smothered them to death. I lurched back as a group of Goblins went chortling past, climbing atop each other to launch themselves at the Farungals like chubby, deadly acrobats. I spun and sliced, narrowly avoiding a clawed hand. Simultaneously, a Glastig stomped his hoof on the same Farungal's tail, stopping him from striking me with it.

"Thanks," I panted after stabbing the monster in the heart.

"Care to team up?" The Glastig grinned. "I can't find my usual partner."

"Fuck, yeah! Let's do this!"

The Glastig and I made our way through the camp, going back to back when necessary, but mostly tag-teaming every Farungal we came across. Between his hooves and my sword, the monsters didn't stand a chance. Not that he wasn't armed with more than nature had given him. He had a thin sword that he was skilled at using, but it was those hooves that gave him the advantage. That is until we were surrounded.

We'd made our way to the end of camp nearest the beach, driving the monsters back to their boats, but had gotten separated from the rest of our troops. We wound up in the sand within a circle of Farungals, and I knew my time had come. Did I have regrets? Abso-fucking-lutely. At the prime spot on my regrets list was refusing Tae's offer. Not because I would have had a greater chance of surviving this, but because I would have had *him*. I would have had another day with Taeven before I died, instead of spending it drinking with Daron and wading through nightmares. But the good news was that I wouldn't regret it for long.

"If you survive and I don't, can you do me a favor?" I called to the Glastig over my shoulder; we were fighting back to back again.

"What?"

"Tell the Falcon Lord that I love him. My name's Shane."

I could feel the man's confusion, but you don't deny a dying man's request. "You got it, Shane. I'm Marthos."

"Thanks, Marthos." That made me feel better. At least Tae would know how I'd felt about him.

I slashed and stabbed, intent on going down swinging, but the amount of Farungals surrounding us was increasing while my strength was failing. I didn't think either of us would live through this. Not even Marthos's immortality would save him. Which meant that I wouldn't have survived this battle, even if I had become a valorian. That thought gave me some peace. When it's your time, it's your time. But it would mean that Tae would never know how I felt about him, and so my peace was ruined with an acidic burn in my heart. I should have told him. Why hadn't I just told him?

Then, suddenly, a shrieking came from above. A rush of wings thundered in my ears and a breeze battered me. We all, including the Farungal, squinted against the sand that rose like a blossom around us. Then came a sharp pain as something pierced my shoulders. Blood seeped down my leather armor as I was lifted—Marthos rising beside me—and the Farungals shouted in frustration as we were carried to safety.

First, I glanced at the Glastig, who was bleeding as much as me but wore a relieved grin on his face. Then, I looked up at the feathered breast of our savior. An enormous falcon head cocked to look down at me, one glassy eye focusing on my face, and I knew instantly who held me. I grinned at the Falcon Lord, then whooped in joy, Marthos joining me.

"Yes! Fuck you, Farungals!" I punched my sword down toward them before sheathing it.

Below us, the combined armies drove the Farungals toward their waiting rowboats. The aerial view allowed me to see just how fucked Marthos and I had been. We'd somehow managed to get in the thick of it, right in the middle of the horde as they retreated. Monsters swarmed over the spot we'd been in just moments earlier, a location several yards away from any other fae or human soldier. There had been no way we would have survived. If nothing else, we would have been trampled.

Tae set us down in the Unsidhe Camp, then rose to land a few yards away from us. Still in falcon form he screeched, "Both of you, get to a medic now!"

"Yes, my lord!" Marthos bowed. "Thank you for saving us."

"You're welcome," Tae gentled his tone for the Glastig.

"Marthos," I held a hand out to him. "You're a badass motherfucker. It was an honor to fight—and nearly die—beside you."

"You too, Shane." Marthos shook my hand and chuckled. "We did well. Until we did *really* poorly."

"We were overrun." I shrugged. "I don't think it was our fault. The important thing is that neither of us wavered. We would have gone down fighting, and I'm damn proud of that."

"There is that. See you around, Shane." Marthos looked me up and down in a way that implied just how much of me he'd like to see.

That startled me. I'd never thought of having sex with an Unsidhe. But why not? I'd bet the guy was incredible in bed. If only there wasn't an enormous Falcon who I happened to be in love with, standing just a few feet away. I grinned at Marthos anyway and said, "See you around."

As soon as he was gone, the Falcon Lord lowered his bird

head to me. "Are you fucking kidding me?!"

"Tae, I—"

"I save you from being slaughtered and you flirt with another man in front of me?! What the fuck is wrong with you?"

"That wasn't . . . aw, fuck, Tae. I didn't mean anything by that. I was just being nice. And thank you for saving me. It looks like we're even now."

"Even?!" Taeven shrieked. "Is that why you think I saved you? To make us even?"

"Tae—"

"Stop calling me that! Only my friends and family call me that, and you are neither."

"Excuse me?"

"A friend wouldn't treat me like this. Coming on to another man like that, knowing how I feel about you." He shook his head. "I can't—"

"Taeven!" I shouted to stop his tirade.

"What?!"

"I'm not into Marthos. I fucking love *you*, you asshole!"

There were very few faeries in the area, most of the troops were still at the beach, but those who were there stopped to gawk.

"Do you mind?" I glared at them, and they hurried away. Then I looked back at Taeven, who stood stock-still, gaping as much as a Falcon could gape. "Are you going to say anything?"

"We need to get you to a medic," he murmured. Then he shrieked, "Medic!"

I started gaping at him as that nervousness in my chest,

the one that had risen when I'd shouted my feelings for him, hardened into a rock. No, a knife. It sliced at me as the Falcon Lord shouted for help. I mean, what did I expect? That after three days, most of which he'd spent angry with me, he'd return my feelings? That was stupid. I was stupid. I shouldn't have said that. I'd thought when he said that thing about me knowing the way he felt about me, that it meant he loved me back. But of course, he didn't. It was too soon for most people to fall in love. It was too soon for *me* to fall in love. But I'd gone and done it, and gone and said it. Now things would get weird between us. Fuck. I was screwing up with Tae left and right.

"I'm a medic," a Goblin hurried over. "Where's the patient?"

I gaped at him. A Goblin medic? Yeah, sure. Why not?

"There." The Falcon Lord nodded at me. "I had to carry him off the beach without a harness. He has puncture wounds at his shoulders, both front and back."

"Not fatal. Not yet at least." The Goblin grinned at me. "But we'd best get you cleaned up and get those wounds closed before they get infected. Talons, especially those used to fight Farungals, can be filthy."

"Thanks," I said as I followed the Goblin. Now that the adrenaline was leaving me, my shoulders started to hurt so badly that I—

I stopped suddenly as a wave of dizziness overtook me, dropped my shield, and bent over to retch. At least I hadn't broken my fast yet; there was nothing in my stomach but bile. And hey, my other injuries didn't hurt at all.

"Shane!" Tae shifted in seconds and steadied me.

"I'm all right," I panted and spat to clear my mouth. "It's just..."

"Puncture wounds are fucking painful," the Goblin medic declared. "They can leave you woozy."

"I've got you," Tae said gently and lifted me into his arms.

"It's all right," I protested. "Put me down. I can walk."

"No." He started following the Goblin.

"My shield."

"I'll send someone to fetch it later."

"But you're naked."

Taeven chuckled. "I'm not shy."

"No, I guess you wouldn't be, not with that body," I muttered.

"I could heal you instantly, you know," he whispered.

As I looked up at his beautiful face, my battlefield regrets came back to smack me. Suddenly, I knew that it was worth the risk; *he* was worth it. If only . . .

"You didn't answer me," I said. "Give me an answer, and I'll give you mine."

Taeven stopped walking. "One moment, Doc," he said to the Goblin.

"I'll be in the hospital tent," the Goblin said. "It's just up ahead."

Taeven nodded, his gaze locked on mine. When the Goblin was gone, he let out a long exhale. "I don't feel the same."

My heart plummeted, and I looked away so he wouldn't see how much that had hurt me. I had to bite my lip to keep from making a pained sound. Stupid. So stupid. Of course, he didn't love me. I had known that. If he had felt the same, he would have responded immediately.

"But I'm getting there," Taeven went on. "Shane, look at me."

I lifted my gaze back to his.

"I care deeply for you," he said firmly. "I know it's not what you want to hear, and I probably should lie and tell you that I love you, but I don't want to lie to you just to get you to accept my offer. I can't do that. I refuse to bind us together under a mantle of deception."

"Thanks," I whispered.

"But I can tell you that I've never felt like this about any-one. One day spent without you, without knowing what you'd choose, has put me into such a horrible state that I'm afraid to make any important decisions."

"I guess that's something."

"Shane," Tae said in a chiding tone, "that's more than something. Stop pouting. I may not love you yet, but I'm nearly assured that love will grow from what I do feel. Will you risk taking my soul without having my heart first?"

I swallowed roughly and thought about those dying re-grets again. "Yeah, I'll risk it for you."

Taeven grinned brilliantly and started walking again.

"You're going the wrong way," I noted.

"No, I'm not. I'm taking you to my tent to make you my valorian. You won't need a medic after that."

Oh fuck, what was I doing?

Chapter Twenty

Daron was posted at the tent flap when Taeven reached it. Upon seeing us, his expression became a mix between relief and sharp envy. I looked away; I was still a little mad at him for the fear that, even now, twisted my gut. But then something occurred to me. Where had Tae's knights been when he'd saved Marthos and me? Had he broken away from them for me? And they let him? The only thing I could conclude was that he'd left them behind to carry us to safety. And he hadn't just left them. The Falcon Lord had left the battle for me. Left his entire army to fight without his leadership.

As I pondered that, Tae carried me back to his bedroom and laid me carefully down on his bed.

"I'll get the blankets filthy," I protested.

"They can be washed." He sat down on the mattress beside me and took my hand.

"Wait!" I said anxiously, causing my wounds to start seeping again.

"Calm down, Shane." He squeezed my hand. "It's still me. I promise I won't change suddenly once you have."

"But what if you don't like me as a faerie?"

He gave me the look that question deserved.

Then I asked what was really worrying me. "What if you

don't like my soul?"

"What?" Tae frowned. "What do you mean?"

"I heard that you'll see my soul when you put a piece of yours into it. What if you don't like what you see?"

"That is not possible," Tae said firmly.

"What if—"

Taeven cut me off with a kiss. Despite the throbbing, nauseous pain, my whole body responded to that kiss. In a good way. In a heart-pounding, thrilling, breathtaking way. I groaned and slid my hand into his hair to feel the silk run through my fingers, then clenched my hand in it. Pulled him closer with it. It had been only a day since I'd kissed him, but it felt like coming home after being away for years. It felt like . . . heaven. Just as Daron had described it. And he was right about something else too—it was worth risking hell to have it.

"Better?" Tae whispered as he eased back.

"Yes."

He grinned. "Just try to relax."

I let out a shaky breath as the Falcon Soul, that large trillium-cut jewel that hung from Tae's neck, began to glow. Its pale crimson light encapsulated us, sealing Tae and me in an orb of magic that then sank into me. I felt it tremble along my skin as it pushed deeper—a glittering sensation that made me want to laugh. But then Taeven turned into an angel and that bright feeling shifted into awe.

I gaped up at a translucent version of the Falcon Lord— a brilliant thing of sublime beauty. His eyes were stars and his hair lifted on a breeze that wasn't there. Like a crystal figurine in the sun, he seemed to be made of light and within that light swirled all that he was. Gleaming facets of strength, bravery, resilience, loyalty, and honor colored by hints doubt, fury, and jealousy. The good and the bad, but they were just aspects of Taeven, not the real him. His soul was at the center of those worldly facets—a thing that couldn't be altered by anything as petty as self-doubt. A core of pure white that burned with a fire that was the true Taeven.

Fuck, there was no way this amazing man, this being of beauty and magic and light, could ever love me. I had doomed myself—I realized it right then and there—but it was too late. I had seen him, and he had seen me. I wanted to sob and hide from him.

Miraculously, Taeven didn't cringe away but instead, smiled. Smiled as he laid his ethereal hand on my chest. Smiled as if he wanted nothing more than to touch me. I looked down and saw my body in a similar state to his—spectral and glowing. Kind of pretty, actually. But nothing like Tae. And still, Taeven went through with it. He pushed his translucent hand into my chest, and as I gaped at our merged souls, I felt him inside me. Not in a sexual way, but a profound, life-altering way. And I *was* altered, not just by the magic but also by the beauty of Taeven Rumerra. By seeing and *feeling* his true self. When he removed his hand, I still felt him there. That piece of him was mine now; the greatest gift I'd ever received. And all I wanted to do was weep because compared to that brilliant speck of a soul, my soul felt dull and unworthy. As if a diamond had been tossed in the muck.

But I couldn't focus on that for long. Suddenly, a rush of bubbling energy pulsed through me. My shoulders itched as my wounds healed rapidly, my cheek stung, and the ache in my side vanished. I tried to focus on Taeven, but the light of my soul brightened until I was blinded by it and my ears stopped working too. No, wait, I could still hear, but it was strange. Hollow.

A woman's voice lifted through the whooshing silence and the calls of animals echoed in the background—in particular, the cry of a falcon. Her words drifted away as soon as they were spoken, but they nonetheless put me at peace. The fear of Tae's rejection vanished along with the feeling of being worthless. She banished them like the brush of sunshine on my soul. When the light dimmed and the voices faded, I was left smiling.

"Dear Goddess," Taeven whispered, his expression one of sublime wonder. "Shane, you . . . I've never seen anything so beautiful."

My smile turned into puzzled amazement. Me? He thought I was the most beautiful thing he'd ever seen? "That magic must have really done a number on me."

"Not your body, you fool," he said affectionately as he removed the bandage from my cheek and brushed away the thread that had been pushed out of my skin. "Though your body is . . ." he looked down and grinned. "Magnificent." His stunning amethyst gaze returned to mine. "I meant your soul. *You*, Shane. Your fear was unfounded; you are beautiful. And I was right; you were meant to be mine, *Falcon Valorian*."

"Thank you," I whispered. "Thank you for not giving up on me."

"Never." Tae had my hand again and squeezed it tightly. "I swear that I will never give up on you. Even if you act the fool again."

I snorted a laugh. I was about to say more when a wave of exhaustion swept over me. All I got out was, "Tae," and then my eyes fluttered closed. As I succumbed to slumber, I could have sworn that I heard the cry of a falcon.

Chapter Twenty-One

I woke up to delicious smells. Mouthwatering smells. My stomach rumbled as I sat up, yawned, and stretched. The arms that rose above my head looked thicker. I brought them down and peered at them, turning them this way and that. It wasn't just my arms, but my entire body. I was thicker, firmer, and more sculpted. My biceps looked fucking incredible. I glanced at the mirror over Tae's dresser and got to my feet with a grin, eager to see my new face.

And promptly fell on it.

Laughter drew my attention to the left. Tae stood in the bedroom entrance, fully dressed, with his arms crossed as he laughed boisterously at me. Oddly enough, I was now the naked one.

"What the hell is wrong with me?" I growled as I stood up. "I feel weird."

"Your new body . . . is . . . stronger," he trailed off as his stare wandered over me. Then he stepped forward, his hands going to his belt.

"Hold on there, lover." I held up a warding hand. "I have a few questions about all this."

"You're fae, that makes you stronger and heavier. You can't go swimming anymore. Faeries are prone to drowning because of our muscle mass. Your face is more fae as well, though it's still you and there are human aspects to it—which I love, by the way. Your jawline is divine."

"My jawline?" I stepped carefully to the dresser, then gaped at my reflection. "I really am a faerie."

I ran my fingers over my sharper facial bones. My cheekbones, in particular, seemed to have lifted and angled upward at the outside, where before, they'd been heavier and wider. My nose was more refined and my jaw was more angular but still had the width of my previous face. And my eyes—fuck, they were gorgeous. The green had turned vibrant and the golden-brown had turned into pure gold like the striations in Tae's eyes. But Tae was right, it was still me, just fae-er.

"I will be taking you to Varalorre tomorrow, where you will learn to shift and use basic magic," Taeven went on rapidly, as if trying to give me as much information in as little time possible. "My hope is to get you proficient enough in magic that when we return, I can take you to train with the Wolf Valorian, who has been instructing valorians on working with emotion magic. After you shift, your senses will sharpen, becoming more like your falcon's—"

"Tae!" I turned toward him with a lifted hand. "I'm never going to remember all of that. Reel it in, babe."

Taeven grinned. "I like it when you call me babe."

I snorted and chuckled. "Why am I naked?"

"Your clothes, which weren't loose, to begin with, were too tight after the change settled in. I had to undress you," he said it dramatically, as if it were a hardship.

"All by yourself. You poor thing," I said sympathetically. "That must have been awful."

"You have no idea," Tae's voice dropped as he stepped closer.

Before he could reach for me, I held up my hand again. "I smell food."

Taeven sighed deeply. "Word has gotten out about your transformation. Your friends have brought gifts to congratulate you."

"They have?" I grinned. "Man, I love those guys." I started past Taeven.

"Shane." He grabbed my arm and stopped me. "Not that I mind, but I get the feeling that you might be embarrassed if someone walked in while you were gorging at my war table *naked*."

"Oh." I blinked and looked down at myself. "But my clothes don't fit."

"That's why you'll wear mine." Tae slid his hand around my waist and moved me gently away from the dresser so he could step up to it.

My cock rose from that one touch. "Holy shit," I whispered brokenly. "Is increased lust a normal part of the transition?"

Taeven grinned at me over his shoulder before he opened a drawer. "Not that I've heard, but I don't imagine most warlords would share that information." He chose a tunic, pants, and a pair of undershorts, then handed them to me. "Get dressed before I take you up on the offer your cock is making."

"Fuck." I palmed my dick and stroked it. "I know I implied that I wanted to eat first but . . ."

"Now you have other hungers?" He lifted a brow. "Thank the Goddess."

Tae yanked me against his chest and slammed his mouth over mine. I groaned and growled, savage sounds coming up my throat as I clawed him closer. I don't know how we got him undressed so quickly, but his clothes were gone in seconds, even his boots. With a rumbling sound of arousal, Taeven moved me onto the bed. I went to my hands and knees eagerly, but he shoved me down flat and pressed his body over mine. We sighed together as he rubbed his front to my back and nuzzled the sensitive skin on my neck.

"I'm going to fuck you so hard that you'll be grateful you have fae healing," he whispered in my ear. "So hard that even with that rapid healing, you'll be limping away from my bed."

"Oh, God, yes!" I wriggled my ass against his cock. "Do it before I fucking explode all over your pretty blankets."

Instead of spreading my legs, Taeven slid down and laid his legs along the sides of mine, pressing mine together. I felt utterly surrounded and so fucking desirable that my whole body twitched with zings of excitement. The pressure of his body eased, and I felt him moving his hand between us, likely getting his cock nice and slick for—*oh, fuck!* His wet tip slipped between my ass cheeks and firmly prodded my hole. That alone had my cock aching, but then he pushed deeper, moving in and out gently until I opened to him.

When Tae was firmly seated inside me, he laid his body back down on mine and started to grind. Undulating erotically, Taeven worked that thick dick into my ass until I was whimpering in need. I could feel the pebbles of his nipples against my back, along with the hard pressure of his muscles, but I needed more. Needed to get even closer. I writhed, my whimpers rising in volume.

"Shh, easy now," Tae whispered, back at my throat again. "This is just the beginning. I know how you like me to start slow."

"Fuck slow!" I shouted. "Give it to me rough, babe. Fuck

that ass like a warlord!"

With an echoing, aroused shriek, Taeven lifted me onto my hands and knees, grabbed my hips, and started slamming into me savagely. I cried out in rapture and triumph as I pushed back onto him. The slap of flesh echoed in my ears, and pleasure rose from below to spread up my chest and emerge from my mouth in panting cries.

"Is that rough enough for you?" Tae's voice had gone low and feral. Fucking sexy.

"Not even close," I said over my shoulder. "Give me all you've got, Tae. Get that beautiful cock in as deep as it can go!"

He made a sharp growl and nudged my legs apart. Then he was thrusting like a wild thing, hitting all the right spots so rapidly and firmly that I started to tense for my release in minutes.

"Don't you fucking dare!" Tae snarled. "Don't you dare come without me after working me into this state!"

"You can keep fucking me after I come," I panted, sweat breaking out on my forehead as I tried to hold back my climax.

"I want to come with you again," he said breathlessly, his tone gentling. "Almost there, sweetheart. Just a few more moments. Wait for me. This is our first time as warlord and valorian. I need it to be special."

"Don't pull out," I urged. "I want to feel that hot cum inside me."

"Oh, fuck, I'm coming!" Taeven shrieked again as he emptied into me.

I grinned as I let go as well and came all over his pretty blankets, just as I'd warned him I would. And he was right; it was worth the wait. Feeling him fill me as I emptied myself was another layer of pleasure that made the moment special.

Tae bent over me, still inside me, his hot breath stroking my cheek. "That was the best sex of my life."

"What was it that you said?" I looked back at him. "Oh, yeah—this is just the beginning."

Taeven laughed, loud and free, and the sound did something to my heart. I had the Falcon Lord; he was all mine, and I had no doubts about my worthiness anymore. But there was one problem; even after seeing my soul, he still hadn't said that he loved me.

Chapter Twenty-Two

I stuffed myself on the treats my friends had brought me while Taeven planned our trip to Varalorre. I was wearing his clothes and the smell of him was nearly as distracting as he was. He was standing right before me, talking with Nelos, another knight in his Guard. Nelos was a golden brunette with tan skin and brilliant turquoise eyes. In short, a beautiful man. It's a shame that beauty was marred by the nasty looks he kept giving me.

Yeah, it was going to take some time before Tae's guards forgave me for refusing him. There were only five left, and they took their duty even more seriously now. Evidently, guarding Taeven included his emotional wellbeing. And then there was the way he'd ditched them on the battlefield to save my life. From what I'd overheard earlier when I was getting dressed, they were not happy with Taeven about that. One of them, I think it was Tasothor, said that Tae had prevented them from doing their jobs and had abandoned his army for one soldier. To which Taeven had replied that their jobs were exactly what he told them they were, and that he was right to save me since he'd also been right about me being his valorian. If I had died, the whole war could have been lost so, in essence, he'd been supporting all the armies when he'd left his to save me. And they hadn't needed him at that point anyway; the battle had been nearly over. The Falcon Guard couldn't say much to that, but they could continue to glare at me and took every opportunity to do so.

"Hey, I'm gonna go tell my friends goodbye and thank them for the food," I said to Tae as I headed out with a platter of bite-sized chocolate cakes in my hand. "You guys want any of this before I take it?"

"No, thank you," Nelos said stiffly.

Taeven lifted a disapproving brow at his knight before taking a cake. "Don't be long. We're leaving soon."

"All right." I grinned at him.

As I walked away from the tent, I heard Tae say, "You need to let it go. He's my valorian now, and that makes him your valorian too."

"It took him long enough," Nelos muttered.

"It was three fucking days!" I called back to Nelos, making him blush and Taeven snicker.

I snorted to myself and headed around back to the cooking tent where Tod and Vanessa worked. I found Vanessa prepping vegetables while Tod cleaned a fish.

"You can probably stop all that," I drawled. "We're leaving for Varalorre soon."

"Holy fuck turds!" Tod shouted as he pulled off his gloves. "Look at you! You're so fucking fae! Look at your eyes! That's wild, man. Wild."

Vanessa set down her knife and came over to peer at my face. "Shit, you *are* fae. But you still look like you."

"Weird, right?" I grinned. "Cake? Evan made them. And thanks for all the fancy food you sent me. I almost licked the plates, it was all so good."

"That's the best compliment." Tod slapped me on my shoulder, then grabbed me there. "Fuck, you're ripped. Feel these muscles, Van."

Vanessa didn't need any encouragement, she started running her hands over my chest. "Oooo nice. Mr. Big, Strong, Faerie Valorian."

"Thank you." I preened, then noticed that the rest of their crew was gawking at me.

Tod followed my stare to his crew and shouted. "All right, fuck-faces, get back to work. Just because the Falcon Lord is leaving doesn't mean we let this food go to waste."

"Yeah!" one of them cheered.

The rest grinned and went back to cooking. Not letting food go to waste was chef code for "it's all ours."

"Congratulations, Shane," Van said as she took a cake. "I'm really happy for you."

"We'll see how long my happiness lasts," I muttered.

"Are you still worried about him chucking you to the side?" Tod rolled his eyes. "You're his valorian now; he's not going to do that."

"Being a valorian doesn't make me immune to dump-ing."

"Uh, I kinda think it does." Tod smirked. "I mean, let's go with the worst-case scenario. Say he does miss pussy and decides to wander. That'll suck, but do you think he'll cast you aside? His *valorian*? No way."

"If he keeps me just to save face, I'd leave him," I said firmly. "Fuck, if he fucks around on me, I'll leave him. I'm not gonna put up with that shit."

"Seriously?" Tod grimaced. "I thought you gays were more open-minded about sex?"

"Open-minded doesn't mean we let our lovers cheat on us," I huffed, knowing he didn't mean anything by it. Tod was just, well, just a straight man. He didn't get it. He thought that having two guys in a relationship meant lots of sex and no games. "I want something real with him, not just to fuck around."

"All right, man, I get that," Tod toned it down. "But if you care about him, wouldn't you try to forgive him if he slips? I mean, it must be harder on him if he likes guys and girls."

"*Harder* on him?" I gaped at Tod. "Why would liking both sexes make it harder to be faithful? Loyalty is about one person; it shouldn't matter what sex I am."

"Tod, you're an idiot." Vanessa shook her head sadly at him.

"So I've been told." Tod grinned. "Sorry, Shane. I didn't mean to step on your little faerie toes."

"It's fine." I handed the tray to Van and hugged him, then switched the tray to Tod to hug Vanessa. "I just came by to thank you for the goodies and tell you goodbye. I don't know how long I'll be in Varalorre."

"I'm so jealous," Vanessa exclaimed. "You have to tell us everything when you get back."

"I promise. And I'll check out the chef scene for you guys."

"Yes! That's what I'm talking about." Tod slapped my shoulder again. "You're the best, bro."

"That's Falcon Valorian to you," I said primly, then we all burst into laughter.

"What changed your mind?" Vanessa asked once we settled down. "You were so adamant against this."

I sighed and glanced back toward the Falcon Lord's tent. "He did. I almost died in the battle. I was out on the beach, fighting beside a Glastig, when the Farungals started to retreat. We got caught in the swarm. We were done for, but then I heard this shriek and there he was. Taeven swooped down and picked us both up, then carried us to safety."

"He carried *two* men?" Tod's eyes went wide. "Isn't that a lot for a faerie?"

I blinked. I hadn't thought of that. "Yeah, I guess it is."

"Adrenaline can give you extra strength," Vanessa said softly. "Fear for a loved one can especially do it."

My jaw clenched. "He doesn't love me. Flat out told me so after I confessed that I love him."

"What?" Vanessa gaped at me. "And you still agreed to be his valorian?"

"Two things convinced me. First, he admitted that he didn't share my feelings, but he does care deeply for me. He didn't have to do that; he could have easily lied to get me to accept his offer. And he told me he's never cared so much for anyone before; that although he doesn't love me now, he's certain he will."

"Sounds like a load of shit to me," Tod growled, fingering a knife on his belt.

"Could be," I conceded. "But I don't think so. I saw his soul, Tod. When he gave me a piece of his soul, I saw it. He's . . . he's a good man. I know I can trust him."

Tod grunted thoughtfully.

"What's the second reason?" Van asked.

"When I was staring down a horde of Farungals, my thoughts were all about him," I whispered. "I regretted not accepting his offer, if only because it would have given me one more day with him."

Vanessa made a soft whimper. "That's so fucking beautiful."

"Saps," Tod said affectionately.

"After he saved us, I knew I had to accept his offer," I concluded. "Even if I didn't get to have him forever, I still wanted whatever I could get. It was too late to reject him. I love him."

"You sure do fall in love fast," Tod muttered.

"Not usually," I protested. "But that day we spent together was pretty amazing. I'll tell you guys about it later, though. I've still got to say goodbye to the others, and I don't have much time."

"Good luck, Shane." Vanessa kissed my cheek. "And remember, even if he doesn't fall in love with you, that doesn't mean you're unloved or unworthy. We all love you."

Tod cleared his throat and said gruffly, "Yeah, man, we love you. Like a brother, you know? So don't go falling apart over a faerie, all right? If he turns out to be an asshole, you just come home, and we'll take care of you. We'll take care of him too . . . if you know what I mean." He grinned viciously.

"Fuck." I sniffed and tried to laugh off the tears that stung my eyes. "You guys are the best. Thanks."

"We're family, bro," Tod declared. "Family takes care of each other. And I don't care if he's a warlord, if he fucks you over, I will fucking cut him into tiny pieces and serve him to his knights—Taeven tartare."

I grinned. "That so fucking psychotic, Tod. Thank you."

"That's chef love, buddy. Embrace the crazy."

Chapter Twenty-Three

When I got back to the Falcon Lord's tent, it was to find Taeven in a meeting with his generals—both the human and fae.

He smiled at me as I stepped up. "Were you able to say goodbye to all your friends?"

"Yeah, I found them." I glanced at the generals and greeted them, "Generals."

"Valorian," they both said respectfully.

Yeah, that was going to take some getting used to.

"I had Daron fetch your things," Tae said to me. "They're in the bedroom. I left a satchel on your trunk for you to pack whatever you'd like to take."

"Oh." I started thinking about what would fit me now. I'd gotten significantly bigger, so it was doubtful that any of my clothes would fit. And yeah, all right, I admit it; I wore my clothes on the tighter side to show off my ass-ets.

"Don't worry about the clothes," Tae said as if in response to my thoughts. "We'll get you a new wardrobe in Varal-orre. I've already requested a few new uniforms to be made for you here."

"Thanks." I grinned. Could the guy be any more thoughtful?

"I have to look after my valorian." He took my hand and gave it a squeeze. "I'll just be a few more minutes with the generals, and then we can leave."

My stomach twisted with excitement. Flying. To Varalorre. Fuck, this was really happening. "All right," I murmured as I headed toward the bedroom.

I have to admit that I was pleased that Tae had moved my things into his tent. I didn't want to assume that we'd be living together, but I had hoped. So, I went through my trunk with a grin on my face.

The only things that still fit were my belts and boots so I packed extras of each. Then I was left looking at my meager belongings. My most treasured possession was my guitar, and although it was there, propped against a fabric wall, I wasn't about to cart it with me to Varalorre. That left my collection of yeast and bread starters, some exotic spices from Lek, and the pictures of my family. Again, I wouldn't want to take any of that with me. I ran a fingertip over my mother's face adoringly before I set the photograph of her and Dad back in the box I kept it in. They both knew about my sexuality and though they had advised me to keep it a secret here, they were very supportive. It was my father who had suggested that I eventually move to Lek, where I could live freely. Damn, I loved them; they were phenomenal parents.

I blinked. I was fae now. I could be open about my sexuality without worrying about getting mobbed. I could even bring Tae home to meet them. Something brightened and burst inside my chest—a knot of anxiety that I hadn't realized I carried. I shuddered through its release, a tear sliding down my cheek, and then took a deep breath. To be able to be myself in my hometown would be incredible.

But then I reconsidered. I could be free with my parents, but not around their neighbors and friends. If the villagers knew I was gay, they wouldn't do anything to me, but they might ostracize my parents. It wouldn't matter that I was fae now; I had once been human, and my parents would be blamed for bringing up an . . . what was it that man had called me? Right, an abomination. Fuck, there went my good mood.

"What is it?" Tae was suddenly there, crouching beside me with a hand on my shoulder. "What's wrong?"

"Nothing. I was just thinking that I could introduce you to my family and be honest about who you are to me." I grimaced. "But I can't. I mean, I can introduce you to them like that, but not anyone outside of the family."

"You're stronger now, Shane," he said firmly. "And you have me. Against the two of us, no human would stand a chance."

I grinned at him. "Thanks for the vote of confidence, and it's good to know you have my back, but I'm not worried about us. My parents would pay the price after we left. They'd probably be scorned. Cut off from the community."

Taeven let out an angry huff. "I'm still trying to accept that humans can be so hateful."

"They can also be kind and loving," I protested. "There are good and bad people in every group. Unfortunately, here in Stalana, the main religion preaches against homosexuality. It turns even the nice people into assholes. Faith can be a powerful thing, so I try not to take it personally."

Tae sighed and nodded. "I will endeavor to do the same. But I would still like to meet your family."

"You would?" I grinned.

"Yes. Maybe after we get back from Varalorre, depending on what's going on with the war."

"All right." That good mood came rushing back.

"Is that all you're taking?" He lifted his brows at my boots and belts.

"Well, you said not to worry about the clothes and there's nothing else I need. I assume they'll have soap and towels in Varalorre?"

"Yes, they have soap. They have shampoo and conditioner too." He chuckled and reached into my trunk to brush a finger over the little bottles I'd taken from the hotel. "Are you ready to leave?"

"Ready when you are."

Taeven stood and held a hand down to me. I took it, and he pulled me to my feet.

Pressing in close, he stroked my cheek and murmured, "There's a flight harness on the bed. Put it on."

"That sounded kinky, Falcon Lord."

"It will be kinky when I use it as a handhold to fuck you later."

I shuddered so violently at his words, that he had to steady me.

"Oh, I like that response," he whispered in my ear before kissing my throat. His hands slid down to knead my ass, then spread it as if he were about to fuck me. "I can't wait to see you in nothing but those leather straps."

"I think maybe we should do that now," I suggested breathlessly.

Taeven pulled away from me, grinning. "We don't have the time."

"You just deliberately aroused me, knowing that you

weren't going to have sex with me!" I accused him.

"Yes, I did." He grinned, utterly unrepentant.

"You are a cruel man, Falcon Lord," I declared, but I did so smiling. "I'm going to be hard the entire flight to Varalorre."

"Hopefully, the entire flight to Wynvar."

"Wynvar?"

"That's the royal city of the Falcon Kingdom."

"How far is it?"

"By air, it's still many hours of travel. We'll be crossing the width of Stalana, going slightly at an angle to take us on a direct path to Wynvar, but the Falcon Kingdom is only two kingdoms away from the northern tip of Varalorre."

"So we'll be crossing nearly the entire continent."

"Yes. We'll stop for lunch either in Coyote or Fox to rest our wings. Those kingdoms are at the halfway point for us. But I plan on having dinner in the Falcon Kingdom."

"Then we'd best be off." I frowned.

"What is it now?"

"I think I'd better pee first."

Taeven laughed uproariously.

Chapter Twenty-Four

Tae was right; the flight was long. Although, once we crossed through the magical mists that protected Varalorre, the sights below my dangling feet were enough to keep me from getting bored. Even from that height, the landscape of Varalorre was amazing—the colors brighter and richer than those in Stalana, the architecture luxurious and fascinating, and the scents pure. Above me, Taeven bent his head often to check on me as he flew. I grinned up at him and gave him a thumb's up every time. He'd told me to let him know if I needed to take a break, either to stretch or pee. But I made it to the village of Frehan in the Coyote Kingdom without issue.

Tae set me down, then landed a few feet behind me. Suddenly, I was surrounded by naked faeries, but no one made a big deal out of it. They just pulled their clothes out of their satchels—worn around their necks during the flight—and got dressed. I limited myself to ogling Taeven. He was the only one I wanted to look at.

The Falcon Lord grinned as he stepped up to me. "I thought you'd be more interested in your first up-close look of Varalorre than me."

"Babe, when you're naked, nothing else matters. Not even a magical country." I smirked.

He chuckled and took my hand. "Welcome to the Coyote Kingdom, Shane." He waved a hand at the clearing. "Up ahead is the village of Frehan. They're sap farmers, I believe."

"Sap?" I asked as I looked around. "Like for syrup?"

The trees were perfect, almost too perfect, and some of them towered over the rest, higher than I'd ever seen a tree grow. Through the scattered trunks, I glimpsed the village that I had spotted before we landed; it had been hard to miss since it gleamed with the shine of polished gold. Even from a distance, I could tell that the homes were finer than any in Stalana, even those in the cities. They had square bases but their roofs were domed and gilded so that the sunlight reflected off them and set the village aglow. And this was a farming community?

"Yes, precisely," Tae answered as he led me toward the village. "The sap of the amaronth trees is sweet and can be harvested without hurting the trees, making it a relatively low-labor endeavor. But the farmers of this village also refine the sap and turn it into syrup."

"So, amaronth trees are similar to maples?"

"Yes, though I think you'll find that amaronth syrup is unique."

"I'm sure it is," I murmured as I stared at the gleaming leaves and vibrant flowers. I could practically feel the magic in the air. "Great balls of fuck!" I jerked to the side, knocking into Taeven as I released his hand.

"What is it?" Tae asked as everyone went on high alert.

"I saw this glittering thing zip through the trees!" I pointed in the direction of the object.

The knights relaxed with irritated and slightly amused expressions while Taeven chuckled.

"What?" Then I saw it again. "There it is! It's . . ." I trailed off.

"A Pixie," Taeven finished for me. "Several, from the look of it."

A faint giggling carried over to us.

"Greetings!" Taeven called to the Pixies. "It's my valorian's first time in Varalorre. Forgive his ignorance."

I gaped as a swarm of tiny people with iridescent wings burst up from a thick carpet of wildflowers and zoomed over to us. They welcomed me to Varalorre with high-pitched voices and light brushes of their hands on my cheeks as the tiniest of the bunch—children, I assumed—showered me with flower petals. I stood there, feeling my smile turn goofy, and held my hands up to catch the petals. A child took it as an invitation and landed on my palm.

"Thank you. I'm Shane. What's your name?"

"Elissa," the little girl said. "I like your eyes, Valorian Shane. They are the color of leaves in the sunshine."

My heart melted.

"I like your wings," I countered. "They're like diamonds but very thin."

She giggled, jumped into the air, and hovered beside my face to kiss my cheek. Then the whole flock rose and flew away with spiraling acrobatics.

I stared after them in wonder.

"They're just Pixies," Tasathor muttered.

I tucked the flower petal into my satchel with a side-glare at Tasathor. "I'd wager to say that there is nothing in Varalorre that should be preceded with 'just,' especially not those magnificent faeries."

"Well said." Taeven nodded approvingly as he reclaimed

my hand.

Tasathor flushed as the other knights frowned at him.

A few minutes later, we stepped out of the forest and onto a stone sidewalk. We strolled into the foot traffic of Sidhe and Unsidhe citizens, several of whom looked surprised to see us. They nodded respectfully to the Falcon Lord as he passed, his retinue of knights marching in formation behind him. But I didn't have time to glance at Tae's guards; I was too busy taking in the people of Frehan, especially the Unsidhe. There were races I'd never seen before, including more of those amazing Pixies. The Pixies weren't allowed to serve in the armies for obvious reasons. Though, I had a feeling that a swarm of them could do serious damage if they put their minds to it.

"Oh my God!" I stopped at a store window and peered in. "Is this a spice shop?!"

Taeven peered over my shoulder. "It appears to be. Would you like to go in?"

"Do they take Stalanian coin here?" I asked hesitantly.

"No." He leaned down to whisper in my ear, "But I'm happy to buy you whatever you desire. You can work it off later in bed."

"Did you just suggest that I whore myself to you for spices?" I asked with a broad grin. "Because I totally will. Whatever you want me to do. *Anything.*"

Taeven laughed and turned toward his knights. "Go ahead without us. Get a table at Grannelt's and order their special for both of us. We'll be along shortly."

"Yes, my lord." Daron bowed, gave me a heavy look, and left with the others.

"He thinks you're upset with him," Taeven murmured as

he opened the shop's door for me.

"Who, Daron?" I asked in surprise. "I thought he was upset with me."

"He . . . I'm not sure how he feels about you. Daron can be secretive. But he mentioned that he feels guilty for telling you about the glimpse of souls."

"He told you about our talk?" I asked, but I was distracted, and my voice trailed off as I stepped into the shop.

A U-shaped counter formed a barrier between the center of the shop and the walls, which were lined in shelves, many of them filled with square drawers, labeled with the names of spices I'd never heard of. Another counter ran down the middle of the central space, with enormous glass containers in fanciful shapes atop it. Chunks of raw spices filled the containers and silver sample plates of the ground spice sat before them. The floor, ceiling, shelves, and counters were all made of the same, reddish-brown wood, polished to a dull shine, and the scent of all those spices combined to become a heavenly smell that was like an aromatic hug.

I went up to a counter in a daze. "By all that's holy," I whispered as I stared at the hundreds of jars of spices on the shelves above the drawers. "I didn't know there were so many."

"My lords!" A Glastig woman with dark hair down to her hips sashayed over to us, her hooves clicking on the floorboards. "Avians *and* soldiers? How unusual. Welcome to Frehan."

"Thank you." Tae nodded. "I'm the Falcon Lord, Taeven Rumerra, and this is my valorian, Shane."

"A warlord and his valorian in my shop!" She clapped her hands in delight. "The Goddess smiles upon me today. How may I help you?"

"My valorian is a baker," Tae explained. "He's a little overwhelmed by your selection."

"A baker?" She cocked her head at me. "I have many spices that do well in bread and some better suited to desserts."

"Actually, I was hoping to bring back presents for my chef friends too. Only one of them is a baker like me."

"Human chefs," she said pensively. "You'll want the most exotic of my spices; things that can't be found in Stalana."

"Yes, Ma'am."

"Oh, darling, you don't have to call me that. Please, I am Revana. Now, you just wait there, and I'll put together collections of spices for you and your friends. How many chefs are there?"

"Um." I did a mental count. "Five chefs, one baker, not including me." I looked at Tae. "Is that all right?"

"As I said, whatever you desire." He grinned.

"In exchange for whatever you desire?" I lifted a brow.

"Indeed."

"Oh, my, how *luscious*," Revana purred. "I'll be right back, lovebirds."

With that, she twirled away, and I gaped after her. I knew that faeries were accepting of any lifestyle, but I hadn't expected such outright approval. Sure, Tae and I had held hands as we'd walked down the street, but having a stranger make such a comment to me, so freely, was . . . well, it was fucking liberating. I grinned broadly at Taeven.

"You can be whoever you wish in Varalorre," he said softly, accurately interpreting my look. He brushed a hand over my ponytail. "Why don't you wear your hair loose here?

You won't be baking."

"Oh, uh." I ran a hand over my slicked-back hair self-consciously. "You like it down?"

"I like being able to run my hands through it. And grab a handful."

I yanked my leather tie out of my hair and it fell heavily to my shoulders. I'd expected Tae to laugh at my eagerness, but instead, his eyes widened in appreciation, and his fingers instantly slid into my shoulder-length locks.

"Beautiful," he murmured and weighed a hank of it in his palm.

"Says the man with golden hair."

Taeven grinned and brushed a lock of my hair behind my ear. "I'm glad you like it." His finger trailed along my jaw, then down my throat to rest in the hollow at the top of my collarbone. My heartbeat sped up as he began to lean down toward me.

"Here you are, my lords," Revana declared.

Tae straightened, giving me a smug smile when I made a disappointed sound.

Revana set a small wooden case on the counter before me. "I've packed the spice bottles in this to protect them since I assume you're continuing on to the Falcon Kingdom."

"Yes, we are, thank you, that was thoughtful," Taeven said. "And do you have any bottles of amaronth syrup?"

"Yes, of course. How many would you like?"

"Enough for my valorian and his friends. So, that would be seven, right?" He looked at me.

"Yes, seven. Thank you." Emboldened by Revana's behavior, I stretched up to kiss his cheek.

Taeven grinned broadly. "You're welcome."

With a delighted smile at our interaction, Revana spun around and took seven bottles off a shelf behind her, then tucked them into the box with the spices. I sighed in delight when I spotted the little bottles bundled into groups for my friends. Once the box was closed and latched again, Tae paid Revana with Varalorrian coins.

"They're all labeled and grouped." Revana tapped the box. "The two that are different are for you and your fellow baker."

"Thank you, so much," I said. "This is fantastic."

"Wait till you try them." She winked at me. "The gerris powder is so delicious that it practically turns every dessert into an aphrodisiac."

"Well, I guess that means I'll have to make you a dessert," I said to Tae.

"The way you said that makes it sound as if *I'm* going to be the dessert," Tae teased.

I lifted a brow at Revana.

"Oh, yes, go ahead and sprinkle it on him as well," she said. "I guarantee you'll *love* the result."

"You're naughty!" I declared in delight. "You must be a chef."

Revana laughed. "I am at that. And I'm thrilled that my spices will be traveling to Stalana, straight into the hands of a valorian's friends."

"Not as thrilled as they're going to be to receive them." I tucked the box into my satchel. "Thank you again."

"My pleasure, my lords."

"Thank you, Tae," I said to him again as we stepped outside.

"My pleasure," he repeated Revana's words but in a low, sensual tone. "Or it will be." He put his arm around my shoulder.

I looked at him in surprise.

"After buying you presents—and presents for your friends—I think I should get to hold you closer." He winked at me.

"Hold me as close as you want, babe." I slid an arm around his waist as we strode off. "I think I'm going to love it here."

Chapter Twenty-Five

"Before we leave, you should put this on." Taeven pulled a thick jacket out of his satchel and handed it to me as we stepped back into the clearing we'd arrived in earlier. We had an amazing lunch in a little cafe—a meal I would never forget. The food was incredibly delicious, everything tasting exotic but also simply better. For instance, a carrot in Varalorre tasted more carroty than one in Stalana. I don't know how else to describe it; the flavor of everything was more intense.

"Why?" I frowned at it; the jacket was lined in fur.

"This time of the year, Wynvar is cold."

"How cold?" I asked warily.

"It will likely be snowing," he said with a soft, wistful smile.

"Snowing?!" Part of me was intrigued; I'd never seen snow. But most of me was wary. The upper portion of Stalana got cold, but never cold enough to snow, and I was from the lower region—where the Falcon Camp was. "I'm Lekian, we're a tropical people."

"I believe Lek is considered too arid for that description," Tae mused. "To be tropical, there has to be—"

"All right, we're a desert people."

"No, it's not desert either. I thought you've been to Lek?"

Tae's knights snickered.

"Well, what do you call it then?" I huffed.

"I believe it's somewhere between the two."

I rolled my eyes. "Whatever it is, that's what I am. I'm not good with cold."

"Technically, you're fae now, so you should be fine," Tae said calmly.

"I've never seen snow," I whispered.

"Then this will be a treat. Put on the coat, Shane."

"Don't I need a hat too? I've heard that people wear hats in cold weather."

Tae frowned at that.

"He's right; hats are just as important as coats," Azla, the only female knight in Tae's Guard, said. "He'll lose a lot of body heat through his head, my lord."

Taeven sighed. "Could you run back into town and get the Valorian a hat, Az?"

"Yes, my lord." Azla turned and started for the village.

"I thought you'd been to Wynvar," I tossed at him teasingly. "How do you not know about hats?"

"I've never bothered with them. But now that I think about it, I do recall a lot of faeries wearing them." Tae cocked his head at me. "Are you truly worried about being cold?"

"A little." I grimaced. "You said a lot of Avian cities are in the mountains, right?"

"Yes."

"Is Wynvar?"

"Yes."

"Then the air will be thinner too."

"Your new lungs will handle it just fine, Valorian. Come here." Tae pulled me further away from the other men, off into the trees a bit. "What's really bothering you?"

"I don't want to live in a place where it snows," I whispered.

"This will only be temporary."

"Yes, but—" I stared at him, willing him to understand so I wouldn't have to say it.

"But you're worried that after the war, I'll want to live there?" He asked softly.

"Yes."

"I own property in Wynvar; it's been my home for many years, and it isn't cold all the time. Winter is merely a season, Shane."

"I know, but if I'm miserable throughout it—"

Taeven let out a sigh that sounded a bit annoyed. "Why must you always worry about things before they happen?"

"What?"

"You've never seen snow or Wynvar." He waved a frustrated hand at me. "Yet, you've already decided that both will make you miserable. You've taken it even further to a future that could change at any moment. I don't know where I'll want to live when the war ends, beyond it being in Varalorre, but if I'm living with you and Wynvar does make you miserable, don't you think that I would move us to somewhere you'd be happy?"

I gaped at him. "I . . . you'd move for me?"

"I wasn't born in Wynvar; I'm not that attached to it. I moved there from one of the valleys—a farming village."

"You were a farmer?" My jaw dropped even further.

Taeven nodded. "Leeks and Carrots. My father purchased the farm after he retired from the Falcon Army. I was raised in a warmer clime like you. But I grew to love the cold. Seeing the snow coat everything is magical. There's a beauty in *all* that nature offers; you shouldn't snub it before giving it a chance."

"In my defense, giving you a chance meant a complete life and body transformation," I muttered.

"Yes, you were right to be cautious about that," he conceded, but his tone was a tad patronizing.

I rolled my eyes at him. "Fine, I'll give your city a chance; you don't have to be an ass about it."

Taeven laughed, then looked up. "Az is back with your hat. Now, will you put on the damn coat so we can finish this journey?"

"Yes, Falcon Lord," I huffed.

He leaned down and kissed me. And it was hot enough to keep me warm all the way to Wynvar.

Chapter Twenty-Six

We flew over spiky forests of pine, spruce, and fir (though maybe they were Varalorre versions of those trees and had other names entirely), wide valleys of farmland, and snow-capped mountains. The Falcons didn't seem bothered by the chill, but I was glad for the hat and coat as soon as we started gaining altitude. Not only would I have lost precious body heat, but my ears would have gone numb. I know this because my entire face nearly did; I had to tuck it down, into my collar several times to prevent it from happening. I should have asked for a scarf too, and, more importantly, a pair of gloves. I had to cross my arms and press my hands into my armpits to keep them warm. By the time we reached Wynvar, I was not in the mood to appreciate the view. That being said, the city was spectacular.

Taeven was right about the snow. It lay over Wynvar like a coat of fresh paint, reflecting the city lights to nearly blinding proportions. Poking out of that layer of brilliant white were the spires of palaces the likes of which I'd never even dreamed of. And I do mean palaces plural. There wasn't merely one but many of them, spotting the sprawling city that sat tucked within sheer spikes of glittering rock like a falcon in her nest. A glowing falcon. Wynvar was a beacon in the night, shining across the dark valleys below. As a whole, it looked like something out of a children's story—a place untouched by any of the petty traumas that the rest of the world suffered. And at its center, the largest palace of all dominated, its spires sporting pennants that gave spots of color to the scene, like drops of blood in the snow.

"Welcome to Wynvar," Taeven called down to me. "What do you think of it, Falcon Valorian?"

"It's beautiful, but I think I'd appreciate it better on the ground with a hot beverage in my hand."

Taeven laughed and it came out as a high-pitched falcon shriek. He angled his body sharply and circled the massive plateau. From up there, the plain looked unnatural, as if it had been carved out of the center of a single mountain peak, creating numerous, thinner and sharper peaks to ring it like a deadly necklace. Below us, warmly dressed faeries strolled down the sidewalks and magnificent carriages rolled down the streets, pulled by horses that snorted steam into the frigid air. There were fewer Unsidhe there—from what I could tell from the sky—and I saw no Pixies at all. I suppose their wings wouldn't do so well in the cold.

Tae descended toward one of the palaces, its gleaming spires connected by arching bridges with gold railings. One of its many towers was not a spire, but instead had a flat top bordered by a stone railing. He headed for that one, though it seemed too small a space for us to land. It turned out that it was merely my perspective. As we drew closer, I saw that there was more than enough room for all of us. Tae set me on my feet there, then shifted to Sidhe. He got dressed a lot faster than he had at Frehan, but when I offered him his coat back, he waved me off.

"I'll be fine once we get inside," he said as he went to a hatch in the floor.

Taeven lifted the wooden panel to reveal a set of stairs. Down we went, into a dark corridor. I had to go slowly, with a hand on the chilly wall to guide me, but no one else seemed to have a problem with the lack of light. We made it to a landing and suddenly, there was light. I frowned as I watched a panel finish sliding into the wall, revealing a tiny room that was the source of the light. Tae led me into that little room, and I glanced up to see fae lights—magical stones that glowed brighter than any fire—set into a glass case on the ceiling. The others crowded into the room with us, to the point where I couldn't lift my arms without touching someone, then they turned to face the doorway.

"What are we doing?" I asked Tae as I turned as well.

"This is an elevator," he explained as he hit a numbered button on the wall. There were many buttons, set in descending order, and he hit the ones labeled 15 and 1. "It will transport us to the floors we select via these buttons."

The panel slid shut and the entire room shivered. I slapped a hand on the wall to brace myself as I felt us move downward.

"This is a magic, moving box?" I asked in shock. "Like a dumbwaiter for people?"

Tae's knights snickered, and he shot them a silencing look before he explained, "It's not magic, just pulleys and such, very much like a dumbwaiter, though I believe the mechanism is powered by magic." He frowned and looked at his knights. "Isn't it?"

They all shrugged.

"Could be, my lord," Azla said. "Honestly, I've never asked."

"No, you just accepted it as a part of your world." I shook my head in wonder. "I can't even imagine being raised to take such amazing things for granted. To become so accustomed to them that even a brilliant feat of magic and engineering becomes mundane."

That shut them up. The knights glanced at each other guiltily. *Yeah, maybe count your blessings instead of deriding others for not having them.*

"We do become immune to the little miracles," Taeven mused as he ran a hand over the metal casing that housed the buttons. "It is a wondrous thing, isn't it?" He smiled at me. "Thank you for giving me a new perspective, Shane. I can't wait to see the rest of the city through your eyes."

Before I could reply, something dinged, and we came to a halt. The panel opened and Tae took my hand to draw me out, past his shifting knights.

"Notify Halfrin that we're home and ask him to send up some hot chocolate for Shane and me," Taeven said to his knights. "Also, send a message to Their Majesties that we'll be attending them soon. We'll leave for the palace in an hour."

"Yes, my lord," they said in unison.

The panel closed just as Taeven hit a switch on the wall. Around us, fae lights came on, illuminating a corridor. We strolled down it, me gawking at the amazing artwork on the walls—landscapes, battle scenes, portraits, and still lifes, all framed in intricately carved and gilded wood. The frames alone were worth a fortune.

"Um, Tae, where are we?"

"Oh, I . . . I'm sorry, Shane, I assumed you'd know. This is my home."

I stopped walking. "You live in a *palace*?!"

"It came with the warlord position," he explained. "Gifted to me by the Crown."

"You were *given* a palace?!"

Tae chuckled. "Yes, but most nobles have them here."

"But . . . are you a noble? You said you were a farmer."

Something sharp and painful zipped across his expression. "No, I wasn't born noble, though my status as warlord is considered such."

"So . . . you think this place is pretty fucking awesome too, don't you?" I grinned knowingly at him.

Taeven burst out laughing. "Yes, it is spectacular." His laughter faded, his expression softening into something tender as he lifted a hand to my face. "You can be so pessimistic and yet, you have a lightness to you that transforms darkness into something beautiful."

I laid my hand over his, then lowered our hands together so I could weave my fingers with his. "I'm not a pessimist, I'm a realist, and that doesn't have to be a bad thing. A realist sees things as they are and accepts them so that he can be happy. I may not be blissfully ignorant, but with awareness comes appreciation, and that is a lasting joy that cannot be hurt by the truth since it is born of truth."

"Dear Goddess, who are you?" Taeven grinned and shook his head at me.

I shrugged. "The product of my parents, I suppose. They taught me how to live and appreciate life, but they also taught me to be careful. I'm sorry if my wariness annoys you."

"No, I'm sorry I said those things to you. You were wise to question the life you were offered before simply jumping into it. Very few men would have."

"Thanks."

"Now, come along; we need to get dressed to present ourselves at court."

Tae started leading me through the corridor again, taking so many turns that I was lost in minutes. We eventually went into another elevator and stepped out onto the 25th floor. My grip on his hand loosened and then I let go entirely as I stepped forward into a grand room lit by a glittering chandelier the size of my old tent. The huge space was broken up into several areas by furniture placement and rugs, but its focal point—in addition to the chandelier—was a massive fireplace.

"This is our sitting room," Tae said. He gestured toward the right. "Across that bridge is your tower, should you wish to stay in it, but I'd prefer you stay with me here, in my bedroom." He waved his hand to the left.

"I'd prefer that too." I grinned. "As if I'd want to sleep across a fucking bridge from you."

Taeven grinned back brightly, but then, suddenly, frowned. "We should have purchased some clothing for you in Frehan. It slipped my mind."

"You don't want me borrowing yours?"

"No, it's just that my clothes are a little big on you." He waved a hand at the bunched fabric at the tops of my boots and the billow of it over my belt. "That's not appropriate for court." He sighed. "I'll just have to find my smallest pieces. I believe I have some leather breeches that are a little tight on me."

He turned and headed through a doorway. I followed him into a room of silken fabric, polished wood, and faceted crystal. A vaulted ceiling made it feel even larger than it was, as did the enormous mirror atop the heavy dresser. Plush rugs covered the stone floor, adding color to a neutral palette of indigo and silver. Crystal shards, larger than any I'd ever seen, formed bedposts around the behemoth of a mattress that reigned on a circular platform. Plush, dark blue velvet covered the bed and puddled on the dais. Above us, fae lights twinkled in a chandelier of silver stars, and off to the left, a pair of glass balcony doors presented a view of the night sky that made it feel as if the room were merely a continuation of it.

"Whoa," I whispered.

Taeven looked back at me as he reached for a silver door handle. "I'm glad you like it, but you can look around later. We need to get you dressed."

"My lord?" A sweet, feminine voice called from the other room.

I went tense, staring from the doorway to Tae.

"It's a servant with our drinks." He gave me a chiding look. "I have no lovers stashed here, Shane."

"Of course not." I cleared my throat. "I was just startled."

Tae gave me a skeptical look as he called out, "In here, Evella."

"Falcon Lord, welcome home!" A stunning woman exclaimed as she came striding into the room on transparent legs —a Sylph. She carried a silver tray with two steaming mugs and several little pots on it. And . . . a paintbrush? "I have your drinks here and Halfrin sent the paint with me, in case you'd like to adorn your valorian." She cast a bright grin at me. "We've heard the joyous news. Welcome home, Falcon Valorian."

"Thank you." *Home?*

"Thank you, Evella," Taeven said as well. "Put the tray down on the dresser. I think I will have you adorn him, but first, I need to find him appropriate clothing. Unfortunately, his are now too small for him, while mine are too large."

Evella frowned pensively as she set the tray down. She absently took a mug and offered it to me with a, "You look chilled, my lord."

"Thank you." I sniffed at the drink, the scent of sugar and chocolate making me sigh. It was actually warm enough that I should have removed my coat and hat, but I was too eager to sip the drink and did that first.

"Perhaps I could pin a garment to temporarily take it in?" she offered. "I have some sewing pins that latch shut so they won't hurt the Valorian."

"Evella, you'll be getting a bonus for that!" Taeven declared. "Good thinking! Fetch your pins."

"Yes, my lord." She bobbed a curtsy and hurried out.

"Oh, damn," I murmured.

"What is it?"

"This hot chocolate is amazing. Try it before it gets cold."

"I've had it before, and I know it's wonderful. That's why I ordered it for us." But he nonetheless took his mug and sipped at the drink, then made a pleased sound. "I admit, it's better than I remembered."

"Um, what's all that about adorning me?" I shucked out of my coat while transferring my mug from hand to hand so I didn't have to set it down, then laid the coat on a chair.

"Oh, it's a tradition started by the first valorian. Or rather, his warlord," Tae explained. "Evella will paint a design on your forehead to denote your status. Since we're Avians, it'll likely be a pair of wings."

"She's going to paint my forehead?"

"And outline your eyes in kohl." He nodded. "Think of it as a type of circlet. I will be wearing one to announce my status as warlord."

"A crown?"

"No, a circlet—a band of gold without jewels. The monarchs wear crowns that have jewels in them; we're a step below them in rank." He frowned at me. "But if you don't wish to be painted, you don't have to."

"No, it's fine." I shrugged. "A little paint never hurt anyone."

"Good." He grinned. "Now let's go find you something that Evella can take in."

Chapter Twenty-Seven

Evella worked her non-magical magic on Tae's clothing and took in the seams with her sewing pins so that our chosen pieces looked as if they'd been made for me. With a fur-lined cloak topping the velvet and brocade ensemble and painted gold wings arching over my kohl-lined eyes, I looked like another man. Only my boots were out of place. Tae's boots were way too big for me, and the last thing I wanted was to fall on my face in front of the King and Queen, but Tae said that my footwear could be overlooked far easier than an ill-fitting tunic. I agreed; I mean, who'd be looking at my feet when I had gold paint all over my face?

Once we were dressed, we headed downstairs. We stepped out of the elevator and into an enormous hall over four times the size of my parents' house. Tae's knights weren't waiting there as I'd expected. The vast space had nothing in it beyond a few plinths holding ancient statuary and a single man.

The dark-haired man bowed to Taeven as we approached. "Welcome home, Falcon Lord," he said warmly.

"Thank you, Halfrin." Tae waved a hand toward me. "This is our valorian, Shane Rumerra."

I blinked at that. *Had he just given me his last name?*

"It's an honor to meet you, Valorian." Halfrin bowed to me. "If there is anything you need, do not hesitate to ask."

"Thank you. I appreciate that."

"And may I say that you look dashing with the gold markings of your status?"

"Thanks." I grinned, one hand lifting to touch my temple. I did like how the gold looked against my skin and the kohl made my eyes so bright that they seemed to glow.

"My lord, your carriage is waiting," Halfrin added to Taeven.

"Very good. Thank you, Halfrin." Tae took my hand and led me toward a pair of grand, double doors.

Outside, the night was brightened by moonlight reflecting off snow. Gardens surrounded Tae's palace, but the plants were just lumps of white split by a circular drive that had been cleared for travel. At the bottom of a flight of stone steps, a carriage waited, the emblem of a falcon on its door. The horses stamped and huffed steam as the driver opened the door of the carriage for us.

Inside, thick blankets waited on the padded benches. I slipped under one and Taeven joined me, settling in beside me to wrap an arm around my shoulders. I tucked him in beneath the blanket with me as the carriage started to move.

"All right, I do like the snuggling part of being cold," I admitted.

"Just wait until I show you the other wonders of Winter," he whispered in my ear.

"Oh, that sounds promising."

We rolled through a pair of massive gates, then out onto the city streets. Fae streetlamps lit Wynvar but so did the softer glows filtering out from the windows of palaces and then, once we left the residential area, shops. Snowflakes drifted by the carriage windows like dandelion fluff, and I leaned against Tae as I watched them.

"It's pretty but I don't think I want to go walking in it," I said.

"It's not so bad when you're bundled up and you don't have the frigid air blasting in your face."

"I suppose."

"Here's the Royal Palace," Tae murmured.

"That was fast." I lifted my head from Tae's chest to peer out the window.

"Yes, my proximity to the palace is another symbol of my status."

The gates we passed through were a pair of gold wings that split at our approach. Soldiers stood beside them, thick coats worn over their uniforms; they saluted our carriage as we rolled by. We went up a long drive then around the side of a roundabout and parked before a set of stairs. The double doors at the top of those stairs opened as soon as we stopped, as if someone had been staring out the window, awaiting our arrival. A man hurried out to us to open our carriage door. He bowed as Taeven and I climbed out.

We went up the stairs and into the soaring edifice that was home to the monarchs of the Falcon Kingdom. I caught only a glimpse of the main keep, outdoor lights shining up its stone walls, before I was inside. This entry hall was even larger than Tae's, but it was also full of people hurrying to and fro, several bearing silver trays and most wearing red uniforms. As we stepped across the room, the bustling people expertly navigated around us. Tae barely paid them any mind, moving straight forward, certain that a path would be cleared for him.

"Why didn't your knights join us?" I asked him.

"They're not necessary here. For the entirety of our visit, they're on leave. Well, partial leave. They'll stay with me in case they're needed to send messages to camp."

"Is there anything I need to know about the King and Queen?"

Tae turned down a corridor and the rush of bodies lessened. Here, there was surprisingly less artwork than in Tae's home. In fact, the corridors we strode through were empty of all but the occasional statue. Doors were closed as well, making it feel even more stark, but the way was wide enough for several faeries in falcon form to walk through it at once. It seemed a waste to me.

"King Dehras and Queen Siarra are fair rulers," Tae answered. "The King was born to the throne, which means that his take precedence to his wife's. He is a warrior, as is his daughter, Princess Sanasenne, so they are more sympathetic to us soldiers than the rest of their court."

"What does that mean?" I frowned at him. "People don't like soldiers here?"

"No, that's not it. There are those in the court who opposed a non-noble being appointed as warlord," he lowered his voice to say. "I'm not openly scorned, but you'll notice that I'm not warmly received by everyone either."

"Idiots," I huffed.

Taeven's eyebrows rose. "That's all you have to say?"

"You want me to kick someone's ass?" I offered. "I can totally make it look like an accident."

Taeven chuckled. "That won't be necessary. I . . . I was merely surprised that you're not worried about being snubbed."

"Why the fuck would I care what a bunch of uptight faeries think of me?" I lifted my chin. "I'm the fucking Falcon Valorian. Doesn't that make me noble too?"

"Actually, you outrank all but the royals and myself,"

"Great balls of fuck." I gaped at him. "Are you serious?"

"Yes."

"Then I *really* don't give a shit what they think." I grinned broadly. "They should be kissing our asses."

"You know, you're right; they should." He lifted our joined hands and kissed the back of mine. "We're going to stay as late as we like, eat a lot of food, drink a lot of wine, and dance right in the middle of them. And they can kiss our asses."

"Dance?" I lifted my brows. "You dance? I can dance with you?"

"I insist on it," Tae drawled. Then his gaze veered away. "We're here. All right, we go in and wait at the threshold to be announced, then I'll take you to the royals. Once I introduce you, kneel. I'll help you up when they finish speaking with you. Oh, and refer to the King and Queen as 'Your Majesty' but the Princess is 'Your Highness.'"

"Got it." I nodded.

"Prepare yourself; the throne room is a feast to the senses."

Then Tae stepped up to another set of double doors. A pair of footmen opened them for us simultaneously, and a rush of sound and scent hit me like a slap in the face. The drone of voices was peppered with laughter and the aroma of perfume, flowers, and food. It was also warm. We stepped into the room, and I knew immediately that my cloak was going to get stifling in seconds.

"Welcome, Falcon Lord," a man near the door said respectfully. "Their Majesties have been eagerly awaiting your arrival."

Another man stepped forward with an outstretched hand as Tae swept off his white cloak. Beneath the brocade and fur, Taeven wore an apple-red tunic that matched the Falcon Soul and a pair of white, leather breeches. His broad shoulders stretched the brocade and a hint of sculpted chest peeped through the V neckline. With his golden hair swept back beneath a circlet that was nearly indecipherable from it, and a thick belt slung low on his hips, he looked like a prince—a warrior prince. Tae handed his cloak to the footman and motioned for me to do the same. I gratefully removed my cloak as Tae continued speaking to the first man.

"I'm here with my valorian, Shane Rumerra."

"Yes, my lord. I will announce you."

He'd done it again—given his name in place of mine.

I was about to ask him why when the man he'd spoken to bellowed, "Taeven Rumerra, the Falcon Lord, and Shane Rumerra, the Falcon Valorian."

The faeries filling the throne room—both Sidhe and Unsidhe—turned to face us. There were too many of them to focus on and since Tae had already warned me that their reception wouldn't be cordial, I ignored them and checked out the room instead. Tae had said it would be a feast for the senses, and he hadn't exaggerated.

Especially after the bare hallways, the throne room was a sensory rush. From floor to ceiling, it was alive with texture and color. Bright rugs covered every inch of stone, overlapping indolently. Sheer silk panels hung from the ceiling, outlining a central space and breaking up the massive room into sections, much like the panels in the Falcon Lord's tent. The central portion was dominated by a dais at the far wall, upon which three people sat enthroned, but the rest of the space was filled mostly with people—both courtiers and servants who carried trays of goblets among them.

Along the lines of the silk panels, potted plants added more color and freshness to the room, and through the translucent fabric, I could see more faeries moving about. In the space to the right, those faeries danced to effervescent music, light enough to lift your feet from the ground, and to the left, they dined at little, round tables. Above us, enormous chandeliers hung, adorned with crimson jewels. They gave a pink cast to the room that imparted a healthy flush to pale, winter skin.

A path cleared before us, courtiers drawing back to form it, and Taeven escorted me down the channel, chin lifted and gaze fixed ahead. At the opposite end, the royals waited, their gazes serene. The Falcon King sat in the center, his wife and daughter flanking him, and a crown sat atop his head, circled with stones that matched the Falcon Soul in both color and shape. His jewels pointed up as well, giving his crown a sharp appearance. Beneath that vicious head-jewelry, his strawberry-blond hair flowed down his broad chest nearly to his waist. The color went nicely with his golden tan, which also went well with his green eyes, the irises ringed in dark brown. He was slimmer than I'd expected of a warrior, but between his delicate wife and daughter, he looked downright bulky.

"Taeven." The King's expression shifted into pleasure. "It's good to have you back with us."

"He has been so excited ever since we received news of your valorian," the Queen added, her hand on her husband's forearm.

In contrast to her husband, Queen Siarra was pale, with eyes in a bright shade of blue. Her dark hair was braided elaborately beneath her crown, and her slim shoulders looked too frail to carry the weight of her heavily embroidered gown. The Princess was even paler than her mother, with that rare version of blonde hair that I'd only seen on faeries—so light that it was as white as the snow that covered the city—and her skin nearly matched it. She wore an ice blue gown that brightened her coloring to a nearly blinding state and matched her eyes. She was practically translucent. Her hair, unlike the Queen's, hung unbound past her hips in a shining cape. Her crown offered a spot of bright color, and even though it had only a single jewel at center-front, it stood out sharply against her pallor.

"Thank you, Your Majesties." Taeven bowed. "I'm delighted to present your valorian to you. This is Shane Rumerra."

I stepped forward and knelt at the base of the dais. "Your Majesties." I inclined my head to the King and Queen, then to their daughter. "Your Highness."

"Welcome, Falcon Valorian, beloved of our Goddess," the King declared. "We are honored to have you with us."

"Thank you, Your Majesty. The honor is entirely mine. Your home is magnificent."

The King's grin broadened. "Funny that you should mention homes. I have a gift for you, Valorian. An estate in Wynvar, near your warlord's."

"An estate?" I gaped at him. "Are you saying that you're giving me a house, Your Majesty?"

"I am indeed." He was obviously delighted by my shock. "And for you, Taeven, a property on the Avalar coast."

"I'm overwhelmed by your generosity, Sire," Tae said as he stepped up beside me. "Thank you."

"You have served us well these many years, Tae. The reward has been earned," the Princess declared.

Tae. She had called him Tae.

"Thank you, Your Highness," Taeven said with a soft smile.

"It has indeed," the King said. "I will speak more with you tomorrow when you give me your report. For tonight, enjoy your accomplishments and the *honor* they have brought you and your *already esteemed* line." The King's sharp gaze flicked around the room almost in challenge, and I instantly liked him for it. When he looked back at Tae, his gaze softened. "I notified your parents of your valorian and just received word back from them. Your father is extremely proud and asked me to convey his congratulations and love to you."

"Thank you, Your Majesty." Tae swallowed roughly. "That was very kind of you."

"Nonsense. You know I keep in contact with my old General. I try to give him updates on you regularly."

"I appreciate that, Sire."

I looked back and forth between the King and Taeven with a soft smile. So what if some of the nobles didn't like Tae? His royals did, and that was far more important.

"This celebration is in honor of you both," the Queen added, setting her gaze on me. "Feast and make merry, Falcon Valorian. You have found your way to your true home at last."

The room cheered at this, though I couldn't fathom why, and Taeven helped me to my feet. Tae tugged on my arm as he started to bow, so I followed suit. Then he backed us away from the thrones. The crowd closed in around us, but as we turned, I saw the Princess stand and start down the stairs. A man waited for her at the bottom of the dais. His skin was a shade darker than the King's, speaking to time spent outdoors, and his golden-brown hair was pulled back in a severe braid. He glanced over at us, his gaze roaming me critically and then Tae with familiarity. I blinked at that. It wasn't a look you gave an acquaintance. But then he pulled the Princess close and kissed her passionately. Perhaps I had misread them both.

Taeven nodded to courtiers as we passed, several inclining their heads respectfully, but none appeared worth the time for Tae to stop and speak to. Instead, he led me out of the central section entirely and into the dining area. Once past the translucent partitions, I got a look at a banquet table set with the most beautiful food I've ever seen.

"Holy shit," I whispered as Tae led me over to it. "Look at the finish on that braided loaf! It's perfect!"

Tae chuckled and escorted me to the bread section at one end of the table. It was laden with crusty rounds, glossy loaves, and fluffy rolls. Some were speckled with herbs, others fruit, but the focal point was a centerpiece of a falcon in flight, all done in bread. The intricacy of the pointed feathers blew my mind.

"I feel as if I should kneel," I declared.

"It is rather like an altar to bread," Taeven noted as he handed me a plate. "Try a piece of all of them."

"But . . ." I trailed off as I looked down the length of the table at the feast done in appetizer size so that people could eat without worrying about utensils. Every single offering was beautiful and displayed a level of skill that I could only dream to achieve one day.

"Yes, that can be a problem." Tae nodded as if he'd heard my thoughts. "I recommend these two." He pointed at a round tinted green and then a loaf with a shiny top. "The green one is flavored with an herb similar to dill and the loaf is a savory sweet bread that's my absolute favorite."

"Thank you," I said in relief and sliced myself a piece of each.

"My pleasure. I can advise you on the rest as well."

Tae took me down the table, pointing out his favorites as he snagged them and stuck them on his plate. By the time we reached the dessert section, our plates were full, and I wound up pouting at the cream puffs.

"We can come back for more." Tae patted my shoulder reassuringly.

"All right." I followed him to an empty table—a tiny round thing that only sat four.

A servant brought us drinks, and we set to enjoying our meal of appetizers. We were halfway through our plates—me groaning in pleasure—when the pale Princess and her critical boyfriend stepped up.

"Do you mind if we join you?" Princess Sanasenne asked.

"Of course, Your Highness." Tae started to stand.

"Oh, don't be like that, Tae. You don't have to stand for me." The Princess set her hand on Taeven's shoulder and pushed him back into his seat.

"He could have been standing to greet me," the man chided her.

"Oh, how rude of me," the Princess declared. "By all means, let the reunion commence. The Terrible Two back together."

Terrible Two?

Taeven grinned and got to his feet. "Thalsar, how are you?" he asked as he shook the man's hand.

"Excellent, thank you."

"As am I," Sanasenne declared brightly, her tone warming her cool coloring.

"But look at you—the conquering hero, returning with a valorian on his arm," Thalsar said and turned his bright green gaze on me pointedly.

"Thal, this is Shane," Tae waved a hand toward me and then the man. "Shane, this is General Thalsar of the Royal Falcon Army."

"General?" I asked in surprise.

"I'm his replacement," Thalsar said with a nod toward Tae as he held out a chair for the Princess. "Someone has to watch over the troops while this guy is off saving the continent."

The General took the seat across from Sanasenne as Tae resumed his. I stared from princess to warlord to general, trying to process what was happening. Taeven had prepared me for the worst, but he didn't mention that he had a friendship with the princess and her boyfriend general. That felt odd to me. I lifted a brow at him.

"We became friends during our training," Tae explained.

"The three of you trained together?" I asked. Then added, "Your Highness."

"Don't worry about all that." Princess Sanasenne waved off the title. "Call me Sana."

"Oh, I don't know if I should—"

"I insist," she cut me off. Then, to Taeven, she added, "He's beautiful. His skin is amazing."

"Yes, he is, and it is," Tae said. "But you can compliment him directly instead of saying it to me as if I had anything to do with it."

I had to hold back my snort.

"But you did have something to do with it," she protested. "Giving him a piece of your soul made him pretty, didn't it?"

I stiffened.

"No, Shane was attractive before the change," Tae said firmly. "In fact, we were together before I made him my valorian."

"Are you saying that you were lovers *before* he proved his valor to you?" Thalsar asked in shock.

"No." Tae shot me a grin. "Shane saved my life first. I was compelled to change him, but he refused."

"Refused?!" Thalsar nearly shrieked.

"That's right." Tae's grin turned into a smirk. "He didn't want to be immortal or fae. I had to convince him to accept."

"You seduced him into being your valorian?" Sanasenne asked, then appeared to remember Tae's chiding and looked at me to repeat the question, "He seduced you into becoming valorian?"

"I wouldn't call it a seduction," I said. "It was more about us getting to know each other."

"But you said you were lovers," Thalsar said to Tae.

"We were. We *are*. But that came after we spent some time together as friends."

"How fascinating," Sanasenne murmured, then studied me as if I were an oddity. "Why wouldn't you want to be immortal?"

"I'd rather not get into it. Let's just say that I believe mortality has its perks."

"Perks?" She was horrified. "What could—"

"Sana!" Tae said sharply.

"What? I just don't see—"

"Remember that he was human," Tae growled. "And that half my army is human as well. Do not insult them."

Sanasenne sat back. "Well, you've changed."

"It's been over twenty years. It happens," Taeven said dryly.

"It's been over twenty years since you've been home?" I asked Tae in surprise.

"I've been busy." Tae grinned at me.

"And you've forgotten all about your old friends it seems," Thalsar drawled.

"Of course, I haven't," Tae protested. "But I *have* changed."

"Well, we've missed you, old friend." Thalsar set a hand on Tae's shoulder. "Let's go out tomorrow night—dinner and the usual."

"No," Tae said in a way that had me wondering what the usual was.

"Fine." Thalsar rolled his eyes. "Dinner at your place. Would that make you feel safer?"

"Safer?" I asked. "What is it that you three used to do together?"

"Nothing," Tae said with a pointed look at the General. "It was a long time ago."

"Yes, I suppose it was," Thalsar drawled as he stood.

Wow, well that was a short reunion. I blinked at the General's abruptness.

"We'll see you tomorrow night around seven, Falcon Lord," Sanasenne declared in a tone that wouldn't be refused. Then she nodded at me. "Falcon Valorian."

"Your Highness," I replied warily. Something was off, and I had a feeling that I didn't want to know what it was.

"Princess." Thalsar extended a hand to help Sanasenne up.

She took it but kissed Tae's cheek before she stood. The couple strode off, courtiers bowing to them respectfully.

"Wow." I shook my head. "You must have some interesting stories about them. The Terrible Two?"

"Sana came up with that, but it was usually Thal getting us into trouble." Tae rolled his eyes. "Being a general and consort to the Princess gives him a lot of leeway."

"Ah, I see." I didn't really. "Would you hate me if I said the Princess was kinda bitchy?"

Tae laughed brightly. "Sana can be very arrogant, especially when it comes to being Sidhe. She's never ventured out of Varalorre, so her image of humans isn't the most accurate."

"And that means what exactly?"

Tae shrugged. "The facts are that humans are mortal, physically weaker, and less advanced both magically and technologically than the Fae. Certain assumptions can be made from those facts."

"You sound as if you made those assumptions yourself."

"I did," he admitted readily. "I was just like them once. But then I became the warlord of an interracial army, and I realized that those things are generalities. They describe physical conditions and limitations that have nothing to do with who humans truly are."

"Well said. And thanks for saying I was attractive before the change."

"You were."

"But not as attractive as I am now?" I lifted a brow at him.

"Are you trying to start a fight with me?" Tae scowled. "Yes, I think you're more attractive now, and I believe you think the same thing, so why are you giving me shit about it?"

"Sorry." I grimaced. "Maybe I feel guilty for thinking that."

"Beauty is subjective and shallow; it only goes skin deep and yet it can be transformed by what lies beneath. Look at Sanasenne for example. She's stunning, but after hearing her speak so callously, even knowing that she wasn't trying to be malicious, her beauty faded for me."

I almost asked him about the General; if his beauty had faded and how close they'd been in the past. What kind of trouble exactly they had gotten into. But whatever had happened between them, it was over now. Twenty years had passed without them contacting each other, so they couldn't be that close. And, frankly, it might be best if I never knew what they'd been to each other, be it close friends or more. I didn't need those images in my head when I was kissing Tae. And it was his business, not mine.

"Are you ready for dessert?" Tae asked.

"Does it include sprinkling gerris powder over your cock?" I whispered.

Tae burst out laughing. "Later, Valorian. We're going to dance, remember?"

"Oh!" I exclaimed. "I forgot about the dancing."

"Why don't we dance first, then have dessert?" Tae suggested. "Hopefully, we'll work up an appetite."

"Oh, I'm counting on it, Falcon Lord," I declared as I got to my feet.

Chapter Twenty-Eight

I've danced before, but it had been with a woman and always of a more casual nature. Loud, joyous music, that sort of thing. Nothing like dancing at the Royal Palace with Taeven.

When we reached the dance floor, I stood at the edge of it and just gawked like the bumpkin I was. The couples were practically embracing as they glided across the polished marble floor to the romantic music. It was the only section of the room where the floor had been left bare, and when I saw how the faeries drew their feet across it, it became obvious why. This was not a clapping, stomping barn dance. Far from it. I don't know why I had expected anything but.

"Um, I don't know how to dance like this," I whispered to Taeven.

"We can dance however we wish." He held his hand out to me. "Just follow my lead."

I took Taeven's hand, and he pulled me against his chest. With one hand on my waist and the other still holding mine but lifted, Tae exerted enough push and pull to guide me in the direction he wanted me to go. I followed his sliding foot movements, and soon, we were moving as elegantly as the rest of them.

Swept up in the music and the floating dance, I stared up at Tae and smiled. "This is amazing."

"You're a natural," he said approvingly. "Very graceful."

"Thanks." I glanced around. Then I whispered, "There are women dancing with women."

"And men with men, like us," he said matter-of-factly. "There is no limit on love in Varalorre."

"That's . . ." I trailed off when I caught an imperious stare —directed not at me but Tae.

"What is it?" he asked.

"Nothing." I stroked his cheek, feeling blissfully free to be able to do that while dancing with him.

The only other place I could be this open about my sexuality was in camp, which is another reason why I enjoyed my job. But my friends would laugh their asses off if they saw me dancing like this. The fact that Tae was looked down on by some of these idiots bothered me but it also, in a way, made me feel closer to him. It was yet another thing that made him more real and less god-like. It was reassuring to know that not everyone worshiped him. Still, I didn't like their snobbery.

So I drew him to a stop in the middle of the dancing couples, grabbed the back of his neck, and pulled him down into a kiss. Tae tensed in surprise at first, then melted against me, his arms circling me to pull me closer. I put all of my love for him in that kiss and let the faeries around us see it. I wanted them to know that their new valorian adored the Falcon Lord. To remind them that it was he who chose me, and the Goddess who had approved of *his* choice. That to both her and me, noble blood didn't mean shit.

Give me a buff farm boy over a simpering nobleman any day.

When I eased back, Tae's stare was tender. He stroked my cheek and pressed his forehead to mine. Around us, the faeries danced, but I saw their wide-eyed stares out of the corner of my eye, a few of them disapproving. Let them gawk and sneer; they couldn't hurt us in Varalorre. For that matter, no one could hurt us anywhere. Not off a battlefield anyway. I may not like the notion that faeries were better than humans, but by making me fae, Tae had given me the world. We could go anywhere, well almost anywhere, and dance just as freely as we did here. We could hold hands and go to dinner alone, like any straight couple. Or even stand in the middle of a dance floor and kiss. No one would tell us that we couldn't, and the only nasty stares we'd get would have nothing to do with our sexuality. I don't know why that felt better, but it did.

"I find myself in desperate need of dessert," Tae said as he lifted his head.

"Nuh-uh." I shook my head and stepped back to settle into a dancing pose. "You said we were going to enjoy the shit out of this party, and that's what we're going to do. It's in our honor after all."

"More yours than mine," he said as he began leading me around the floor again, but there was no bitterness in his tone. In fact, he sounded pleased.

"Will I be attending the meeting with the King tomorrow?" I asked.

Tae blinked at the sudden shift in conversation. "No, you will be in school."

"School?"

"The Falcon Academy, where young Falcon Faeries learn how to shift and perform magic."

"Will I be in a classroom with a bunch of kids?" I grinned.

"No, I believe they'll assign you a private tutor."

"Aw, bummer. I would have loved to see all the baby faeries."

"You'll still see them." He swung me around a gawking couple. "You just won't be in a classroom with them."

I glanced around, making sure the Princess wasn't anywhere near us before I asked, "Would you be upset if I asked to postpone that dinner with the Princess and General? I would have liked to spend my first night in Varalorre with just you, but since we had to come to court, I was hoping that maybe tomorrow night could be ours."

"Welcome to status." Tae grimaced. "As a valorian, just as it is with a warlord, certain things are expected of you and one of them is entertaining royalty. I can try to put off Sana, but she can be pushy, especially when she gets the impression that you're pushing back. If I make an excuse, they'll likely show up anyway."

"We'll be out." I shrugged.

"We'll have to come home sometime," he shot back. "Let's just get this out of the way and then we can have the next night together. It's not as if we won't be alone later tonight and after they leave tomorrow night."

"You make a convincing argument, Falcon Lord." I smirked.

"I'll also make it up to you with butter and gerris powder," he promised, a twinkle in his eye.

"I suddenly like your friends a lot more."

Tae burst into laughter.

Chapter Twenty-Nine

We danced to several more songs before we had our dessert, and I was surprised when people started to approach us. A few of them were snide but most seemed genuine when they welcomed me to Varalorre and Taeven home. We spoke with them over delicate cups of tea and tiny plates heaped with beautiful and decadent desserts, and it was then that I began to feel truly at home. I understood how a few nasty people could ruin a group for someone, so I didn't blame Tae for not making the effort with the courtiers, but he'd discounted them as a whole when it was only a handful who were assholes. Judging by Tae's lifted brows, he had come to that conclusion as well.

The Princess and her General came by again after a large group had formed around us, and although they were offered seats, they chose to remain standing—flanking Taeven's chair like a couple of birds on perches. The way they casually touched him and the lazy looks they gave me told me that I was the outsider there, and I was still on probation. Instead of bothering me, this put me at ease; it was similar to the way my friends would have treated Tae if he hadn't been a warlord. I concluded that the Princess and General were merely trying to watch out for their buddy, and that made me like them more. I smiled and nodded to them in acknowledgment, content that I understood them better now. Maybe it wouldn't be such a bad thing to have dinner with them. After all, Sana hadn't been horrible, just a bit arrogant as far as the Fae were concerned; I could get over that.

At the end of the night, Tae and I both left lighthearted, with grins on our faces. I didn't even mind the blast of cold air that smacked my face when we stepped out of the palace. We snuggled in the carriage on the way back to Tae's home and were met at the door by a maid, who offered us mugs of tea as if she'd been keeping a pot warm just for us. She probably had.

The luxury of the way Tae lived was astonishing, but I felt comfortable there knowing that he hadn't been raised to expect this either. He had fought for it and earned it. He deserved these things, and I got to enjoy them because he chose to share them with me. That made it special instead of offensive.

"Mari, could you have a pot of tea and some toast sent up?" Tae asked the maid.

"Yes, my lord."

After we were in the elevator heading upstairs, I asked, "Toast? I mean, the tea is nice." I lifted my mug. "But aren't you full?"

"Toast comes with *butter*, Shane." Tae gave me a wicked look. "I didn't want to ask her to send up a bowl of butter and nothing else. That would have the entire staff talking."

"Oh!" I started to smile. "Smart thinking, Falcon Lord." Then I remembered what I'd kept forgetting to ask him. "Hey, why do you keep introducing me with your last name?"

"Oh, I should have explained that to you." Tae's naughty look faded into a serious one. "Giving you a piece of my soul also means that I've given you a piece of my magic. That magic is what the Goddess used to transform you. Therefore, you are of my line."

"Like a son?" I grimaced.

"Similar but we aren't related, the magic is. And so you

take my name."

"Whoa," I whispered.

"Is that all right?"

"Yeah, it's fine. I was just wondering what it was all about." I thought about it and added, "Maybe don't mention it to my parents when you meet them."

"You can still be Ruhara in the human world."

"If we ever get married, you could take my last name among the humans, then we can have both," I said without thinking.

"Married, eh?" Taeven lifted a dark-gold brow. "And you want me to take your name?"

"I was just, uh, it was . . . it just came out." I flushed.

Tae chortled, then pulled me into a kiss. A very hot kiss —both in passion and temperature. We held our mugs of tea to the side as our lips melded, but he pulled me close with his free arm, holding me tight to his chest. Then the elevator chimed, and the panel opened.

Tae pulled back and smiled softly at me. "You're allowed to think about the future, Shane, as long as you don't worry about it. And I'm glad that you see me in it."

He took my hand and led me through the dark sitting room, into his bedroom, then let me go to turn on the bedside lamps, leaving the chandelier off to give the room a soft illumination that enhanced the moonlight instead of competing with it. I followed him into the dressing room where we disrobed, then re-robed in, well, robes. Tae handed me a thick, cerulean velvet garment, embroidered with gold at the cuffs, while he slid on a black one that turned his hair into shining ribbons.

Taking my hand, he led me into the bathroom—an expanse of pale marble, snowy porcelain, and silver fixtures. For a moment, a glittering view of the city appeared through the picture window behind the tub, drapes pulled open to frame it, but then the lights came on and mirrored the glass. Above us, glass globes hung from the coffered ceiling like a bunch of grapes, each one containing a fae light, and silver-framed mirrors hung over the counter that ran half the length of the room, crowned by falcons with spread wings. The massive tub had a spigot in the shape of a falcon as well, but Tae didn't head toward it. Instead, he went to the shower stall—large enough to fit five—and turned on the spray.

As we shrugged out of our robes, I noted, "Your tub has a spitting falcon."

"My tub has a what?" Tae looked at the tub and cocked his head in consideration. "I suppose it would be more of a vomiting falcon."

"Gross." I squished my face at him while he laughed.

"My lord?" A voice came from the bedroom.

"Just leave it on the dresser, Mari," Tae called out to her.

"Yes, my lord."

"Our butter has arrived." Tae waggled his brows at me. "But first, I want you squeaky clean."

"I will scrub until I squeak," I promised. "Then you can get me dirty again."

We stepped into the shower, and Tae closed the glass panel behind us. As soon as he did, the back wall of the stall lit up and a painting came to life. A forest scene at midday—sun shining onto a meadow in the distance—had been painted on the thick glass wall, unseen until it was illuminated. As I gaped at that, the sound of birdsong came from above me.

"What the fuck is this?" I looked from the painting to the ceiling and back again.

Tae laughed his ass off.

Finally, he said, "This is the ultimate shower system, the Forest Glen 3000, complete with birdsong and scented mist settings." He hit a button on the wall and warm steam, scented lightly with pine, filtered in through vents at the bottom of the walls. "It also has twenty spray settings." He pushed another button and the water—coming from a huge disc-shaped showerhead hung directly above us—began to fall stronger, then in thicker drops, then in a gentle spray. "When I furnished this place, I had it installed. It makes me feel as if I'm showering outdoors."

"This is fucking ridiculous," I declared. "I love it!" I started pushing buttons, and the scent changed to wildflowers while the spray shifted direction.

Tae chuckled and stepped into the water while I played. But then he was wet and running his big, warlord hands over all those big warlord muscles, and I forgot about the buttons. I was grateful we were in the shower because I was on the verge of drooling. Then his hand reached out and grabbed a sea sponge hanging from a ribbon on a hook. He held it beneath the pump of a blue glass bottle set on a silver ledge and dispensed some liquid onto it. A few squeezes and the sponge got soapy. Then his body got soapy.

I whimpered.

"Come here," Tae's voice dropped to a low, sensual tone.

I stepped forward, and he began to wash my chest. With a sigh, I leaned my head back to enjoy his touch. His hands swept around to my back and pulled me forward as he ran the sponge over me from shoulders to ass. And as Tae washed my back, he rubbed himself against my soapy front. The slippery feel of him was so surprisingly erotic that my cock rose to nudge his. A gentle spray of water sent the soap downward to collect there and soon, the slippery feeling extended to my shaft.

"Oh, fuck, I don't think I can wait for the butter," I whispered.

"You *will* wait," Tae said into my ear before he nipped it. "*I've* been waiting to suck your buttered cock for days, and I will not be denied."

He stepped back, breaking contact with me completely, and finished washing himself.

"But . . ." I whimpered again.

Tae grinned and handed me the sponge. "Squeaking clean, Captain."

I started scrubbing myself rapidly and a bit roughly as he rinsed off. Taeven's grin turned devilish as he leaned his head under the spray to wet his hair. He stepped out of the water so I could rinse, but took his sweet ass time washing his hair, then conditioning it. My hair was clean in thirty seconds and when I was done, I didn't wait for him or bother with conditioner. Instead, I hurried out, dried off, and practically ran into the bedroom. Tae's laughter followed me out.

"We'll see if he's laughing in a few minutes," I murmured to myself as I went to fetch the gerris powder out of my satchel.

When I returned, I heard the water cut off. Cursing, I hurried to the tray of tea and toast. The butter was there all right—a little ramekin of it, whipped and piped into pretty peaks. I dipped a finger in, then rubbed the stuff over my cock as I ran to Tae's enormous bed, water dripping down my back from my damp hair.

Cock buttered, I sucked the remnants off my fingers

before opening the bottle of powder. A sweet, almost vanilla scent hit my nose. It had a tinge of caramel to it, or maybe almond. I sprinkled the pink powder over my dick, capped the bottle, and set it on the bedside table. My erection glittered at me tauntingly, and I couldn't help but swipe my finger over it and have a taste. The flavor of fresh cookies, berries, and cream hit me, sending me reeling back onto the pillows with a moan of delight.

"Dear Goddess," Tae whispered from the bathroom doorway. "Now that's a sight I wouldn't mind seeing every night."

I managed to open my eyes and swing my head to face him, but my gaze was heavy lidded and my body twitching in pleasure.

"Have you been playing with yourself while you waited for me?" Tae grinned as he strode to the bed, his naked body gleaming in the moonlight and his damp hair clinging to his glorious chest in golden ribbons.

"Nope." I sighed. "I just had my first taste of gerris powder."

"That good, eh?" His gaze went to my cock and he licked his lips. "Spread your legs for your warlord, Valorian. I'm suddenly ravenous."

As my heartbeat sped up, I spread my legs, bending them at the knees to give him even more room. Tae wasn't the only one looking forward to this. I felt as if the pleasure had been snatched away from me that day in Fellbrook. Now, at last, I would feel his mouth on me. I caught my breath as Taeven settled his body between my legs, his broad shoulders pressing into my thighs, and, with his gaze locked on my cock, lowered his mouth to me.

Heaven. Pure, zinging bliss. I cried out brokenly as the wet heat and firm grip of Tae's mouth consumed me. But I couldn't look away, couldn't close my eyes and toss my head as I wanted to. Not with those sexy lips tightening around me and that beautiful man between my thighs. Tae held me steady with just a ring of his fingers at my base so he didn't waste any of the flavoring. He groaned in rapture as he sucked his way down, nearly to the base—further than any man had gone with me. He drew upward, sucking me hard, then angled his head to lick the base of my cock free of butter and powder.

"You really like that stuff," I murmured as I slid my hand into his hair.

"The flavor is addictive." Tae glanced up at me, his amethyst eyes dark in the low lights but glittering with those gold striations. "But combined with your cock, it becomes irresistible. We're going to have to buy a vat of this powder."

I chuckled as he went back to licking my base clean, then returned to my weeping tip to lick the bead of moisture forming there. It set him to groaning again, and he dove over my cock, sucking me avidly. It was all I could do to keep from thrusting up into him; he was that fucking good. Instead, I sprawled beneath him, twitching uncontrollably under the lavish attention of that strong tongue and even stronger lips. Alternating between rapid strokes of his hand and strong sucking, the Falcon lord had my body tensing toward completeness in a matter of minutes.

"I could suck your cock all night," Tae declared as he stroked me.

"No, you can't," I panted. "If you don't stop, I'm going to come in a few seconds."

"Are you now?" He grinned and eagerly sucked me back into his mouth.

"Tae! Tae, I'm going to come!"

He kept going.

My body convulsed as the Falcon Lord worked his magic on me, and I erupted into his talented mouth, his deep moans ratcheting my orgasm to a higher level. I couldn't look away from the sight of his rapturous expression and his throat working as he swallowed. My legs flopped open further as I panted my way down from the heights he'd taken me to, and Tae lazily sucked his way off me.

Then he rose to his knees—this glorious man who'd given me more pleasure than any man had before him—and he took his cock in hand. As he stroked nectar over it, he commanded, "Pull up those legs, lover. Pull them up and out as high as you can. I want to see it all."

I groaned, shivering from his words alone. As I grabbed the back of my knees and yanked my legs up and out as far as I could, my cock gave a twitch, already coming back to life.

"You are so fucking sexy," Tae murmured as he leaned forward and drew a finger over my hole, coating it with nectar. "Look at that pretty, pink hole, puckered like a pair of lips ready to be kissed."

I groaned. "Fuck me!"

"Not yet." He slipped his finger inside me and started a gentle pumping. "I want you hard again."

"I just came," I whined.

"Yes, I know." Tae grinned wickedly and started playing with my balls.

"Oh, God," I whispered.

His finger twirled, stretching me open, then he added a second. "Get that dick hard, Captain," he ordered. "I want to see it dripping onto your chest while I fuck you."

And damn if my cock didn't obey.

"There we go," Tae said approvingly as he worked his fingers deeper. "Nice and hard and so fucking thick."

"Now, fuck me!"

He leaned down and licked me from base to tip. "So delicious."

"Damn it all! Fuck me, Tae!" I yelled.

"You don't have to shout, Shane," Tae purred as he removed his fingers. "Just ask *nicely*."

"Please side that big dick into my ass and fuck me deep, Falcon Lord." I gave him the look I used when I sang.

"That's better."

That thick, slick plum tip nestled against my aching hole and eased inside with an almost audible pop. My muscles clenched around Tae and drew him in as I pulled my legs even wider apart, bringing my asshole into a prime fucking position. And Taeven made use of it. He shoved in fully with one thrust, making us both cry out, and then went still for a moment. I was about to start begging again when he leaned forward, setting his palms to the mattress on either side of me, and began a steady thrusting.

"Oh, yeah," I moaned. "Just like that, babe. You're hitting spots no one has before."

"Am I?" Tae asked breathlessly, his stare raking my body. "You like that?"

"You know I do."

"Tell me. Say it."

"I love that big cock inside me," I said eagerly. Dirty talk done right was one of my turn-ons. "Stretching me wide, fucking me deep. No one does it like you, Tae."

"You squeeze me so tightly," he groaned, stretching his neck luxuriously. "Like a fist. The perfect fit for me." He looked down at me, his expression softening. "I'm so glad you're mine, Shane. You are mine, aren't you?"

"Heart and soul, baby," I whispered.

Tae shuddered, then started a faster pace. His hair, even damp, lashed about him with his wild thrusts, his expression sliding into savagery again. I grinned wickedly and rested my legs on his shoulders so I could stroke the bulging muscles of his arms. He bent further over me, nearly folding me in two, and lost his damn mind. But it was all right; I was sane enough for both of us. I held on tightly as my warlord went feral, and then I was shouting again, this time his name, and coming all over myself. Tae's eyes widened appreciatively, then he gave one last pump before pulling out and adding his release to mine.

My legs flopped down onto the bed as Tae eased back, then he dropped onto the pillow beside me with a serene look on his face. He was out in three seconds flat, his chest rising and falling gently with his deep breaths. I chuckled at his exhaustion and slipped out of bed to go rinse off. When I got back, he was just as I'd left him—naked across the covers, his cock limp and glossy. I folded the comforter over him and slipped beneath the sheet and lighter blanket beneath. Tae snuggled into his cocoon with a sigh, and I watched his face as I drifted off to sleep, hoping he'd follow me into my dreams.

Chapter Thirty

I woke to rosy sunshine streaming in through the balcony doors—perfect for my mood. Sighing, I slipped out of bed, giving the puffy roll that was Taeven a grin. I shrugged on the robe I'd discarded at the foot of the bed and headed into the bathroom. After taking care of the morning's business, I thought about climbing back into bed with Taeven, but the allure of seeing Wynvar in daylight drew me to the balcony.

With a grand motion, I yanked the double doors open and breathed in deeply of the crisp air. That's when I remembered that it was fucking freezing outside. I cursed and slammed the doors shut, then shivered as I pulled my robe more tightly around me. Muffled laughter came from the bed.

"Shut up, you!" I said affectionately.

A hand pushed back the comforter, revealing the grinning face of the Falcon Lord. "Did you forget where we are?"

"No, I wanted to see the city in the sunshine," I huffed and turned back toward the doors, to peer through them at Wynvar. "I forgot that it was cold. It's so warm in here."

Tae came up behind me, not bothering with his robe, and wrapped his arms around me, covering my hands with his to rub them briskly. "Better?"

"Oh, yes." I snuggled closer to his heat. "And warmer too."

Taeven grinned against my skin, moving his lips up the curve of my shoulder to my throat, then lifted them to kiss my cheek. His whisper tickled my ear, "We need to get dressed."

I unbuckled my robe and spread it so he could see my erection. "Are you sure?"

Tae groaned, one hand going to my shaft to stroke it while he rubbed his against my ass. "Maybe we could make it fast."

I pushed him back, dropped my robe, and bent over, bracing myself against the glass. "Fast, slow, in between. I don't care, just fuck me."

Instead of laughing, Taeven growled in arousal and quickly rubbed nectar over himself. Seconds later, he was working himself inside me, and I pressed my face against the glass, enjoying the chill on my flushed cheek as I lowered one hand to start stroking myself. Tae began to make primal grunts behind me as his skin slapped mine and my breath fogged up the glass. Through the hazy pane, I saw movement that didn't register at first. Then I realized it was a Falcon—a faerie one, not a regular bird. It was gliding over the city, but I was almost certain that it had spotted us and was now enjoying the view.

And I was surprised at how much that excited me.

"We've got an audience," I said over my shoulder.

"What?" Tae saw the bird and grunted. "Do you want me to stop?"

"No, let's give them something really naughty to watch."

Tae made an approving, delighted sound and leaned forward. "Put your arm back and wrap it around my neck."

I did, and he swept his arms beneath my thighs. I yelped as he hooked my legs and lifted me, spreading my thighs so that I was on full display to the Falcon, who now circled closer. Holding my weight as I gripped his neck and set my feet against the glass for stability, Tae began to thrust up into me rapidly. My cock flopped until I grabbed it with my free hand and started stroking it again. The Falcon flew closer, close enough that I could see his plumage and the way he angled his head to focus one dark eye on us.

"Oh, fuck, this is so fucking hot," I panted. "Look at him watching us."

"I'd rather watch you." Tae met my gaze in our ghostly reflection, laid over the view of the bird. "That strong body spread open. My cock sliding into it. And your dick throbbing in your hand." He groaned. "You like being watched because you're so fucking beautiful. Because we're beautiful together."

"No, I think it's more of a bragging thing." I grinned at him. "I like showing someone else how good I have it."

"You like being mine?" his voice dropped into a low, possessive tone.

I laughed in delight even as pleasure rippled through me. "I like chocolate. Being yours is on another level entirely."

"Better than chocolate, eh?" his possessive tone lightened to amusement.

"Better than chocolate *cake*," I groaned as he slowed his pace, drawing himself in and out with delicious smoothness but punctuating the height of each thrust with a sharp jerk of his hips. "I've never been fucked like this—held like this." I angled my head back for a fast kiss.

"That Falcon is going home to masturbate to thoughts of you. To thoughts of you stroking that huge dick while I fuck you. Do you like knowing that?"

"Oh, yeah. And I like knowing that they can't have you."

I paused as I realized that we hadn't discussed exclusivity. "Right, Tae? You're mine too, right?"

"Of course, I'm yours. There will be no sharing for either of us." Then his voice sank into a growl, "This is all I'll allow others to have of you. Do you understand me, Shane?"

I grinned broadly. "I love you, Tae; I don't want anyone else."

Tae groaned and sped up. No, he didn't just speed up, he slid into that wild lust and began driving into me so fast and hard that my grip on his neck became integral.

With a primal growl Tae demanded, "Stroke yourself faster, baby, I'm about to come."

I stroked faster; it didn't take much. "Tae, I'm coming!"

Tae pulled out and as he climaxed on the floor, I came across the glass. The Falcon outside shrieked, probably in gratitude, and spun in an arch to fly away.

Chapter Thirty-One

"Does that happen often?" I asked Taeven as we snuggled in his carriage on the way to the Falcon Academy.

"What?" He angled his head to look at me.

"Voyeurs flying past windows."

"Ah, Falcons often fly over the city, and our eyesight is very good in that form. I'm sure all sorts of things are accidentally seen, but most faeries would never deliberately spy on others." His expression tightened. "Did you not enjoy it? We don't have to do that again."

"No, I did. I just don't enjoy the thought of someone watching me when I don't know they're there."

"Oh, good." He settled back with a grin. "Was that the first time you . . . put yourself on display?"

"It was," I admitted. "And I'm surprised at how much I liked it. Especially since I don't know who was watching."

"Yes, that makes it more thrilling." Something shifted in his eyes.

"So, you've done that before?" I moved so I could see his face better.

"Shane, you know that I've taken multiple people to my bed at once. That, in itself, is a type of exhibitionism."

"Not really," I protested. "You're all participating. No one's just watching."

"True."

"So?"

"So?" Tae repeated.

"Have you done that before?" I shoved at his chest in exasperation. "Have you had sex while someone else watched?"

Taeven's expression went guarded. "Yes."

"That's it?"

"Did you want details?" He lifted a brow at me.

I blinked. "No, I guess not."

Tae sighed. "Shane, I'm a lot older than you. I've had more time to experiment sexually."

"How much older?" I scowled.

"I'm two hundred sixteen."

"Two *hundred*?!" I gaped at him.

"Sixteen," he finished for me and nodded. "I'm assuming that makes me nearly two centuries older than you."

"I'm twenty-eight," I whispered.

"As I said."

"Holy shit."

"You will live to be my age," he said gently. "At least, if everything goes well."

"Holy shit," I said again, the weight of immortality finally hitting me. I'd been riding high on a cloud of love, ignoring the fact that I had done something I didn't want to do. Ignoring the ramifications of my actions.

"Shane, are you all right?"

"Yeah, I'm fine," I whispered. "I just . . . holy shit. I just realized that I'll likely bury my brother."

"But you'll also be able to promise him that you will look after his children and his children's children," Tae said as he took my hand. "What a gift that will be to a parent, don't you agree?"

A shiver coasted through me. "I hadn't thought of that. I could become the family guardian."

"In a way." He nodded. "You can become whatever you wish, Shane. That's what I've been trying to tell you. Immortality gives you the freedom to work on your dreams until they become reality."

"Thank you." I kissed his cheek. "I feel much better now."

"Good." Tae grinned and looked out the window. "Because it's time for your first day of school."

I followed his gaze to a grand set of stairs leading to an even grander door—single, not double, with golden hinges and a central point. Our driver folded down the carriage steps and opened the door for us, and Tae waved me out ahead of him. I climbed out and stepped forward to stare up at the soaring edifice of the Falcon Academy. Two wings stretched off the main keep, curving out like real wings to surround the roundabout we'd parked on. Towers crowned the keep, that central building rising many floors higher than the wings, and bridges arched from tower to tower. Falcons jumped off those bridges to glide above me in complicated patterns, their massive bodies spotting the pale sky.

"Whoa," I whispered.

"Yes, whoa." Tae took my hand and led me up the stairs. "I'll see you settled, then I have to leave for the Royal Palace. But I shouldn't be long. I'll come back and take you to lunch."

"All right," I said distractedly.

Taeven opened the door for me, and we strode into a cathedral-like entry hall whose soaring, steepled rafters were home to crossbeams, upon which Falcon Faeries perched—some in Sidhe form, naked, with their legs dangling over the sides, casually shooting the breeze with their friends. A skeleton of a Falcon hung from one thick beam in the center of the hall, its giant wings outstretched to show off every bone. Beneath it, robed scholars hurried by us with imperious expressions while younger Sidhe congregated in groups. They hardly noticed us, but I hardly noticed them too; I was too busy staring up at the skeleton.

"Someone you know?" I asked Tae.

Tae tried to hold in his laugh and ended up snorting. "Actually, I do know who that is, though I wasn't personally acquainted with him. That's Gerhan Unvellor, the first Headmaster of the Falcon Academy."

"And you guys stuck him up there because . . ."

"Because it was a way to honor him and, more importantly, he asked for it. Not only asked for, but also provided the spell to shift his body back to falcon form after death," Tae said. "Now, he's forever watching over the Academy."

"I suppose it's similar to the way they have human skeletons for medical students to study. It's kind of incredible and kind of morbid," I murmured, still staring at it.

"I think it leans more toward incredible," Tae said firmly.

"It leans more toward the left." I cocked my head to appreciate the angle of the wings that really brought the skeleton to life—as much as that was possible.

Tae snickered. "When I went to school here, there was a running dare for someone to steal one of the bones."

"It doesn't look as if that would be too difficult. What with all the students flying around it."

"It has a protection spell on it."

I finally looked away from the bird to lift my brows at him. "They actually thought to protect the skeleton from theft?"

"No." He rolled his eyes. "The protection is against the ravages of time. Without the magic that inhabited those bones when Unvellor was alive, they'll eventually decay. It just so happened that the preservation spell is also useful to preserve the bones against tampering. Any attempt to remove one bone from the rest causes a defensive reaction."

"And you know this how?" I smirked knowingly at him.

"Thankfully, I was not the unlucky fool who attempted the theft, but I was with him." Tae snickered in memory. "It knocked him onto his feathered ass."

"Did you try it in the middle of the day?"

"No, we snuck in—"

"Falcon Lord?" A woman approached us, and Tae quickly clammed up about his childhood criminal activities.

The woman's chestnut hair was touched with gold and hung over one slim shoulder in a long braid. Although she wore the robes of a scholar, her feminine form was evident beneath it in a very alluring way, but it was her beautiful face that drew the most attention. Sultry lips, big blue eyes, and long lashes. I glanced at Tae and saw his eyes widen in appreciation.

I hated her instantly.

"Yes?" Taeven smiled at her, making me grind my teeth together.

I had to remind myself that Tae had told me just an hour earlier that he was mine, and we were not sharing. Also, I was not an insecure man. Or clingy. Or cynical. No, he still hadn't said the L-word to me, but he'd basically said that we were in a fully committed relationship. No need to get nervous around ridiculously beautiful women who had body parts that Tae might be lusting for—body parts that I didn't have.

"I'm Mistress Avanla. I've been chosen to be the Valorian's teacher."

Oh, great.

"Nice to meet you." Taeven shook her hand. "This is Shane Rumerra, the Falcon Valorian."

"Hi." I grudgingly shook her hand.

"It's an honor to meet you, Valorian." She looked me over in the way Tae had looked at her. "You have the most beautiful skin."

"Thank you." All right, maybe she wasn't horrible.

"Yes, he does." Tae stroked my back. "The Goddess was good to me."

"Flatterer," I teased, but inwardly, I was overjoyed.

"I have to meet with the King," Tae said to Mistress Avanla. "But I'll return as soon as I'm able. Where will you two be?"

"Oh, in the library, I'd think. I've been advised that valorians learn best through books, so I've chosen a few books on shifting for the Valorian to read before we try anything physical. And, uh, just to warn you, His Majesty has asked me to attempt a rapid instruction."

"What does that mean?" I asked warily.

"I'm to push you to learn as quickly as possible and advance to lessons as soon as you've shown competency in the previous." She made a face. "This is not how I normally teach. I think a student should master each lesson before proceeding."

"Then perhaps a compromise?" Tae offered. "Advance to the next lesson once you feel that he's capable and not just competent."

Avanla smiled in relief. "Yes, that would be much safer."

"Safer?" I asked. "Is learning magic dangerous?"

"Some types of magic can be, yes," Mistress Avanla admitted. "But only if you don't know what you're doing. I will make sure that you are prepared, Valorian."

"Please, call me Shane."

"And you can drop my mistress title too." She leaned in to whisper, "It's so stuffy, don't you think? It makes me feel as if I'm five centuries old."

Five centuries. I blinked at that. "Yeah, totally stuffy."

"Well, I'll leave you to it then," Tae said, then bent down to give me a quick kiss goodbye. "I'll see you soon."

"All right," I murmured as I watched him leave.

"He's absolutely dreamy." Avanla wagged her eyebrows at me. "Well done, you."

I chuckled. "Thank you. We'll see if I can keep him."

Avanla frowned. "It's in doubt?"

I shrugged. "He's not as emotionally invested as I am.

Not yet. But we've only been courting for about five days. Today makes six, I think." I blinked. "Wow, I can't believe it's been less than a week since all this started."

"Time is irrelevant where love is concerned." Avanla stared at me pensively. "I don't know either of you well yet, but you can't get much more committed than giving up a piece of your soul."

"Yes, but that was done out of duty."

"Was it now?" She grinned teasingly.

"Wasn't it?"

"Oh, I'm sure it was. It's supposed to be a human's valor that inspires a warlord to share his soul with them; that's the whole point. It's why you're called a *valor*-ian." She grinned broadly. "But after seeing the Falcon Lord interact with you and going by what I've heard of the bond between a warlord and his valorian, I'd wager that the reasons he chose you are not the same reasons that he continues to choose you. I think you are correct to add the 'yet' to your statement. If the Falcon Lord is lacking in his emotional response currently, he will not be for long."

I chuckled. "So, you're a matchmaker and a scholar?"

Avanla grinned. "Ah, love. Who can resist it?"

Taeven, apparently. But, I knew I was being unreasonable in my petulance, which is why I'd keep my issues to myself. It had only been two days since I'd made my confession; I couldn't expect him to fall in love with me that quickly, even if I had done so with him. And even if he acted as if we were in love. And even if my unrequited love for him was giving me an ulcer—figuratively speaking, of course. I just had to take a breath and relax. Tae wasn't going anywhere. He was mine; he'd said so unequivocally. Just because he'd said it during sex, didn't make it a lie. Ugh! This is why I don't date outside of my hotness zone. Loving someone and not being loved in return can make you crazy, and it makes every minute feel like an eternity.

"But that is not why you're here," Avanla declared, yanking me out of my crazy thoughts. "Come with me, Shane. I have a few books selected and waiting for us at a table I've reserved in the library."

"Great!" I said brightly, eager to distract myself from the insanity of loving Taeven Rumerra.

Avanla led me down a corridor to an elevator but instead of going up as I'd expected, we went down.

"The library is underground?" I asked in surprise.

"That is the best place for libraries." She winked at me. "Sunlight can damage books."

"Oh, I hadn't thought of that."

"The problem with underground libraries is the damp," she went on. "But here, our underground is technically still above ground." She giggled. "It's carved out of the mountain, not the earth, so we don't have an issue with moisture. At least, not as much as if soil surrounded the books."

"Are there many basements like this in Wynvar homes?" I asked.

"I don't know if basement is the correct term for them, but yes, many homes have rooms beneath the first floor. They make good vaults."

"Like treasure vaults?" My eyes widened.

"Precisely so." She flicked a finger in the air as if assigning me a point. "All sorts of treasure is locked away in Wynvar. But, if you ask me, the true treasure is here." She waved her hand as the elevator panel opened, almost as if she had planned her speech accordingly. "Welcome to the Great Library of Wynvar."

Avanla stepped out of the elevator and into a cavernous space—literally cavernous, what with the rock walls and domed, stone ceiling. A reception desk waited just before the elevator, with a man idly reading at it. Beyond him, several rows of heavy, wooden bookshelves stood in rows like an army at attention. I couldn't see the end of the shelves, a glance down one of the aisles ended in a reading area backed by another shelf, but the ceiling arched forward hundreds of feet. From that ceiling hung fae lights in serviceable globes, giving the space a brightness I didn't associate with libraries.

"Master Mallor, this is the Falcon Valorian, Shane Rumerra," Avanla introduced us as she stepped up to the desk.

The man looked up, looked me over, then looked again. Yep, a lot of looking was done. More of an inspection, really.

"Yes, he's pretty, isn't he?" She grinned.

The man cleared his throat and stood up to extend a hand to me. "Master Mallor, Head Librarian."

"Captain Shane, uh, Rumerra," I stumbled over Tae's name, making Avanla chuckle.

Mallor was handsome in a distracted sort of way. He had his blond hair pulled back in a tail but strands had come loose and he didn't seem to care or even notice. His robe was askew, showing an ink-stained tunic beneath, and a pen was tucked behind one ear. Since there was another pen set near his book, I had a feeling that he'd forgotten about the one behind his ear. Despite Avanla's teasing, he didn't seem embarrassed, or even certain of what she had teased him about.

"It's an honor to meet you, Valorian Captain," he said as

if that were a thing. To Avanla, he added, "Your table has been reserved, as requested, Mistress Avanla."

"Thank you, Master Mallor." She nodded primly, then escorted me past him and into the stacks. Once we were a safe distance away, she whispered, "Now, he really is stuffy."

"Like five centuries stuffy?" I teased.

"More like seven."

"What?" I hissed. "That guy is seven hundred years old?"

She blinked at me. "Don't you know that we're immortal?"

"Well, yeah, I do. I just . . . it hasn't registered until today."

"Most scholars live to be much older than Mallor," she said. "We don't venture far from our academies and don't take risks that other faeries do. So, Mallor's age isn't all that impressive."

"It is to me," I huffed.

Avanla giggled again. "It won't be for long, Shane." She took a turn and then another, leading me so deep into the library that I started to worry that Tae wouldn't be able to find us. "Here we are," she said at last, taking a turn into a rectangular space defined by bookshelves.

A heavy table dominated the area but there was also a padded chair in one corner with a small, circular table set beside it—the sort of arrangement you might find in a home library as opposed to a public one. No one occupied any of the seats, not the padded one or the wooden ones around the table. Probably because of the sign that perched atop a pile of books on the table. It read, "Reserved for Mistress Avanla and the Falcon Valorian" in beautiful script.

"Have a seat." Avanla waved her hand at a chair while she took the one opposite. As I sat down, she started putting books before me. "These are my top choices for books on the process of shifting. You may skim through them and choose one for yourself, or if you'd rather I pick, start with this one." She tapped the leather-bound book in the center of the grouping. "You may keep the others in reserve if you wish."

"So, I just start reading?"

"No. I will guide you through the book."

"All right, let's go with your pick."

"Very good." Avanla flipped the book open and began, "Here is a diagram of a Falcon body."

Chapter Thirty-Two

By the time Taeven returned, my brain felt like mush. I knew exactly what a Falcon looked like from the inside out and had the premise of shifting down. Basically, I had to envision myself as a bird and believe that I was in a Falcon body instead of a Sidhe one. That last bit was interesting. I wouldn't know how difficult it would be to believe that until I tried—which I hadn't yet—but I was betting it wasn't going to be easy. I was still trying to accept the fact that I was a faerie now, believing that I could magically transform into a bird was gonna be a hard sell. Avanla explained to me that Falcon Faerie children were told from a young age that they would be able to shift one day, and growing up around shifting adults helped as well. Believing for them was a piece of cake, but for me, it would be another story.

"Oh, you found us!" I declared when Tae walked into our little reading den. "Thank God."

"Goddess," Avanla corrected with a saucy look. "We thank the Goddess here. You, especially, should thank her."

I gave Tae the once-over and grinned. "Yeah, I guess I should."

"You look tired." Tae ran a hand over my hair—I'd been wearing it loose for him, and he couldn't seem to stop playing with it. "How about some lunch?"

"Yes, please!" I got up, then looked at Avanla. "Would you

like to join us?"

"Oh, no. You two have a nice meal together. I'll grab a bite in the cafeteria. There are some things I need to get done while you're gone. But after you get back, we can try shifting."

"I have to come back today?" I gaped at her.

Taeven burst out laughing, earning himself a few shushes from scholars in the stacks. He pressed his lips together and gave me a guilty look but didn't seem at all chastised. "Yes, you have to come back. But this time I'll be with you."

"Oh, good. You can witness my failure."

"You must stop being so negative." Avanla slapped my arm primly before heading off. "Negativity will make magic ten times harder."

Tae's look turned wincing. He had apologized for calling me negative, but now that Avanla had as well, I was beginning to wonder if I was. Just like my father says, we all have very different images of who we are and very few are the truth. Was I truly negative?

"I'll try to be more positive," I said firmly as I followed her out of the book maze.

"Good lad!" she praised, and I grimaced.

To her, I wasn't much older than the children she taught —mature but not at her level of adulthood. Which meant that she called me things like lad, boy, and young one—the last being my least favorite. Tae, seeing my grimace, snickered.

"Come to think of it, Mistress Alvana, we have some things we need to get done today. Most importantly, we need to purchase a new wardrobe for Shane," Tae said. "We're dining with the Princess tonight, and Shane has nothing to wear. Perhaps we could resume his lessons tomorrow?"

Alvana paused to look at us. I could see the indecision hovering on her face. "The King wants us to proceed as fast as possible, but I suppose he'd agree that the Valorian needs to be presentable as well. All right, I'll see you in the morning."

"Thank you," I said to Alvana, but I gave Tae a look to let him know that I meant it for him as well.

"Of course, my sweet boy," she said blithely, making me grimace at her back again after she turned away.

Tae snickered once more.

"Shut up," I hissed at him.

"My sweet boy," he whispered in my ear, making it sound naughty.

I rolled my eyes. Thankfully, he didn't say any more until we were in his carriage, riding away from the Falcon Academy. Unfortunately, he'd been saving up and came out swinging.

"Someone has a crush on you." Taeven waggled his brows at me.

"Who, Alvana?" I asked in horror. "No, she doesn't."

"Yes, she does, *my* sweet boy," he drawled. "I'm calling you that in bed tonight."

"You had better not!" I pointed at him.

"Or what?"

"Or . . . I will . . ."

"Yes?"

"I'll wait till you're asleep and put your hand in warm water!"

"What?" He scowled in confusion. "Why would you do that?"

"Because it makes you pee the bed." I laughed diabolically.

"It does not," he scoffed.

"Yes, it does! I have an older brother, believe me when I say that it does."

"What does having an older brother have to do with it?"

I blinked at him, then realized that he was an only child.

"Siblings play pranks on each other," I explained. "One of the classic pranks is the warm water thing. It works every time."

"And it makes people pee themselves? In their sleep?"

"Yep."

"That's disgusting."

"And it's only one of the reprehensible things I've learned from him. Bwa-ha-ha-ha-ha!"

"What was that?"

"That's my evil laugh. Every criminal must have an evil laugh," I said dryly. "Boy, you really missed out on a lot being an only child."

"A lot that I'm grateful for missing," he muttered.

"Nah, there's good stuff too. Like knowing they'll always have your back. My brother's a good guy. If he had known what his friend had done—you know the one I lost my virginity to—he would have kicked Tom's ass."

"You never told him?"

"No, Brandon would have felt bad for introducing us and probably would have blamed himself for not protecting me. But if it hadn't been Tom, it would have been someone else, and at least Tom was nice."

"Except for abandoning you to marry a woman," he said with surprising bite.

"It happens. I understood. Even more so now. Back then, I had silly dreams of taking him to Lek with me, but Tom would never have left Stalana. He'd rather hide who he is than leave his home."

"That's sad."

"For him." I shrugged. "We all have choices to make. Sometimes others make them for us. At least Tom got to decide for himself. I like to think that I was his one happiness before he had to pretend to be someone else. I hope he still thinks of me and that what we had gives him some comfort."

"I'm sure he does think of you. How could he not?" Tae's hand wandered back to my hair. "But that other part's sad as well, especially because it's true."

"Which part?"

"That others sometimes make decisions for us. I suppose the best a man can hope for is to be the master of his own destiny."

"Ah, but then you have no one but yourself to blame when it goes wrong." I winked at him.

Tae snorted in amusement. "Blame is for the weak."

"A very warlord answer," I noted.

"You disagree?"

"Yeah, I do. Sometimes, blame is properly placed. Sometimes we aren't given those precious choices and people do things that hurts or changes us. I don't think we should whine about it, but I don't think we should be blamed for the actions of others either."

"Fair enough." He glanced out the window when the carriage stopped. "Here we are. Ready for another adventure in fae cuisine?"

"Do you really have to ask?"

Chapter Thirty-Three

After lunch, we went clothes shopping. I don't know how much Varalorrian money Tae spent, but I imagine it was more than I made in five years. He bought me tunics, jackets, cloaks, pants, boots, hats, belts, and more. I couldn't keep track of the number of items the salesclerk presented to us while I tried things on, but Taeven just kept nodding. *Yes, that too. Yes, that as well.* On and on until I was ready for a nap. Luckily, we didn't have to cart it all back to his place; they would send it over later, after they steamed and pressed everything. I guess when you spend that much money, you get some perks.

When we got in our carriage, I thought we were heading home, but we turned in the opposite direction.

"Where are we going now?" I asked.

"I want to show you something."

Our carriage left the city on a lone road, heading into the forest that filled one end of the plateau. The street looped around to head back into Wynvar but instead of turning, we parked at the end of the curve, and Tae got out. I jumped out after him, and he took my hand to lead me off the road and through the woods. Snowfall was light beneath the trees so the going wasn't hard. It was actually lovely—a little sanctuary away from the city. But then we stepped out of the trees and onto a pointed promontory. The cliff hung out over the mountain—a perfect launching point if you happened to have wings.

"Tae, is this . . . ?"

"This is where I came that day," Tae confirmed as he removed his hand from mine in favor of slipping his arm around my shoulders. "I stood right here, the city hidden behind me and the possibility of freedom lying ahead of me."

"And then the falcon came."

He nodded and looked down at me with a soft smile. "And then the falcon came." His words were heavy, weighted with tender emotion.

"Thank you for sharing this with me," I whispered, looking from him to the phenomenal view.

Valleys and mountains stretched into the distance; the horizon an indigo smudge. I wondered what Tae saw with his sharper fae vision. Avanla had told me about the way a faerie's two forms synthesized after the first shift. At first, they'd be separate, only my mind connecting them, but then the heightened senses of the falcon would become mine in Sidhe form. Not as sharp as they'd be in falcon form, but a marked improvement. And a falcon's greatest sense was his sight. She said I'd be able to see much further than I could now; it would seem as if the world had suddenly expanded.

But my world had already grown thanks to the man beside me. He had urged me into this, but now I was grateful for his determination. Standing there on that cliff, looking out across the kingdom of his birth with his arm around me, I didn't want to be anywhere else. This was where I was meant to be, and he was who I was meant to be with. I'd never believed in silly things like fate, but I was rapidly changing my mind.

Because of the Falcon Lord.

"I wanted you to see this," Tae said, drawing my gaze to him again. "Because I believe you are the reason I didn't fly away that day."

Love blasted through me—all of its variables. The sharp ache of longing, the deep well of adoration, the warm zings of desire, and the acidic taste of fear. That last one could turn me into a clinging lover if I didn't rein it in, but I didn't even have to try to let it go or reason with myself that fear was a natural response to being presented with something precious. With the mere desire to rid myself of it, a feminine voice whispered through my mind, banishing that fear before it could take root and tighten into a hard ball. Instead, I took Tae's words as a good sign. He believed that we were meant to be. Surely that meant he was falling in love with me. I didn't need to be afraid. In fact, it was too late for fear. I was his valorian, there was no going back, and we both seemed to be happy about it. So, I denied the negativity, focused on the brighter aspects of love, and slid a hand behind Tae's neck to draw him down into a kiss.

Taeven turned toward me to pull me into his embrace as his mouth covered mine. The heat of his tongue sweeping against mine felt searing in contrast to the cold air on my cheeks, and his flavor was more addictive than anything I'd tasted in Varalorre. But it was the tenderness in Tae's touch and the way he moaned softly as he pulled me closer that made my heartbeat accelerate. If I got only this from him—beautiful kisses and nothing else—I'd be happy forever.

Tae eased back, nibbling at my lips before straightening. With a soft gaze, he slid his warm hands around my face. "I'm so glad I stayed."

"And I'm so glad you convinced me to be your valorian."

"I suppose we both nearly screwed up horribly." His eyes crinkled with his smile and he leaned down to give me another quick kiss before turning back to the view. "But the Goddess had other plans for us. Let's hope she continues to offer us guidance."

"Did I tell you that I heard her? That she still whispers to me, even now?"

"What?" Tae gaped at me. "No, you didn't. As I mentioned before, I've been told that valorians hear the Goddess and the Beasts when they are transformed, but none have ever remembered what she said and only a few have heard her after the change."

"The Beasts?" I recalled the shrieks and roars. "Yeah, I heard animals too."

"They are the Divine Beasts, consorts to the Goddess and the Fathers of the Sidhe races," he explained.

"I heard a falcon, in particular."

"That would make sense. But, Shane, what did the Goddess say to you?"

I grimaced. "I don't know. Even now, when I hear her it's as if she's far away. In another room. But her voice gives me peace. I have to admit, I've never been religious, but hearing the voice of a goddess can change a man's mind."

Tae chuckled. "I imagine it would." Then he went serious. "The Goddess can speak to us in many ways; she may try to reach out in a less direct manner. You must be alert. Watch and listen for her, Shane. If she's trying to communicate with you, it's important that you hear her."

"I'll listen; I promise."

"Good. Now let's get back to the carriage, it's fucking cold out here."

We rode back to his palace and after a hot shower—and a bit of hot shower sex—we curled up on a couch in front of the fireplace in Tae's enormous sitting room that was more of an all-purpose room. Kind of like the communal tent in camp but a lot nicer.

"Shopping is exhausting," I declared. "I'm still tired."

Tae chuckled softly. "That's probably more to do with all the sex we just had than the shopping."

"No, it was definitely the shopping."

"You're a soldier. How can shopping exhaust you?"

"I don't train as much as other soldiers."

"What do you mean?" He pulled back to look at me.

"Chefs and bakers have weekly sword training instead of daily. Don't you know that?"

"No, I don't. I don't handle the training schedule. Why don't you train daily?"

"Because we have other daily tasks. You know, like feeding an army."

"But soldiers don't just train. They each have other jobs to do daily."

"But their jobs don't take as much time as ours do. We have to make three meals every day. We work in shifts, but it still ends up being a full day for all of us."

"Ah, I see. And yet it was you who slew the Farungal who attacked me when even my knights couldn't stop him."

"Your knights were taken unaware while I took the Farungal unaware. It makes a big difference."

"You still struck the blow, Shane," Tae said as he took my hand. "I saw you—watched you the entire time. You never wavered. You could have gone for help, but instead, you took that Farungal on alone."

"As every soldier in battle does." I shrugged. "Except that

I had the advantage on him, and I knew you wouldn't last long enough for me to summon help." I smiled to banish the dark thoughts those words inspired and said brightly, "Hey, let's not get into this again. I'm your valorian. You got me good, babe. You don't have to flatter me."

"No, I don't. But I always give credit where it's deserved." Tae smiled.

"Thanks. And this is nice." I sighed and snuggled closer to him. "I like the cuddling in front of a fire part of cold weather."

"Just wait until we have sex in front of the fire." He nuzzled my cheek.

"Why wait?" I gave him a saucy look.

Tae chuckled and glanced at the clock on the mantle. "Because our guests are due to arrive any time now."

I groaned.

"I haven't seen them in years, Shane," Tae said sternly. "Try to be nice."

"Yeah, I know. I'm sure they're great, I was just really enjoying being alone with you."

"I'll try to discourage them from staying too long."

"No, don't do that. I don't want to be the guy who tries to take you away from your friends. Let them stay as long as they like. Or, rather, as long as you like."

"Thank you."

"Not that you needed my permission," I amended.

Tae burst out laughing.

"My lord?" Halfrin stepped out of the elevator.

"Are they here, Hal?"

"Yes, my lord. I've shown them into the casual dining room."

"Very good." Tae stood and offered me a hand.

I took it and sighed as I got to my feet. I decided to try my best to like Tae's friends. I reminded myself that they had just been looking out for Tae, and were probably good people under their arrogance. I mean, Sanasenne was a princess, I suppose she had a right to her arrogance. Or at least a reason for it. Besides, it was only one night, and we wouldn't be staying in Varalorre long; I could do this.

We went downstairs with Halfrin, then parted ways after we stepped out of the elevator.

"I'll send the first course in now, my lord," Halfrin said as he hurried away.

Although we had gone downstairs, or down in the elevator rather, we weren't on the first floor. Instead, we were on the fifth floor of the keep, and Tae led me through a short hallway before opening a door and waving me into an intimate dining room. The far wall was glass—not a balcony, just a massive window. Beyond it, snow swirled, the closest flakes lit by the fae lights that hung from glittering chandeliers above the dining table. It was a six-seater and two of the chairs, including one of the two on the short ends, were already taken.

Princess Sanasenne looked regal despite her lack of a crown and absolutely stunning in an indigo gown that matched Tae's bed linens exactly—a bit of an odd coincidence. The color made her seem paler and her eyes almost looked blind. She was the one who had taken one of the end seats and to her right, General Thalsar sat, wearing a gold brocade tunic that complemented his skin and her gown.

"There you are!" Thalsar declared as we came into the room.

"You couldn't have been waiting long; we came straight down," Tae said as he stepped forward and hugged the General.

"No, not long at all. I'm just excited to see you," Thalsar said as he released my warlord.

Sanasenne didn't stand, but Tae bent down to kiss her cheek and say, "You look beautiful tonight, Sana."

"Thank you, sweetheart." She stroked Tae's cheek.

During this intimate moment—which I told myself was normal behavior for friends who'd been separated for years, I stood to the side awkwardly. I didn't want to sit down before Tae did because I wasn't sure if he'd choose to sit beside the Princess or take the other end of the table. He did the latter, but since it was a short table, there wasn't a huge space between them. I sat on his right, opposite Thalsar but down a seat.

"Hello, Your Highness. General Thalsar." I nodded to them.

"Now, what did I tell you, Shane?" the Princess chided me. "Call me Sana. I'm sure we're going to be great friends." Then she waved her hands at a bottle of wine and two full glasses in the center of the table. "Pass out the wine, Thal." To Tae, she added, "I hope you don't mind. We weren't sure how long you'd be and your steward left this bottle with us, so we went ahead and poured some drinks."

"As you were meant to," Tae said as he accepted a glass from Thal.

I smiled as I took mine and tried my best to make it genuine, but I could have sworn I'd heard a snide tone beneath the Princess's kind words. The way Thalsar grinned at me as I sipped felt a bit vicious as well. But then servants arrived with our first course and things seemed to mellow. Food always makes things easier. If nothing else, it gives you something to do with your mouth when you can't come up with anything to say.

There were four courses and a dessert, and I enjoyed every one of them so utterly that I had even the elegant Sanasenne laughing like a little girl at my groans. Coffee was served with dessert but after we finished our cake, Tae suggested that we retire to a sitting room to enjoy the rest of our beverages.

There was a room just off the dining room, which I imagined was for this very purpose. It was smaller than most rooms in the palace, but appointed lushly, with thick carpets that squished beneath my boots, jewel-toned velvet upholstering the couches, and a fireplace that was already lit. The lighting was low and a coffee service waited along one wall in case we needed refills. I chose a loveseat by the fire, happily taking the fur blanket from the back of it and laying it across my lap.

Before Tae could sit beside me, Thalsar did. Since it was a loveseat and not a couch, this had him pressed up against me, and he put an arm around my shoulders for good measure. I flinched and drew back from him.

"Thal," Tae said in a warning tone.

"What? You can't hog our valorian, Tae," the General pulled me closer. To me, he said, "Relax, Shane; I don't bite. Not unless you ask me to."

I looked at Tae for help. He grimaced at me in apology but then took the couch across from us with Sana. She slid up next to him and laid her hand on his thigh. I looked from that hand to Tae's face. His expression was tight and uncomfortable, but he didn't remove her hand. I had to finally admit that this was beyond the behavior of friends, and I suddenly knew that I'd been right to be wary of them. These people had been Tae's lovers; I was nearly certain of it.

I make a point of not fighting over men. First of all, I think it's silly. If a man wants me, he'll choose me. If he wants me and doesn't choose me, or doesn't do what needs to be done to be with me, then he doesn't care about me enough. And if a man doesn't care about me enough to do what needs to be done, then why would I waste my time fighting over him? Second, I just think it's embarrassing. Like a form of groveling. I'm all for showing my love for someone, expressing myself, and demanding the same in return, but fighting over him with another potential lover? No. Not happening. That being said, fighting *for* a man I love is something else entirely. If he needs my help or is being attacked, I will have his back. That was not the case here. In fact, it was a little of the opposite. I needed Taeven to stand up for me, but he had taken a seat instead. I can't express how much that disappointed me.

I weighed my options. I could respond in two ways; I could either welcome the General's advances and try to make Tae jealous out of spite, or I could remain as dignified as possible and speak to Tae about this privately later. I chose option two with a twist.

"I'm sorry, Thalsar, but I don't snuggle with men when I'm in a relationship. Especially if the man trying to snuggle with me is in a relationship as well." I took his arm and removed it from my shoulder, then went to sit in the only chair— a big wingback across from the fire. I took the blanket with me.

Sana laughed her ass off. "Sweet Goddess, I don't think I've ever seen you brushed off before, Thal."

"I meant no offense." I held up a hand toward Thal's furious face. "I'm sure you didn't mean anything by it, but I was uncomfortable, and I don't let anyone make me feel uncomfortable. Not even a general."

Thal lifted a brow and nodded to me, his expression shifting to respect. "Maybe you're good enough for him after all."

"Oh, so this was a test?" I lifted my eyebrow too.

The General shrugged.

"Are you even bisexual?" I asked him casually.

Sana burst into another round of laughter, but quieted when Thalsar shot her a nasty look.

Thalsar schooled his features when he settled his stare back on me. "I am bisexual, and I find you very attractive, Shane. Does that shock you?"

"Not at all. Thank you for the compliment."

"Would it shock you to know that I enjoy being both top and bottom? That I would like nothing more than to be between you and Tae tonight—fucking you as he fucked me."

I swallowed past the dryness in my throat as my cheeks heated. The image of him in bed with Tae and me popped into my mind but instead of arousing me, it turned my stomach. I was utterly speechless.

The General smirked at me. "It *does* shock you. How adorable."

"Thal, stop it this instant," Tae said firmly, finally sticking up for me.

"I'm just testing his mettle, Tae." Thal cocked his head at me as he pulled a flask out of his coat. He tossed it to me. "How about something stronger than coffee, Shane?"

"That is enough!" Tae stood up and went to take the flask from me.

"What is this?" I asked him, keeping the flask out of his

reach.

"Knowing Thal, it's something very strong."

"It's just curvou," Thal huffed. "It's not as if I'd poison him. Come now, Tae, you refused to go out with us, at least stay in with us and have a drink."

"I can handle fae liquor now, right?" I asked Tae.

Tae frowned. "Yes, but, you don't have to drink that, Shane."

"It's just a drink, and I like experiencing new flavors." I held it up to him. "Do you want to try it first and make sure it's safe?" I grinned at him.

"Actually,"—he slid a suspicious look Thal's way—"I do."

"I would especially never poison you, Tae," Thal said softly. "You know that."

Taeven opened the flask, sniffed it, then lifted his brows in surprise.

"As if you expected it to be the cheap stuff," Thal grumbled.

Tae chuckled, then took a swig. With a sigh of delight, he handed me the flask. "Just sip it, Shane."

I took a sip.

Chapter Thirty-Four

I woke up naked and face-down on a rug. A heavy arm laid across my back and warm breath brushed my ear. I lifted my head, brain foggy, and looked around as I tried to remember how I'd gotten there. Then I heard the battle shriek of the Falcon Lord.

"What the fuck?!" Taeven shouted.

And if he was shouting, he couldn't be the man lying beside me. Heart racing, I looked over to see Thalsar blinking awake, a confused frown on his face.

"By the Goddess! Tone it down, Tae," Thalsar growled then rolled onto his back, showcasing his nudity.

"Holy shit," I whispered and jumped to my feet.

"How dare you?!" Taeven roared and yanked Thalsar to his feet. "You fucking snake!" He punched the General in the face, and Thal stumbled backward, knocking into a chair as he fell to the floor.

"What is the ruckus about?" The Princess drawled as she came gliding out of Tae's bedroom . . . in his robe.

I gaped at her, then at Tae.

"What the fuck, Tae?" Thal snapped as he got to his feet and swiped blood away from his face.

"Don't you dare fucking look at me like that," Tae snarled at me, ignoring Thalsar completely. His face settled into that primal expression he wore to war. "I didn't fuck her. She passed out in my bed."

"Naked?" I asked.

"As if you've room to talk." He waved a hand at me.

"I wouldn't have fucked him!" I screeched.

"Wouldn't?" Taeven narrowed his eyes at me. "Meaning that you admit to fucking him?"

"No, meaning that I can't remember!"

"Oh, I'm wounded, Shane," Thal said dramatically.

"We couldn't have," I whispered in horror. "There's no way."

"You're pleading memory loss?" Tae growled at me. "Seriously?"

"There had to be something in that drink!" I shouted.

"We all drank it!" Tae shouted back. "And yet, I remember last night. I distinctly remember you conveniently falling asleep on the couch."

"And you just left me there to go sleep with the Princess?"

"No, the Princess slept in my bed while I took yours . . . in the bedroom you'll now be inhabiting."

"Tae, I think you may be overreacting," Sanna said gently.

"It's just sex," Thal huffed. "What's your problem?"

"Get the fuck out of my house," Taeven growled at the General.

"Tae?" the Princess asked warily.

"I'm sorry, Sana, but you need to leave too," Taeven said without looking at her. "Just go, both of you, before I hurt Thalsar even worse."

A horrible quiet descended as the Princess and General collected their things and got dressed. Neither Tae nor I moved as they did, just stood there staring at each other like a pair of beasts about to brawl. The Princess tried to speak to Tae once more before they left, but he only shook his head at her. Once they were gone, he let loose.

"So, this is how you treat someone you love?" Tae sneered.

"And this is how you treat someone you believe the Goddess sent you?" I shot back.

Tae flinched but pressed his lips together and continued to glare. "Perhaps she made a mistake."

"Wow." I shook my head at him. "You won't even consider that I might be telling the truth."

"About what? Forgetting that you fucked Thal? Forgetting it doesn't make it go away."

"I don't believe that I had sex with him. There is no way that I would have betrayed you, especially not with him."

Taeven narrowed his eyes at me. "And yet Thal remembers it."

"Does he?" I lifted my brows. "Or is he saying that to break us up?"

"So now your defense is that this was all a vicious plot to tear us apart? And you wait till Thal's gone before you say it?" Tae gaped at me. "You're a piece of work, Shane. I can't believe I was falling for you."

Oh, that stung.

"And I can't believe I loved a man who doesn't trust me." I shook my head at him. "You swore to me that you'd never give up on me, even if I acted the fool."

"This is a bit beyond foolish," Tae growled. "I never thought you'd betray me. Not for one second did it cross my mind. So, I suppose I'm the fool now."

"Fuck this," I snarled and walked past him. "I need to get to the Academy."

"Where the fuck do you think you're going?"

"To get dressed," I said over my shoulder. "I'll move my clothes into the other room when I get back."

Tae didn't say anything, which drove the wedge of his betrayal deeper into my heart.

Chapter Thirty-Five

"All right, Valorian, out with it!" Avanla declared angrily.

"Out with what?" I asked morosely.

"With the reason that you're flopping about limply like a dying fish when you need to be focusing on shifting."

We were in a classroom now, sitting on a woven mat, Avanla across from me while I tried to believe myself into falcon form. It wasn't going so well. I was fresh out of belief.

"It's nothing."

"Does that nothing happen to be a warlord who is notably absent today?" She lifted a brow at me.

I sighed deeply. "I can't tell you. It involves the Princess."

"Oh, my." Her eyes widened eagerly. "Now you *must* tell me!"

I gave her my first smile of the day. "You have to promise not to breathe a word of it to anyone."

"Yes, yes, all of that. I promise. Spill!"

So, I told her. I mean, fuck it, I had no one else to vent to and boy did I need to vent. I told her about the Princess and her General, their strange behavior, Thalsar's flask, and then my amnesia. Avanla blinked a bit, sometimes very slowly, but didn't interrupt, nor did she exclaim in horror. Instead, she looked pensive.

"Were either the General or the Princess alone with your food or drink at any time?" she asked.

"You're saying that something else could have been drugged? Something other than the curvou?" I scowled and considered this. Then my jaw dropped and I whispered in horror, "The wine."

"Wine?"

"When we got to the dining room, the Princess and General were drinking wine, but they'd poured glasses for all of us. Tae's and mine were just sitting there. I thought that was a little odd. Who pours wine before people show up? But I mean, they do that at the palace, so I didn't think much of it. That being said, Thalsar handed the glasses to Tae and me. He could have easily drugged one of them and made sure to give me the drugged glass."

"I must caution you to not accuse the General and especially not the Princess of suck trickery without proof," Avanla said gently. "It could go very badly for you."

"But how do I get proof?"

Avanla considered this. "I imagine that your glass has already been discarded, which leaves only you as our evidence. Unfortunately, the drug has likely left your system by now."

"Then I'm fucked," I huffed.

"Not entirely." She held up a finger and wagged it pensively. "If he gave you what I suspect he did—hulrine potion—then I know the cure for your memory loss."

"You do?" I leaned forward.

Avanla nodded and stood up. "Get dressed and come with me."

I had undressed in preparation for shifting, but I rapidly pulled on my clothes and then followed Avanla out of the room. She took me to an elevator and then up to the sixth floor. Once there, we went down a few corridors and then, at last, into a strange room.

"What is this place?" I looked around at the glass vials and silver tools crowding atop numerous tables that were scattered about the room.

"A laboratory," Avanla said as she headed toward a bookshelf in the corner.

She skimmed the titles, then pulled out a large volume. I joined her at the central table and watched over her shoulder as she flipped through the pages.

"Here we are." Avanla tapped a page. "Hulrine antidote."

She drew a nail down the list of ingredients, then started bustling about the room, collecting bottles and vials. I helped her by taking the items and transporting them to the table where she'd set the book. At last, we had everything, and Avanla lit a little gas burner with a flick of her finger. Over the flame, she put a metal holder, then set a glass vial into it.

I watched anxiously, my stomach knotting as she added the ingredients, referencing the book often for the amounts. The liquid in the vial changed color several times, going from gold to green to blue before settling into purple.

Avanla lifted the vial, swirled the contents, and handed it to me. "Drink up."

I sniffed it. It was acrid enough to make my nose wrinkle, so I downed it in one go. It tasted nasty but didn't burn or do anything to indicate that it was working. I flopped down onto a wooden stool and grimaced.

"I think he drugged me with something else," I grumbled.

Avanla frowned. "I can't think of anything else that could produce those results. Maybe—"

"Hold on!" I jumped to my feet. "I'm starting to see pictures. Memories!"

"Tell me! Describe them as they come; it will help more to emerge."

"I remember lying on Tae's lap. He was stroking my face and playing with my hair. Saying pretty things that the other two rolled their eyes at. Then . . . the Princess and Thalsar started kissing." I blinked. "They were standing in front of the fire, right in front of us too, and they . . . fuck, they took off their clothes. They started having sex in front of us. Holy shit, Thalsar got Sanasenne on her hands and knees and they had sex as we watched."

"What?!" Avanla's eyes went round. Then she lowered her voice to ask, "You watched the Princess and the General have sex?"

"Yes, and they kept staring back at Tae and me, smiling."

"Oh, how naughty," she whispered. "Tell me more."

I remember . . . Tae had an erection, and I was getting angry." I shook my head. "I left the room. I should have stayed because after Sanasenne and Thalsar finished, they all followed me up to Tae's bedroom. Well, to the sitting room next to his bedroom."

"And then?"

"Then Tae tried to talk to me, but the other two kept butting in. The Princess and General were only half-dressed. They kept making light of what had happened, and Tae kept telling me it was just one of the things they liked to do." I stopped myself before I told Avanla what else Tae had said —that he'd thought I might enjoy watching instead of being watched, and maybe even performing for the other couple. Sort of an exhibitionist swap. My stomach rolled as I went on, "I finally let it go, and everything seemed normal for a while. Tae and Thal were sitting before the fire, just talking, and the Princess sat down beside me." My eyes went wide. "Oh, that fucking bitch!"

"What?" Avanla asked almost gleefully. "What did she do?"

"She . . ." I decided to tell her about what Tae and I had done after all; I couldn't tell her what Sana said without it. "I have to tell you about something intimate first. Try not to judge me."

"Oh, please." She rolled her eyes. "I have had my fair share of sexual escapades. And yes, I've even had sex in front of an audience. A large one, if I'm being entirely honest."

"All right, well." I cleared my throat, trying not to think about my esteemed teacher on her hands and knees before an applauding group of faeries. "Tae and I had sex in front of his bedroom window the other day and there was this Falcon flying nearby. We both liked being watched, so he . . . well, *we* really put me on a show. The Falcon flew closer and saw everything."

"You're not saying . . . was that Falcon . . . no." Avanla gaped at me.

"Princess Sanasenne thanked me for my enthusiastic performance," I growled. "She said she was only trying to repay the favor."

"Holy falcon shit!" Avanla exclaimed. "It was the *Princess* watching you?"

"Yes, and it gets worse." I grimaced. "When I expressed my surprise at it being her, she looked confused. She said that she has very particular markings in falcon form, and she had assumed that Tae recognized her. She said that she loves to watch two men together, something which Tae knows, so she thought he was showing off for her. And she assumed that he had told me who we were performing for."

"No!" Avanla gasped.

"Yeah," I growled getting madder. "She acted so sweet, but I knew she was taking great pleasure in pushing us apart. So, I let that go too."

"You did?"

"Well, I wasn't about to play into her plans, was I?"

Avanla nodded approvingly. "Well done, my lad."

"Yeah, sure, I did great until I passed out on the couch," I grumbled.

"Do you remember what happened after that?"

"I was just so tired."

"A result of the hulrine," she said.

"Someone started to undress me, and I thought it was Tae so I didn't protest. I remember being moved off the couch and then falling asleep again."

"So you didn't fuck the General?"

"No, I didn't," I growled. "He posed me like that and then told Tae that we had sex. He lied. Which means that I was targeted, Avanla."

"Targeted by some very devious and powerful people, my sweet boy." She stroked my cheek sympathetically. "Which means that we must be just as devious to expose their machinations."

"How?"

"We must get one of them to admit their crime. Give me some time to think about this. For now, try telling the Falcon Lord that I've helped you to remember and see how that goes."

"No, fuck that." I shook my head angrily. "He didn't trust me and he didn't stand by me when he specifically said he would. I'm not saying anything to Tae until I have proof, and then I'm going to shove it in his face and walk out."

"But, Shane, you can't walk out. You're needed to—"

"Yes, I know. I'm needed to help end the war, and I will do that. Then I'm moving to Lek with the proceeds I earn from selling the palace the King gave me. I'm not going to let that asshole stop me from achieving my dreams."

Avanla smiled sadly. "I hope you get everything you want, my sweet boy."

"Well, let's start with shifting," I said firmly. I had a goal now, and that made the heartbreak easier to bear.

At least, I hoped it would.

Chapter Thirty-Six

When I got home that night after Avanla helped me recover my memories, it was to find my clothing already moved into the tower that adjoined Tae's. I had to cross a bridge that dangled high over his property to get to my room, but it was nice to have a space of my own where I could avoid him. There was even a little library and a dining room in the massive tower. I had everything I needed there, and it became a sanctuary for me. In fact, I didn't see Taeven for the next several days. I don't know what he did with his days, but when I left for the Academy each morning, he was either gone already or still sleeping—I never checked.

After day three, I started to miss him horribly, but I kept seeing his furious face in my mind and it stopped me from seeking him out. I was still angry, of course, but I often wavered. I recalled that I had mistrusted everything about Tae without reason to, but he had never held that against me. Was it fair for me to be upset with him for not believing me with just cause? There were days when I felt sorry for myself and my anger would surge. On those days, the answer would be yes, it was fair for me to be upset with him because back when I hadn't trusted him, we didn't know each other, but he didn't trust me *after* we had become intimate. Tae should have at least attempted to figure out what happened instead of immediately discounting my protests.

Then there were days when the ache of missing him

would overwhelm me and my anger would vanish. Everyone makes mistakes, and Tae had awoken to find me naked beneath the arm of his ex-lover—an ex-lover who lied about having sex with me. It was easy to understand how Taeven could refuse to believe me after that kind of evidence had been shoved in his face. Especially when all I had to dispute it with was a lame excuse that I couldn't remember. Those were the days when I considered telling him about Avanla's cure and my returned recollection. But I didn't want to face his contempt again. I didn't want to see that savagery fill his eyes without arousal to soften it. When I told him about everything, I wanted him to know that I was speaking the truth.

But Avanla and I were no closer to finding a way to force a confession from Thalsar and Sanasenne than we'd been that first day. How do you make someone admit something they don't want to admit? You must put them in a position where the alternative is worse. The problem was, what could be worse for Thalsar than admitting that he had orchestrated the whole thing? As far as I knew, he could be spending every night with Taeven—him and his princess. Thinking about the three of them together was enough to make me sick. Enough to make me dust off my hands and say "fuck 'em all." But as much as I don't fight over a man, I don't quit when the going gets rough either. I wasn't going to freak out and run off like a child; I'd stay and face what happened like a man.

The good news was that I learned to shift, although that accomplishment was bittersweet without Tae to celebrate with me. Avanla took me out to dinner at a beautiful restaurant on the rooftop of a twenty-story building to celebrate, and I kept thinking about how I could shift and leap off the edge if I wanted to. But I also kept thinking about Tae. That being said, flying is about the most uplifting activity there is, and training to fly with Avanla put me in great spirits. The crisp air bothered me less in falcon form, and soaring over the valleys was one of my favorite things to do after my lessons every day. Up in the clouds, everything else became small. Irrelevant. It was easy to see how Tae had been tempted to leave everything behind and simply take to the air.

The process of my learning to fly had been amusing, and I wished many times that I could have shared it with Taeven. I imagined him standing to the side of the vast classroom, laughing uproariously every time I tumbled off the launching platform and fell onto the pile of cushions below.

Avanla had the flight platform built specifically for me. Evidently, young Falcons are simply shoved off a balcony in the highest tower as soon as they learn to shift. Their instincts take over, and they fly. I, however, had no natural instincts so Avanla took a safer route with me, and I'm grateful she did. If she hadn't, I'd be a smear on the courtyard stones.

Anyway, nearly two weeks had passed since my argument with Tae, and I had progressed in my studies, advancing well into my elemental magic lessons. After the failures of my flight training, I don't think either Avanla or I had high hopes for my progress, but it turned out that I had a knack for magic. I excelled so rapidly that we started to attract a crowd of both scholars and children. Other professors often offered to help with my training, as Master Rundel currently was. He was in falcon form while I held him aloft with air magic, giving him a current to glide on.

Then Taeven walked in.

A rush of love—sad, unrequited, aching, angry, betrayed love—rushed through me at the sight of the Falcon Lord. Unfortunately for Master Rundel, that emotion destabilized my magic, and he got blasted up to bash into the ceiling.

"Fuck!" I shouted and ran toward the floundering Falcon.

But Master Rundel wasn't a professor for nothing; he righted himself and glided to the ground.

"Are you all right?" I asked him, doing my best to keep from looking at Tae.

"I'm fine, Valorian," Rundel said, having no such qualms about eyeing the warlord. "It appears that you're needed elsewhere."

He shifted to Sidhe and slipped into a robe while the other professors ushered the children out of the room.

"Thanks for your help, Master Rundel," I called after him as he left as well.

"I'll just be outside," Avanla said with a heavy look at me, then Tae. "I'd advise you both to keep an open mind."

Tae frowned in confusion at her as she left.

"What are you doing here?" I asked, not unkindly.

"The King has requested that we join him for dinner." He tossed a bag at me. "I took the liberty of choosing some clothes for you to wear."

I looked at the bag on the floor, then at Tae. Part of me wanted to refuse, but this was the first time I'd seen him in thirteen days and the other part of me—the part that was in the majority—wanted to spend time with him, even if it meant enduring his icy glares. I shrugged out of my clothes and into the ones he'd brought me.

"Don't do that!" Tae snapped.

"Excuse me?" I frowned at him as I pulled on my boots. "I thought you wanted me to wear these clothes?"

"I know that you're trying to seduce me, Shane. Stop it."

"I'm trying to seduce you by *getting dressed?*" I gave him a baffled look.

"By the way you're—never mind, just hurry up."

I blinked at Tae, my confusion slipping into hope. I hadn't been trying to be sexy at all, but he thought I was. Which meant that he still wanted me. Enough so that it made him angry. Good. Angry was better than indifferent.

I stuffed the clothes I'd been wearing into the satchel and slung it over my shoulder before I walked out, striding past him without even a side-glance. I heard him make a frustrated sound, then start following me.

"I have to cut the lesson short today, Avanla." I hugged my teacher goodbye. "I've been summoned to dinner with the King."

Tae started walking down the hall, not bothering to wait for me.

"Oh, all right." She pulled me into another hug to whisper in my ear, "Mention hulrine potion to the Princess and see how she reacts."

I nodded to her, though I had no idea how I'd bring that up in conversation.

"Perhaps imply that there's a record of the purchase, and we've found it," Avanla whispered as she stepped away. "Scholars excel at research."

"Thanks, Ava!" I kissed her cheek. "Leave it to you to come up with a plan on the fly."

"I work best under pressure." She winked at me. "Speaking of flying; fly high and strike hard, my sweet boy. No mercy tonight; they deserve to go down in flames for what they did to you."

"No mercy," I agreed, then strode after Tae.

I didn't rush even though I lost sight of him. It wasn't as if Taeven were going to leave me there, not after coming specifically to fetch me. Sure enough, I found him waiting in his carriage at the foot of the Academy stairs, the door open expectantly. I got inside and, for the first time ever, sat across from instead of beside him. I saw the skin around his eyes twitch just before he knocked on the carriage wall to let the driver know we were ready.

"You're doing well with your lessons, or so I've heard," Tae noted crisply.

"Are you blind?" I shot back. "You were watching me hold Master Rundel aloft, weren't you?"

"And I saw you slam him into the ceiling."

"Because I was surprised to see you."

Tae stared at me, his mouth tight. I looked away.

"Have you remembered anything?" he whispered.

Holy shit. I went still. Should I tell him the truth? I couldn't lie to him, but I didn't want to hear him call me a liar again. Then again, lying so I wouldn't be called a liar was a special kind of irony, wasn't it?

I looked Taeven in the eyes and told him the truth, "I remember it all. I've remembered since the day after it happened."

"What?!" Taeven leaned forward furiously. "And you didn't tell me?" Then his face fell. "Because you remember fucking him, don't you?"

That question sent me into such a rage, that I had to take a few deep breaths to calm myself. Tae leaned back, his eyes widening as he beheld my fury.

"No, I absolutely did not fuck him," I said in a low, dangerous tone. "I did nothing sexual with Thalsar at all."

Taeven just stared at me.

I turned my head to stare out the window. I knew it. I knew that he wouldn't believe me. Not without hard evidence.

"And yet you didn't declare your innocence until now?" he finally asked.

"I declared my innocence that very day!" I snapped. Then I took another deep breath and went calm again. "You know what, Tae? That is all I'm going to say about it to you. I refuse to beg you to believe me. I told you the truth and that should be enough. Now you have to decide whether to believe me or not. Take some time. Think it over." I looked back out the window. "Let me know when you've made a decision."

We were silent the rest of the way to the Royal Palace. Silent all through the long walk to the royal residence inside the palace, and all the way to the family dining room. It was empty when we arrived, the long table set with polished silverware, fine china, and crystal goblets. It stood directly beside a window-wall similar to the one in Tae's dining room and there were no seats on the side of the table next to the window so that everyone would have a view with their meal.

And the view was exceptional.

I strode past one of the thrones—there was one at each end of the table—to the glass wall and stared across the sparkling fae city. It looked so peaceful while inside me, harsh emotions churned. I could hear Taeven behind me; it sounded as if he was making himself a drink at the sideboard. A minute later, his hand appeared beside me, offering me a glass of wine.

I frowned at it. "No, thank you. I don't drink wine anymore."

"Why not?"

Before I could answer, the royal family walked in. I turned at the sound of the door and followed Tae's lead to bow to the trio.

"Welcome, both of you," the King said grandly. "Do you like the view, Valorian?"

"It's spectacular, Your Majesty," I said.

"Yes, it is." King Dehras grinned proudly. "Please, sit down." He waved a hand at the table before pulling out a throne for his wife.

Meanwhile, Taeven set two glasses of wine down and hurried to pull out a chair for the Princess. She didn't have a throne, nor did she wear a crown—none of them did—but she sat straight in her seat, her chin lifted regally as if she did wear one. When she glanced at me, I met her gaze with open hostility.

And she flinched.

I looked away, giving her time to process my venom, but also took the seat right beside her, hemming her in between me and the Queen. "How are you tonight, Princess?" I asked in a tone similar to one she'd used on me the night she drugged me.

"Well," she said. "Thank you for asking, Valorian."

"Please, call me Shane. We're friends now, remember? Such *good* friends."

Taeven shot me a confused look at my sharp tone as he sat on my other side, near the King.

I knew there was a possibility that the Princess was completely innocent of any wrongdoing, but I didn't think that was the case. Especially not with the frantic looks she was giving me. There was fear in her eyes. Fuck, Ava was right; I could twist her guilt to my advantage, make her think I had evidence even though I didn't. I just had to be careful. Choose my words specifically. So, I looked away again, right at her mother.

"And you look stunning this evening, Your Majesty," I declared.

"Oh, thank you, Valorian." The Queen preened. "How gallant of you to say so."

"Thank you for having me here tonight. I'm honored."

"Well, we've heard about your rapid advancement at the Academy, and I decided that we should celebrate," the King said as a slew of servants tromped in and started ladling things onto our plates.

"That's kind of you, Your Majesty," I said. "But I owe my success to my teacher, Mistress Avanla. She's amazing. Did you know that not only does she teach flight but also science? In particular, the mystic sciences."

"Mystic sciences?" the Queen asked, her tone light.

Beside me, Sanasenne went deathly still.

"Yes, my dear, that's the study of natural things used for magical purposes, such as potions and the like," the King explained.

"Oh, how fascinating!" the Queen exclaimed as she held her glass out presumptuously.

A servant rushed to fill it.

"It is indeed," the King agreed, then started to eat—a sign that the rest of us could start as well.

"I certainly was fascinated by it," I said dramatically to the Queen. "Especially after Mistress Avanla helped me with her science. I was having trouble remembering something, but she whipped up a *cure* for my amnesia,"—I paused to stare pointedly at Sanasenne, and she paled until she was the color of curdled milk—"and wouldn't you know it, I was right as rain in mere moments. All my memories returned in a flash."

Tae went tense beside me. "You're awfully talkative tonight, Shane."

"Oh, I'm feeling much more comfortable in my new home now, Tae." I grinned at him, then at the King. "Thank you again for my estate, Your Majesty. I haven't gone to see it yet since I've been so busy at the Academy, but I will soon. Perhaps I'll even stay there awhile." I slid a look at Tae that had him gaping at me. Then I looked back at the King to add, "I've never owned my own home."

"Oh, how sad," the Queen declared.

"He's young, my dear," the King said. "I don't believe that's unusual for humans."

"Actually, Your Majesty, at my age, a lot of humans have homes and families, but I have other dreams." I returned my bright smile to the Queen. "But back to the discerning art of mystical science. You should see the equipment, Your Majesty. It's truly amazing what can be done with potions. And the scholars are so meticulous with the records of their potions and the ingredients that are put into them." I turned to spear the Princess with my glare as I asked, "Did you know that the scholars keep track of potions sold around the city, Your Highness?"

Sanasenne shrieked and fell backward in her chair as if I'd physically attacked her.

"Sana!" the Queen exclaimed in shock.

The King and Tae lurched to their feet, but I was there first, gallantly helping the Princess up while I whispered in her ear, "I have proof of your crime."

"It wasn't me!" Sanasenne screamed and scrabbled backward across the rug away from me, startling everyone.

The servants drew back, while the Queen shrieked and clutched at her chest, and Tae just gaped at the display with round eyes. But the King—oh, he was a clever one, and he must have known his daughter very well.

King Dehras narrowed his eyes at the Princess, then shouted at the servants, "Out! All of you get out!"

The room cleared in seconds. As they left, the King went to his daughter and helped her to her feet. Once she was standing, he demanded, "What have you done, Sana?!"

"I didn't do anything, I swear. It was Thal! I begged him not to use the hulrine potion, but he wouldn't listen to me."

Holy shit, I didn't even have to mention it. *Thank you, Ava!*

Tae's eyes went wide and swung toward me. I met his gaze with cool and aloof dignity, taking great pleasure in watching comprehension and then regret fill his expression. After that satisfaction, I dismissed him entirely and turned back to watch the drama unfold.

"Hulrine potion?" The King asked in confusion.

"What is that?" the Queen asked breathlessly, her eyes still wide in shock.

"It's a potion that slowly puts its victim into a stupor—a state from which they cannot be aroused for several hours—and when they awaken, they cannot remember what transpired. It's used mainly for interrogations—we send a supply to our army regularly. I can't for the life of me imagine what Thalsar would want with it."

Interrogations. That was how General Thalsar knew about it. And how Tae knew about it too.

"I can," Taeven growled and started out of the room, his face a mask of fury and his shoulders bunched.

"No, Tae!" Sana grabbed for him, but he shook her off callously. "Please, don't hurt him! He didn't mean for—"

"For what, Sana?" Tae swung back to sneer at her. "Thal didn't mean to make me think that my valorian had betrayed me with him?"

The Queen gasped and swayed on her feet.

"And what about you? You think that just because you didn't dose Shane, you're innocent?" Taeven growled. "You could have told me. That morning, you could have told me that I was wrong. That Thal was lying to me when he implied that he'd slept with Shane. That Shane had been drugged, and that was why he couldn't remember anything."

"I couldn't!" Sana protested. "Thal would have been furious."

"You could have told me during any of the *numerous* times you visited me afterward," Tae snarled. "Or were you too busy trying to seduce me to bother with clearing my valorian's name?"

"How dare you?!" the Queen shouted.

"My love, shut the fuck up," the King said sharply.

The Queen gasped again.

"He's in the dining hall, Tae," the King said grimly. "I will attend you."

The men strode out of the room.

"Thank you for dinner, Your Majesty." I bowed to the

Queen, stuck my tongue out at her daughter, and hurried after my warlord.

There was no fucking way that I was going to miss this.

Chapter Thirty-Seven

The dining hall of the Royal Palace was a vast space of stone and wood, with vaulted ceilings and heavy chandeliers that shed a soft light on the diners. And there were a lot of diners. Courtiers from all the fae races sat at long crystal tables in gilded chairs—or on the floor in the case of the Trolls—with platters of food set in lines down the center of the tables. They laughed and drank, generally having a good time.

Until the Falcon Lord stormed into the room like a vengeful god.

In a wave, silence spread over the space until it reached General Thalsar, who sat at the front of the room, his table right beside the empty high table that was reserved for royalty. The look of fury on Tae's face would have been enough to put a halt to the festivities, but with the King and me on his tail, the very air trembled.

Thalsar peered around in confusion before his gaze found Tae. One look at the warlord and the General's expression hardened. He stood up and came around his table to face the Falcon Lord, hand rising in placation and mouth opening to speak. Tae punched Thalsar in the face before he could utter a single word.

Thalsar went flying, crashing into the high table hard enough to send it screeching backward. He crumpled to the floor but then shook it off and got to his feet. "That is the second time you have attacked me without cause, Taeven. I will not let it go unanswered this time."

"Without cause?" Tae made a rumbling sound of rage. "I know what you did, Thalsar." He stretched his shoulders and neck like a professional boxer preparing for a fight.

Thalsar glanced at me and the King to find both of us glaring at him, but despite that, he decided to give innocence one last try. "I don't know what you're talking about."

Taeven punched him again, this time a sideways blow that caught the General on the cheek. Thalsar righted himself before he fell, shook off the blow, and snarled, his expression settling into fury as blood dripped from his nose. He sank into a battle stance and bared his bloodstained teeth.

"I'm not going to stand here and let you pummel me, no matter what you think I'm guilty of," Thalsar snapped.

"Sana confessed, you piece of shit," Tae hissed. "I don't think you're guilty; I *know* it. She told us all about the hulrine potion."

The courtiers gasped and whispers began to circle the hall.

Thalsar's expression fell. "Tae, that was just to get you back. You were so wrapped up in him." He waved a hand at me. "You weren't yourself. I was trying to help you."

"You thought you were helping me by drugging my valorian and making it appear as if he had betrayed me with you?!" Taeven roared.

Faeries got out of their seats and started to come forward, standing supportively behind their King and me. It looked as if they weren't too happy about an attack on their warlord and his new valorian. Even the faeries who had scorned Tae stood to denounce the general. Tae's bloodline suddenly didn't matter so much. I suppose it was one of those things, like the bonds between brothers. You could fight with your brother and call him the foulest names, but if someone else dared to come at him, you'd demolish them. Regardless of his low birth, Taeven was their warlord, and he'd been betrayed by someone who professed to be his friend.

"I was going to tell you eventually," Thalsar said.

"Tell me what? That you lied to me when you said you had fucked my lover? That you, in essence, called Shane a liar and drove us apart? Or that you assaulted someone under my protection?"

"I didn't assault him. It was just a little memory loss."

"You drugged him with an interrogation potion and when he passed out, you stripped him and laid down naked beside him, posing the two of you to make me think the worst," Tae growled.

The courtiers started to mutter angrily.

"And when Shane swore his innocence to me, you disputed him. You said it was just sex. You made me *doubt* him when it was you who was lying. You discredited a man who saved my life. Discredited and shamed him. A valorian who has proven himself to the Goddess. The first person to truly make me happy, and you made me believe that he was worthless. That I had wasted my soul on a faithless whore. When you are the faithless whore. Disloyal and cheap with your petty machinations. That, Thalsar, is an attack of the foulest sort."

"You were ours first!" Thalsar shouted. "We made you happy before him, but you barely looked at us with him there. Over twenty years and you looked relieved when we walked away from you that first night."

"I was never yours," Taeven said sharply. "I counted you

both as friends, but you never made me happy. Not like Shane does. And now I know why. His beauty, unlike yours and Sana's, goes beyond the surface. He is truly good."

"Don't you dare speak of Sana like that!" Thalsar shouted and dove for Taeven.

The two men rolled, fists slamming into flesh, and blood flying in a spray that not even the gloriously dressed court flinched away from. A circle of faeries surrounded the brawling men, but this wasn't like a fight in the camps; they weren't egging the men on or placing bets. The courtiers watched with the intense air of a jury bearing witness to justice, and the King stood beside me with his arms crossed and expression vicious —a judge who'd obviously made his decision. He watched in approval as Tae turned into the madman I'd seen in that alley back in Fellbrook. With his face twisted into molten rage and eerie shrieks echoing up his throat, the Falcon Lord beat on the General with cruel efficiency, taking every hit Thalsar landed with barely a blink and giving it back tenfold. It soon became apparent that Thalsar was fighting for his life and only his skill and fae speed were saving him.

The men broke apart, both bleeding, and circled each other as they panted like animals. Neither were armed and both were immortal, so death would take a while, but I saw it there in Tae's eyes and knew he wouldn't stop until his old friend lay dead before him. What would that do to Tae? How could he recover from killing someone he had once cared for? No, this wasn't worth my vengeance. I started to step forward, intent on putting a stop to it, but a pale blur raced by me.

Princess Sanasenne settled into a fighting stance in front of her lover, her gleaming sword held expertly—its tip pointed at Tae's throat. "Stand down, Taeven."

"The fuck I will," Tae growled and grinned menacingly. Yep, the man I loved was gone, overtaken by the predator. And the Princess's sword wouldn't make a whit of difference.

"Sana!" the King shrieked. "Get away from that traitor this instant!"

"No, Father. I love him. And Tae's right; I could have spoken up, but I didn't. That makes me just as guilty. So, if he wants to kill Thal, he'll have to kill us both."

"Sana, no," Thal said gently. "This is my fight."

"Thal." Sana's gaze went soft—the first sign of tenderness I'd seen in her.

"So be it." Taeven spat blood onto the floor and started forward.

"Tae!" I shouted and raced forward to stand between him and the couple. "Enough. The truth is out and you've had your vengeance. Let it be enough."

He started to push past me, but I took his face in my hands. "Babe, stop. I don't want this. I just want you back."

Taeven shuddered, blinked, then focused on me. "Shane?" Tae's voice broke and his throat worked convulsively as a sheen covered his eyes. He laid a hand over one of mine. "They hurt you; they hurt *us*. The things I said to you . . ."

"Forgotten." I smiled softly. "I would have been just as furious if I thought you had betrayed me."

"I would never betray you. You're my gift from the Goddess."

My throat constricted as happiness bloomed inside me, and I turned my hand to take his. "You're my gift too."

"No, I'm not. I failed you. I'm supposed to protect you. Instead, I brought them into our home and stood by while they abused you."

"You trusted them. You had no reason not to."

"We lost all that time together." His hand slid around the back of my neck to pull me closer as his forehead lowered to mine. "I'm so sorry, sweetheart. I'm sorry I didn't believe you. I swore to never give up on you and then I did. Forgive me?"

"Just promise to trust me in the future," I demanded.

"I promise."

"Good." I leaned back to look at him. "And you'd best keep that promise because if you don't, I'm dragging this shit out and shoving it in your face." I waved my finger at Sanasenne and Thalsar.

Taeven laughed—a brilliant and slightly horrified sound that ended abruptly. He shook his head at me and asked, "How do you do that?"

"What?"

"Turn tragedy into amusement. Make me laugh seconds after you bring me out of bloodlust."

"It's a gift." I grinned and took his hand to pull him away. "Now, don't kill your friends," I said in a cajoling tone, one you might use with a child. "There's a good warlord."

Taeven chuckled and let me lead him away from Sanasenne and Thalsar, over to the King, who had been joined by the Queen. A glance backward showed me a gaping General and Princess, Sana's sword tip drooping to the floor. I stuck my tongue out at her again. Couldn't help it, had to be done.

"Falcon Lord, thank you for showing my daughter mercy," the King's voice took on a regal tone and volume.

Tae didn't try to protest and say that he wouldn't have hurt the Princess; it was obvious that he would have gone through anyone, including Sana, to get to Thalsar. I knew it too; I'd seen that expression on his face before. That madness. Nothing but blood would have satisfied him. Blood or my hands on his face. A warmth filled my chest at the thought that I had the power to bring Tae back from madness. It was romantic in a way.

"I expect you to grant me justice, Your Majesty," Tae countered, his voice tight.

"Against Sana as well?" King Dehras managed to keep his expression blank and his voice even, but I saw the worry in his eyes.

Tae looked at me, and I shook my head. If the King punished his daughter, it could affect the entire kingdom. And as much as Sana had been a bitch to me, I'd seen real love in her eyes when she looked at Thalsar. Love like that couldn't be felt by a truly horrible person. It could, however, make good people do horrible things.

"I forgive them, Your Majesty," I said. "I don't require further punishment."

"Since my valorian is satisfied, I will accept monetary reparations from the Princess as long as General Thalsar is punished for attacking a valorian," Tae answered a bit grudgingly.

"No!" Sanasenne shrieked. "He didn't mean to harm Shane, Tae. You know Thal isn't malicious. Please!"

"Silence, Sanasenne!" King Dehras shouted.

His daughter went silent. The whole room did.

"For reparations, Sanasenne will transfer ownership of her property in Dreslen to you, Falcon Lord," the King said.

"Dreslen?" Taeven looked at Sana in surprise.

She lifted her chin and met his stare with just as much

love as she'd shown Thalsar. Shit. She loved Tae. She had bought an estate near his parents' home, likely for the three of them to live in someday. I could see the shattered dreams in her eyes and a glance at Tae told me that he saw them too. And that he had concluded the same thing that I had; that Thalsar had done it all for Sanasenne. They'd both been prompted by love. Thalsar had been trying to get Taeven back for both of them, albeit in a nefarious way.

Suddenly, Taeven said, "I am content with that. I withdraw my request for Thalsar's punishment."

The court gasped and several of them started to murmur angrily.

"Thank you, Tae," Sanasenne whispered.

Taeven nodded and put his arm around me.

The King sighed. "Be that as it may, Falcon Lord, I cannot let this go unpunished. General Thalsar, you endangered all of Varalorre with your dishonorable actions. The bond between warlord and valorian is sacred for a reason. The Goddess has spoken through the Hawk Valorian and told us that all valorians will be needed to end the war with the Farungal. Without them, the Farungal will win; they will use their amulets to break through the mist that protects us and take control of Varalorre."

The watching assemblage, including the servants who stood along the walls watching as avidly as the nobility, gasped in horror.

"I . . . I did not—" Thalsar stuttered.

"Do not try to profess ignorance," the King interrupted him. "I told you of the prophecies myself."

"I wasn't going to deny knowledge of the prophecies, Your Majesty," Thalsar protested. "Only wisdom. I didn't think about that. I honestly didn't believe that their bond would be broken. I thought Taeven would eventually forgive Shane. I only wanted some time with him for Sana."

"Do not use our given names ever again," Tae said coldly. "We are the Falcon Lord and Falcon Valorian to you now."

Thalsar winced but nodded. "I am deeply sorry, Falcon Lord." He transferred his gaze to me. "Falcon Valorian."

"I forgive you, Thalsar," I said immediately. "Love can make us idiots."

Tae swung his head toward me and shook it in amazement again. "My cynical but sweet boy," he whispered.

"Hatred only hurts you, babe. I don't expect you to forgive them now, but I hope you will eventually. I don't want to see you suffer further over this."

"Oh, sweet Goddess, what have we done?" Sanasenne lamented, her sorrow peppered by the clatter of her falling sword. "My humble apologies, Valorian. And, Tae, I . . . I'm sorry, my old friend."

"We are no longer friends, Princess," Taeven said crisply, but then he let out a long breath and added, "However, I . . . forgive you."

Sanasenne sobbed in relief, and Thal held her, nodding to Tae in gratitude—to Tae and me.

"I will take all of this into consideration," King Dehras said as he stepped up to his general. He paused pensively, and the entire room seemed to hold its breath. "By threatening the union between the Falcon Lord and his valorian, who are both treasured by the Goddess, you have not only jeopardized the safety of our world, but you have also insulted the Goddess. The forgiveness of the Falcon Valorian and the Falcon Lord, as well as my daughter's love for you, have saved your life, Thalsar. You will not be executed as you deserve to be. But I cannot have a man like you in my army. You are hereby stripped of your rank and discharged dishonorably from my service."

The angry expressions of the courtiers lessened at the King's decree, even as Thalsar's face paled.

"And although I will allow you to remain in Wynvar, you will leave my court, never to return."

"Father!" Sanasenne shrieked.

Taeven's jaw clenched as the court looked more satisfied; Trolls began to loosen their meaty fists and Red Caps sheathed the daggers they'd drawn. It took me a second to work out why this was so significant and satisfying for them, but, finally, I realized what the punishment meant . . . for Sanasenne. She would never be able to marry Thalsar. How could she when he wouldn't be allowed to step foot in the Royal Palace? When the King banished Thalsar from court, he'd also banished any chance of him ever taking the throne.

King Dehras held up his hand. "Be thankful for that mercy, Daughter. And that his punishment doesn't extend to you."

The smug expressions of the courtiers turned into shock. Banishing a princess would mean removing her title and denying the Kingdom its heir. The King was seriously pissed.

Sana went silent again, staring at her father with eyes gone cold. She had just faced a hard truth—that her father's love wouldn't save her from everything. That he wouldn't stand by her no matter what, as most fathers would do. And that loving Thalsar might mean losing her family.

"I accept my punishment, Your Majesty, and I thank you for your mercy." Thalsar bowed to the King, then took Sana's hand and kissed it. "This is not the end of us, sweetheart. I don't need to be your prince, just the man you love."

"Thal," Sana whispered and hugged him tightly. "I'm going with you."

The entire court gasped again.

"No!" the Queen shrieked, then turned to her husband. "Dehras, do something!"

"It is her choice, my dear," the King said stoically. "She must make it."

"Sana, no!" the Queen begged. "Don't give up your throne for a traitor!"

"I love him, Mother." Sana lifted her chin. "He is not a traitor to me."

"And I love you too much to let you give up your family and home for me," Thal said. "Don't force me to break with you entirely, Sana. Please."

"Thal?" Sana's voice cracked. "We can go somewhere else. Down to the coast."

"Yes, we can. We can do that whenever you wish without you giving up your birthright." He stroked her hair tenderly. "It will be all right, my dearest. I am not defeated, just a bit broken, and I will heal."

Fuck, that tore at me, but there was only so much sympathy I could have for people who had conspired against me. I had forgiven them and stopped Tae from killing them, I wouldn't interfere further. Instead, I leaned against Tae and took comfort from him. He held me tighter and kissed the top of my head.

"But, Thal," Sana whispered.

"I'll see you tomorrow," Thal said brightly and kissed her cheek. "Things will look better in the morning." Then he stepped away from the Princess and bowed to the King and Queen. "I will pray to the Goddess for forgiveness, Your Majesties, and hope that someday I might prove myself to you again."

Then Thalsar, ex-General of the Falcon Army, strode out of the dining hall and toward a new life.

Chapter Thirty-Eight

Tae took me home, sitting with his arm around me the entire ride. We went upstairs holding hands and smiling softly at each other, then went straight into his bedroom.

"I'll have your clothes moved back into my dressing room in the morning," Tae said as he led me to the bed.

"I missed you," I said simply.

"Shane," he cried brokenly and pulled me into a tight embrace. "I was furious, angry beyond reason. I've never felt so betrayed in all my life."

"I know." I stroked his silken hair. "Neither have I."

"I'm sorry, sweetheart."

"Just tell me one thing. Did you know it was Sana watching us that day?"

Taeven froze.

"You did," I whispered. "I didn't want to believe her."

"She told you?" he growled, then shook his head. "I should have told you. I noticed it was her, but you were enjoying it, and I knew she was too, so I didn't see the harm. Then, afterward, when you said that thing about not knowing who it was making it more exciting, I decided not to tell you. She didn't make the best first impression, and I didn't want to ruin the experience for you."

"All right. I understand."

"Shane, I'm so sorry," he apologized again. "For all of it. I was a complete imbecile."

"Stop. I've already forgiven you for how you reacted." I eased back. "But you didn't do this, Tae. It was Sanasenne and Thalsar, and they have been punished. It's done. I'm just sorry that you lost two friends in the process."

"Me too," he admitted on a sigh. "To tell you the truth, one heartbreak was just replaced by another, but this one is easier to bear."

"Heartbreak?" I searched his eyes, hoping.

Tae stroked my cheek and smiled softly. "When you stopped me from hurting them, I realized that you were the only one who has ever brought me out of rage. And you did it, despite what they had done to you."

"I knew that hurting them would hurt you," I whispered. "The anger would have gone away and then you would have been left with the guilt. I didn't want you to shoulder that."

"There, that right there." He shook his head in disbelief. "That you could think about how I'd feel later and stop me from hurting them when you deserved vengeance—that is humbling, Shane. You make me a better person. You make me *want* to be a better person."

"There is no better, Tae." I grinned at him. "I like you just as you are."

"Like?"

"Love," I amended.

"And I love you just as you are."

My face split into a brilliant smile. "You do?"

"I think I always have, I just wasn't able to recognize it."

"Well, if it took this for you to realize that you love me, then I'm grateful to them for what they did."

"Perhaps I needed to break a bit so I could see what lay inside me," he mused. "But I wish I hadn't hurt you. That will haunt me."

"Don't let it. I think it worked out as it was supposed to. I'm happy; be happy with me."

Tae kissed me then—gently and thoroughly, putting his love into the movements of his lips and the slide of his fingers through my hair. Putting it into his tongue and hips as they undulated against me. It came through every inch of his body to permeate every inch of mine. When he finally eased back, I felt drunk with it. Drunk on him.

"It's forever now, Shane," Tae said firmly. "There's no going back for me. I hope you know that."

"I love you so fucking much. You're damn straight it's forever!" I grabbed his face and pulled him down into another kiss, this one savage and joyous.

I put my all into that kiss—the pain I'd felt over losing him, the ache of loneliness, and the relief of our reunion. But, most especially, I put my love into those slashing, stabbing, pressing motions. Shoved it into his mouth before luring him into mine. And Tae growled victoriously.

Our clothes were gone in moments, then he had me on the bed, his body caging mine and hands stroking my face as he continued to kiss me. But *he* gentled *me* this time. With those tender hands and loving lips, he brought me down from my wild joy into sweet languor. Into rolling waves of emotion so deep and vast that the Bellor couldn't compare. I shivered uncontrollably as my body and heart opened to him. As my soul reached for his even though a piece of it was already inside me.

And Tae gave me exactly what I needed.

Kisses trailing down my jaw. Across my chest. Fingertips outlining my muscles and trailing over my thighs. Strong, warlord body settling between my legs. Flashing amethyst eyes adoring me. I sighed and sank into bliss with him, hands tangling in his hair and kneading at his shoulders.

"Tae," I murmured, "I need you now."

"But I need *this*, Shane," he insisted. "I need to settle the falcon inside me; to assure it that we have our mate back."

"Your what?" I frowned at him.

"Every faerie has one person chosen for them by the Goddess," Tae murmured as he kissed his way down my belly. "The bond between mates is even stronger than that between warlord and valorian. More binding than marriage. You're my mate, Shane, and I need to claim you."

"Mates. That is so fucking sexy," I whispered. "Claim away, babe."

Tae chuckled and nuzzled my straining cock. "This might take a while."

I whimpered in both anticipation and frustration.

Then his mouth was on me, those beautiful lips stretching around my shaft, moving down my length slowly as his amethyst stare held mine. His powerful hands touched me expertly, working my sacs and the base of my cock before slipping even further down. Teasing. Tickling. I felt his fingertip go slick against my hole, then nudge inside.

"Oh, fuck," I moaned. "Tae."

He drew off me and gave me a long lick before saying, "Roll onto your belly. I need to touch you everywhere."

I made another whimpering sound of need as I rolled onto my stomach. His large hands swept over my back, followed by kisses and flicks of his tongue. The warm brush of his face made shivers run through me, his breath stroking me like feathers. When his tongue found the dip of my lower back, I nearly came off the bed. But Tae held me down gently and nibbled his way over the crest of my ass.

"I love your ass," Taeven growled and bit it. "So thick." He palmed one cheek and massaged it. "So pert."

I buried my face in the pillow and groaned. It was all I could do not to beg him to stop playing with my ass and fuck it. But then he was kissing his way down my thighs, his hands stroking them as if he'd never seen legs before. I wriggled anxiously, trying to find some relief against the mattress. Finally, Tae pulled me up onto my hands and knees. I spread my legs eagerly so he could get into position.

But when Tae eased my cheeks apart, it wasn't his cock that invaded me. I shrieked in delight as his hot tongue speared my hole. Tae held me firmly apart as he pressed his face into that stretched space, sliding in deep. He flicked his tongue over the outside, laving it, then shoved inside, over and over, until I reached for my cock and started stroking.

"Not yet, darling." He said as his hand went to mine. He eased me away from my cock, but then stroked a layer of nectar over it. "Let me get inside you first."

"All right," I whispered. "Just get the fuck to it already."

He chuckled in that way that men do when they know they have you just where they want you.

"Is this what you want, baby?" Tae slipped the head of

his cock in.

"Yes!" I shrieked and tried to push back on him.

"Easy now." He stroked my lower back before gripping my hips. "Let me take you. This is a claiming, remember?"

"Then fucking take me, mate!"

Tae growled at my words and shoved into me with one thrust.

"Oh, fuck, yes!" I screeched and arched my back. "Claim that ass, Falcon Lord!"

"Tell me this ass is mine!" Taeven demanded as he began a steady thrusting.

"Oh, babe, it is."

"And I can take it wherever and whenever I wish."

"Tae, you can fuck me in the middle of camp if you want," I declared. "Or the middle of court. However you want me, I'm yours."

That drove the Falcon Lord wild and he began to speed up. The sounds coming out of him were bestial and his hands clutched me tighter. I could practically see his arousal billowing in the air around us.

"You like that, huh?" I panted over my shoulder. "You like the thought of showing me off? Of letting people see how your thick cock slides into my ass and how I beg for it?"

Taeven roared wordlessly and began slamming into me.

"But not tonight, Tae," I snarled possessively. "Tonight, it's just you and me."

Tae's wild gaze met mine over my shoulder and softened instantly. His savage slamming slowed as he bent over me to angle his head and kiss me. "I love you, Shane. It will always be just you and me. Fantasies are fun, but *this* is real."

"I love you too, Tae. And I need you to take this realness and shove it into me. Make *me* real again."

Taeven groaned and started thrusting once more. I set my hand to my cock and rubbed eagerly, losing myself to the feeling of him inside me.

"No!" Tae growled and pulled out.

"What?" I turned to gape at him.

"I need to see your face." He flipped me onto my back.

I grinned broadly at him and lifted my legs. "I need to see yours too."

Tae grabbed my thighs and used them to pull me sharply to him. "That's better." He slipped inside me and resumed his steady thrusting.

"Yeah, it is." I began to stroke myself as I admired his powerful body, tightening and releasing in those erotically beautiful movements.

Tae's gaze wandered back and forth from my face to my cock. "You're so fucking beautiful."

"Come inside me," I urged. "I want to feel you in me all night."

"Next time," he growled in a deep, primal voice. "Right now, I need my scent all over you."

"Oh, I like that idea too. Come on my chest, and I'll rub it in." I groaned and panted, "But it will have to mix with mine. I'm . . . I'm coming!"

Taeven shuddered violently, every muscle in his body going taut, and pulled out to empty across my chest as he shouted my name to the night.

Chapter Thirty-Nine

"No, don't go." Tae clutched me close when I tried to leave the bed the next morning.

"Unless you want piss all over your bed, I suggest you let go of me," I teased him.

"Return immediately," he commanded in his warlord tone as he released me.

"Yes, Falcon Lord!" I got out of bed and saluted him before hurrying to the bathroom.

I did my business, but also took a quick shower, just to freshen up. A night of marathon sex can leave a man feeling rank, especially when you have a lover who wants to "cover you in his scent." I also took the time to brush my teeth.

"That was not immediately," Tae grumbled when I climbed back into bed.

"No, but don't I smell better?" I snuggled up to him.

Tae made a pleased sound. "Good enough to fuck. Which I'll have to do since you washed my scent away."

"I have to go to the Academy soon."

Tae turned me in his arms so that I was facing away from him, then hooked my top leg over his. "The Academy can wait," he said as he slid into me.

I moaned and bent my arm back to grab his hair. "Tell me again, Tae."

"I love you, mate," he whispered in my ear.

"I love you too," I smiled as I said it. I was giddy with it—with that joyous relief of having my love returned. I could have listened to him profess his love to me all day. But hearing it while he was inside me—moving with lazy undulations as he held me tightly—that was a whole new level of bliss.

"Can I come inside you?" Tae asked, driving himself deeper.

"Oh, babe, not this time. I can't be going to class with an ass full of cum."

Tae chuckled. "Then I'll come *on* your ass. As I said, I need my scent on you."

"I didn't think birds had much of a sense of smell."

"They don't, but I'm not just a falcon, I'm also a man, and I like smelling me on your skin. It instantly summons the memory of fucking you, and that reminds my falcon that you are mine."

"Ugh, you're so fucking sexy; I can't stand it!"

I felt him grin against my neck. "Sexy enough to come inside you?"

"You brat! No, come *on* my ass."

Taeven laughed and sped up. I sped up my strokes on my cock too, and soon, we were coming together—him on my ass as promised. And we laughed as we came.

Tae rolled away, crossed his arms behind his head, and grinned at me. "First laughter during sex, now a laughing orgasm. I didn't think it was possible."

"Me either, but it was fucking brilliant." I slipped from bed to rinse off again.

"Don't you dare wash that off," he called after me. "Just wipe it."

"You're such a pervert!" I teased, but I did as he asked.

When I came back into the bedroom, he was still smiling and lazing in bed.

"Get up! You're coming with me, aren't you?"

Tae sighed dramatically. "I suppose."

"Oh, please." I rolled my eyes. "As if you aren't eager to see what else I can do."

"Oh, I am most eager for that." His grin turned wicked, and he sat up with a hunter's look.

"Cut it out!" I pointed at him before heading out of the room.

"Where are you going?!" He started after me.

"My clothes are in the other tower," I reminded him.

Tae grimaced. "I forgot."

"I'll be right back." I pulled him into a hug and nestled close for a moment. "I really missed you too."

"You have no idea how tormented I was," Tae whispered. "You haunted my dreams."

I kissed his chest and looked up at him. "I hope you won't stop dreaming of me now that I'm back."

"Never," Tae groaned and kissed me soundly before setting me away from him. "You'd best get dressed or I'll have you bent over the bed."

I ran away, his laughter following me.

Chapter Forty

"So, truth has prevailed," Avanla said smugly as Taeven and I strode into the classroom.

I winced. "It was . . ."

"Traumatic," Tae finished for me as he went to hug Avanla. "Thank you for standing by Shane and helping him when I could not."

"When you *would* not," she corrected him, but she did it gently. "You're welcome, Falcon Lord. I'm glad to see that you have your valorian *and your senses* back."

"The Royal Army will have to assign a new general," I added.

"The General has been removed from duty?" she asked in surprise. "I would have thought he'd be executed."

"Ava!" I gaped at her.

"She's right, Shane," Tae said gravely. "You saved his life. He was proven to be a traitor to the crown and his kingdom. The punishment for that crime is execution. That's why the King stood aside and watched while I fought Thalsar. He expected me to kill Thal. Expected and approved of it. Maybe even hoped for it so he wouldn't have to punish his daughter's lover."

"You fought him?" Avanla lifted a brow. "Good. I hope

you beat him soundly."

I sighed. "Can we forget about this now? I just want to get back to my lessons."

"He's doing well, I've heard," Tae said to Avanla.

"He's doing miraculously," Ava clarified. "The Goddess is doubtless behind it. That both gladdens and troubles me."

"Why does it trouble you?" I asked.

"If she is interfering in your training, things must be dire," Tae concluded.

"Yes, Falcon Lord, those are my thoughts exactly," Avanla confirmed and led us out of the room. "I think we should study in the library today. You need a break from physical manifestation."

"But . . ."

"She's right," Tae said. "You've been through a lot emotionally and physically. Your body needs to rest."

"Well, I am a little tired after our . . . reunion last night," I admitted.

"You don't have to speak in code around me, lad. I know exactly what you two were up to after being separated for so long." She strode out of the classroom, and I grimaced at her back. "And I know exactly what face you're giving me right now."

My grimace dropped into a gape.

Taeven chuckled, took my hand, and dragged me after her. "She's a teacher, Shane. She knows students."

Two hours later, I was regretting my agreement. I would rather have been practicing magic than reading about it. I groaned, got to my feet, and stretched, clasping my hands behind my head and pushing my elbows back. After rolling my neck, I went for a walk in the stacks to stretch my legs too. I was halfway down one aisle when a book fell into my path. It didn't just topple, which would have been startling enough; it shot out from the shelf and dropped right in front of me.

"What the fuck?!" I jerked back.

"Shhh," came from several directions at once.

"A book just flew off the shelf at me; I think an exclamation is appropriate!" I snarled back.

Footsteps came from everywhere as several scholars and one warlord converged on me. We all stared at the book—a heavy leather tome that could not fall off a shelf even were an earthquake to rock all of Wynvar, much less propel itself off one as it had. It had fallen open, facing me.

"Are you certain it fell?" Avanla asked.

"Am I *certain*?" I lifted a brow at her. "Since it fell right in front of me, yeah. I saw the damn thing fling itself off the shelf as if it were trying to attack me." I pointed at a space between books.

The other scholars looked skeptical but they drew closer and tried to peer at the pages that the book had opened to. No one dared to touch the thing. Then the pages started to move.

We all jumped back, which I thought was pretty damn hilarious considering that most of us were teachers of magic. The pages rustled as if in a sharp and very precise breeze, then fell open. I started to approach the book, but Tae grabbed my arm.

"It's just a book, Tae. It's not going to hurt me," I said.

"If you think that, then you haven't been paying attention," Avanla snapped and swept past me.

She held her hands over the book, closed her eyes, and concentrated. After a few seconds of this, she bent and picked it up. Whatever she'd done, the other scholars trusted it because they drew closer.

"What does it say?" I asked.

She flipped the book to glance at the cover, keeping her place with a finger, then handed me the thing. "It's a book on the Unsidhe races—*The Ultimate Unsidhe Reference* by Almand Henris."

"That's a good book," one of the scholars noted. "Very comprehensive."

"Goblins have two hearts," I read the first line, then glanced at the sketch of a Goblin's anatomy on the page beside it. "Goblins have two hearts?" I asked.

"Yes, they're highly adapted to war," Avanla said. "A blow to one of their hearts puts them into a death-like stasis. Enemies believe they have died when in actuality, they are healing, their second heart keeping them alive while the first is repaired."

"Impressive," I murmured. "But what has that got to do with me?"

"Only the Goddess knows," Avanla whispered reverently, and the other scholars bowed their heads.

Tae took the book from me and skimmed the pages. "It must have something to do with the war." He looked up at me. "I think we need to return soon, Shane."

I looked at my teacher. "The other valorians are learning to use emotion magic, and I'll need to start training with them. How long do you think it will be before I'm ready for that?"

Avanla glanced at the other scholars, and they nodded.

"We will combine our efforts to accelerate your progress. But first, I think you need to finish reading those pages. And don't just read them, lad, memorize them. Those words could mean the difference between life and death."

"Uh, can't I just copy them down?" I asked.

Avanla blinked, then looked sheepish. "Yes, I suppose that's a good idea. But you must also learn them. Who knows when you shall need this knowledge? It could be in the midst of battle and then you won't be able to refer to your notes."

"Fair enough," I conceded.

"I will read them too," Tae offered. "I think it may be important for both of us to know these things."

"Well, that didn't sound ominous at all," I grumbled and headed back to the table with *The Ultimate Unsidhe Reference*.

Chapter Forty-One

After the day the book landed—I refer to it that way to give it the gravitas it deserved—my training took on an intensity that left me groaning every night, and not in a good way. I would hobble away from the classroom with Tae supporting me, his worried gaze my only comfort, and nestle in against him during the ride home. As far as the book, we'd read the whole section on Goblins and transcribed the pages it had opened to for future reference. My head was full of Goblin facts and my body full of magic. It only took a week for the scholars to declare that I was ready for emotion training.

"I suppose this means that we'll be leaving today," I said as I stared out the window at Wynvar.

"Do I detect a note of sadness in your voice?" Tae teased me.

We were at the small dining table in his sitting room, having our breakfast near a view, just as we Falcon Faeries liked it. And yes, I had finally begun to accept that this was who I was now. It was nice to be able to sit down with Taeven to enjoy the first meal of the day instead of grabbing something on the way to the carriage. But he was right; leaving Wynvar would be rough.

"It's grown on me," I admitted.

"I'm glad. If all goes well, I'd like to come back here to live after the war is over. We can always spend winters in Dreslen."

"Not the entire winter," I said with a soft smile. "I've even come to appreciate the cold."

"A changed man," Tae murmured.

"In many ways." I looked at him pointedly.

"We're not leaving today," he declared.

"No?"

"No. We've both been working hard, and we deserve a day to ourselves. Our army can survive another day without us."

I grinned and cut into my breakfast with more gusto. "What shall we do with ourselves?"

"Anything you like," he offered grandly. "We could go shopping—there are a few stores that sell baking tools and the like. Or we could just stroll through the city. Or we could go flying."

"Flying?" I perked up.

"We'll be flying for hours tomorrow," Tae warned me. "So we couldn't go for a long flight today, but we could do a quick tour of the valley."

"I'd like that." I grinned broadly. "It will be our first time flying together."

Taeven nodded. "That's why I suggested it. I'd like to have you to myself for our first flight."

"Babe, you can have me to yourself wherever and whenever you wish," I teased. "I made a promise, remember?"

"You joke now, but I'm holding you to that promise," Tae took my hand to say. His eyes gleamed with mischief as he added, "I'm going to wait until I screw up royally and then insist on making love to you."

"You scoundrel," I said dramatically, but I also squeezed his hand. Then, in a much softer tone, I added, "This feels like a dream."

"Breakfast with me?" Tae grinned.

"*Life* with you," I whispered.

"For me as well," he whispered back. Then he went grave. "Losing you would turn it into a nightmare. So you must promise me to be careful, Shane. When we go to battle, do not leave my side."

"I promise."

"Thank you. Now, before we leave, I have a gift for you." He leaned over and pulled something out from behind the heavy drapes. It was a guitar case. He handed it to me with a shy smile. "A mating gift."

"A mating gift?" I whispered as I scooted my seat back and laid the case on my lap. "I didn't get you anything."

"You gave me yourself; I want nothing more."

"I'm going to kiss you for that," I promised. "But first, I want to see what's in this case."

I opened the lid and revealed a gorgeous guitar of astounding craftsmanship. The wood was golden, enhanced by the slices of amethyst that formed the fretboard and bridge. I ran my fingers adoringly over the golden tuning pegs, down the gleaming neck, and across the golden pic guard that was shaped like a wing. Amethyst and gold, just like his eyes. It was a treasure, not just an instrument.

"I've never seen a guitar like this," I whispered and drew my nails across the strings. A rich sound rolled out from its belly. "Tae." I looked up at him. "Thank you. I love it."

"I love you, mate," Tae said, his amethyst eyes glowing in

a shaft of sunlight.

Yep, just like a dream.

Chapter Forty-Two

I rolled through the air, laughing, as Taeven chased me.

We had left the city to dive into the valley, where a warmer temperature ruled. It wasn't tropical by any means, but the pines and spruce were bare of snow and the gleaming streams that ran through their midst flowed free of ice. The air was crisp but not frigid, and I didn't even need to fluff my feathers.

I shrieked in joy as I leveled out, wings extended to glide for a bit. Tae settled beside me, one eye focused on me as we flew above the spiky treetops. That was the hardest thing to get used to—the split vision of a bird. Luckily, the avian brain that came with my falcon body helped me deal with it, even if that brain held a mind that had once been human. If you could even label minds in such a way. In fact, if you could, my mind would probably still be human. Mostly, at least. I may have accepted that I was fae now, but my thoughts hadn't changed; I was still me.

But those were musings for another time. It was impossible to focus on any concerns for long with the wind lifting me and my mate calling to me. Yes, mate. This body knew what that meant more than my Sidhe one did. It held knowledge of the falcon, guiding me in many ways, not the least of which were my interactions with Tae. All of my aerial acrobatics were performed at the insistence of my falcon—a way to show off for my mate. I kept making these strange sounds, a sort of chup-tuk chup-tuk noise. Every time I did, Tae cried back in a similar manner. And I had the strangest urge to kill something and drop it on his head. I resisted that one.

Tae dove suddenly, and I followed. He aimed for a clearing between the trees, through which a clear stream flowed, glinting in the sunlight. Snapping his wings out, Tae glided into a landing, and I did the same. Once on the ground, we set down the satchels we'd been carrying in our claws—and my new guitar—and shifted to Sidhe. I would have happily stayed naked with Tae, but as much as it was warmer in the valley, it wasn't warm enough to stand around in my birthday suit. I got dressed as I ogled my man. Mine. All mine. I could hardly believe it.

I was still getting my boots on when Tae pulled a blanket from his satchel and spread it on the bank of the stream. He removed packets of food and a flask as well, setting them on the blanket.

"A picnic?" I asked in surprised pleasure. "When did you pack all that?"

"I asked Halfrin to pack it for us while you were in the bathroom." Tae grinned.

"Sneaky." I nodded in approval and took a seat on the blanket. "Well done, babe."

"Thank you." He preened and settled beside me. "You know it's a primal urge for me to provide food for my mate."

"Is that why I kept wanting to kill something and drop it on you?"

Tae laughed boisterously. "That would be why, yes. Falcons do that when they're courting—the birds, not the faeries, though, as I said, we feel the urge. We just channel it into things like picnics."

"Much better than a dead mouse dropped on your head."

"Indeed." He pulled a large canister out of the satchel and handed it to me. "Hot chocolate."

"Oh, yum!" I unscrewed the lid.

Tae set out two little mugs, took the canister from me, and poured the thick, rich liquid into the cups. They steamed in protest of the cold.

"This is perfect." I held my mug in both hands and sipped, sighing from the warmth and the sweet flavor. "How about we fly away like you wanted to do that day?"

Tae's eyes widened.

"I'm joking." I leaned against his shoulder and looked out at the forest. "I'm just sad to be leaving."

"We will come back soon, sweetheart," Tae promised as he put an arm around my shoulders.

I smiled and chuckled a little.

"What?"

"No one but my mother has ever called me sweetheart," I admitted.

"Should I stop?" He looked wary.

"*Never* stop." I lifted my face for a kiss.

Taeven eagerly obliged me, tasting of chocolate and love. I moaned, seeking more of it before I eased back to nibble at his delicious lips. Tae's free hand came up to brush my hair back and tuck it behind an ear.

I leaned into his touch. "I love it when you stroke my hair."

"I see that." He sank his fingers in the ends to clench and

release the strands. "It's so thick."

"Like my mother's hair." I nodded. "It's one of the reasons I keep it shoulder-length. It gets heavy, but I like it a little long and this length is just long enough for me to tie it back when I'm working."

Taeven's expression went naughty. "I never did put you in that flight harness as I promised, but I think I'll use your hair as a handhold instead. Would you like it if I pulled your hair when I fuck you from behind?"

His sudden crude words rocked through me, hardening me. "Oh, now you've done it."

"Uh-uh." He leaned back when I tried to kiss him. "We have lunch waiting."

"Let it wait."

"Shane," Tae chided and took my hand. "I want to spend some time alone with you without being inside you."

"Ugh, when did I start dating a woman?" I groaned dramatically.

Taeven laughed his ass off—so violently that he had to put his drink down. When he settled, he began opening the packs of food and portioning them out on the waxed cloth they'd been wrapped in. "Come now, you'll need fuel if we're going to fuck in the cold."

"Don't you know that you need to rest after eating?" I grumbled. "You could get a cramp."

Tae chuckled again. "I'm not going to get a cramp and neither are you; we're faeries."

"But my stomach will be full and then I'll want to take a nap," I tried again.

"I think I can rouse you."

"Ugh, Tae, you're supposed to eat *after* sex, not before."

"Then we shall be rebels." He leaned over and kissed my cheek. "Or we could relax awhile and you could play your new guitar for me before we have sex."

"What?! You want me to wait even longer?"

"I need you too, but I feel as if all we've been doing lately is training and fucking."

"And eating," I added. "Usually *after* fucking."

"Here, put some of this in your mouth." He placed a cloth full of roasted chicken, chunks of cheese, and a hunk of bread on the blanket before me.

I sighed and started nibbling, then ate with more gusto. It was, as everything I'd eaten in Varalorre, exceptional. The best roast chicken I'd ever had. Tae smiled smugly when he saw me enjoying the food, then set to his own meal.

He set a flask between us. "Water, if you'd care for some."

"Thanks." I took a swig.

"I want you to meet my family," Tae said softly.

"You do?" I asked, my heart shivering.

"Yes. We don't have time on this visit, but during the next, I'm taking you to Dreslen."

"The next visit," I murmured. "I like the sound of that."

"Will you take me to meet your family?" Tae asked hesitantly.

"Of course, you're going to meet my family! We already talked about this, remember? My parents are going to love you. Dad will probably interrogate you for a bit, but then he'll be thrilled."

"You think so?"

"Why wouldn't he be?"

"Because I've changed you in a very physical way." He stroked a finger over my cheekbone. "You don't think they'll be upset to see you so altered?"

"I think they'll be happy that I'm happy," I said confidently. "They might have some concerns, as I did, but it's too late now, and they're very practical people. They'll accept it and make the most of it."

"Good," he said in relief. "I was worried I'd have another fight on my hands."

"If you did, you wouldn't be fighting alone," I said softly.

"Even against your parents?" Tae asked in surprise.

"When it concerns us? Yes, even against my parents. Now, if it were about something that could hurt them, it would be another story. But otherwise, I'll have your back, Tae. Always."

"And I will have yours, mate," he said firmly as he took my hand. "I would never do anything to endanger your family. I will protect them with you because they are important to you, and you are the most important person in my life. I never want you to doubt that. I never want you to worry about your place in my life and my heart."

"This is sounding serious," I murmured as I turned to face him more fully. "Tae, we're going to make it through the war."

"I believe that too; I must believe it or I won't be able to take you back there. You are too important to me now. I'd forsake them all to see you safe."

"Holy shit," I whispered. I moved to kiss him, but he squeezed my hand and leaned back.

"I'm not done, sweetheart."

"All right," I sat back warily.

"I can't go back without at least asking you to be mine."

"What are you talking about? I am yours. I thought I was pretty damn clear about that."

Tae grinned and glanced to the side. I followed his gaze to see a flower sprouting from the earth beside the blanket. It grew in seconds and when it unfurled its petals to the winter sun, it revealed a gold ring lying in its fluffy stamens.

"What the fuck?" I whispered in wonder.

"Shane, you're my gift from the Goddess, the greatest love of my life, and I never want to be apart from you. Will you marry me?"

I looked from Taeven to the flower ring and back. "How did you do that?"

Tae's smile went shaky. "I slipped it into the ground with a seed while I was laying out the blanket."

"Amazing." I gaped at the flower. Among its vibrant petals—a shade of red to match the Falcon Soul—the gold band gleamed, showing off an intricate carving of falcons in flight. Two falcons, to be precise.

"Shane?" Taeven's voice took on a note of anxiety.

I blinked. "Oh!" My breath caught. "Fuck, this is really happening."

"Yes." Tae chuckled. "This is real. I am real, and I'm waiting for your answer."

"My answer?" I gaped at him. "Are you fucking kidding me? It's yes. Of course, it's yes. It's yes *forever*." I snatched him to me and kissed him thoroughly.

After we finally eased away from each other, Taeven grinned brilliantly and plucked the ring from the flower. "We don't have time for a ceremony today or I'd marry you before we left. But know that in my heart, this is our wedding."

Tae removed another band from his satchel and held it out to me. I took it with wonder—a duplicate of mine, though slightly larger. *Great balls of fuck, this was happening now. Right now.*

"Shane, I promise to always love you and put you first in my heart and my life. I will be true to you no matter what may befall us. You are my mate."

The words had weight to them—the feel of ceremony— so I repeated them. "Taeven, I promise to always love you and put you first in my heart and my life. I will be true to you no matter what may befall us. You are my mate."

Tae smiled bright enough to light my world. "Together?" He held up my ring.

I nodded and held out my hand. Tae held out his and, in unison, we slid the rings on each other's fingers. Something shivered in the air around us, like the displacement made from the flap of wings, and I briefly felt a warm hand on my shoulder. Taeven's eyes widened, and I knew he felt it too. She was with us.

Tae's broad palms bracketed my face, and he stared at me a moment before saying, "You are my mate and my miracle."

Then he kissed me, and I knew that the true miracle was him. This wondrous man who, by some stroke of luck and magic, had become mine. Who loved me just as much as I loved him. Enough to risk everything for my safety. I started to tremble, and when we finally drew apart, my vision was blurry.

"I love you," Tae whispered and brushed his thumbs over my cheeks, wiping away my tears.

"I love you too, Tae, but if you don't *make love* to me right now, I'm going to scream."

Taeven burst out laughing, and another epiphany hit me. This was what our life would be like, whether we were fighting Farungals or having a picnic in a Varalorre forest. Love and laughter. That's what he was for me, and that's what I was for him. Forever. Or as long as the Goddess allowed us.

Since she was with us, I said my first prayer, though I did it silently. *Thank you. Thank you for choosing me and choosing to give me to him.*

A shiver rushed over me, like feathers against skin, and I heard her voice clearly for the first time.

You're welcome, my sweet boy.

Chapter Forty-Three

We had to stop twice on the way back to Stalana the next day. My wings weren't up to flying for such long spans yet. We used it as an excuse to linger in Varalorre a little longer, first having a drink in a Wolf pub—set in a town built around the base of massive trees—and then lunch in a Coyote cafe. Early that evening, we flew through the sparkling mists and left Varalorre.

We rested twice more in Stalana, and I felt like a horrible drag, but no one made me feel that way. All the nasty looks I'd been getting from Tae's knights had vanished overnight, and they now treated me with great respect. It was especially strange from Daron, but at least he had enough nerve to tell me why. Simply put, they had heard about the shit that went down with the Princess and the ex-general, and they finally saw me as deserving of their precious Falcon Lord. I wouldn't be hanging out with any of them, but I did appreciate their improved attitudes.

Finally, with the moon high above us, we landed within the Falcon Camp. We were instantly approached by guards who welcomed us home and then ran off to inform the Generals of our return. Taeven and I strode through the camp side by side ahead of his knights, the familiar sights and smells reminding me that this place was a type of home to me and there were reasons to be happy about returning to it. As we came within sight of the Falcon Lord's tent, Tae sent Nelos off to request dinner for all of us. Then we split up further, some of his guards going to drop their bags at their tents while the remainder went to their posts. Mere minutes after we arrived in Tae's tent, the fae and human generals came in. I was just walking back into the main room after depositing my satchel and new guitar in the bedroom, and my eyes widened at their promptness.

"Falcon Lord, your arrival is most timely," General Gravenne declared anxiously. "Our Falcon patrol returned an hour ago from their nightly flight out over the Bellor, and they've reported a sighting of Farungal ships on the horizon. We anticipate that they'll reach us by morning, perhaps sooner."

Tae's shoulders straightened and, after casting me a heavy look, he slid back into his warlord role. "Have you alerted the Unsidhe Camp?"

"Yes, my lord. They have joined us in our preparations."

"We don't want our soldiers weary for the fight. Let them rest until the ships get closer. For now, we keep a firm watch on the sea and prepare for an early morning. I want a Falcon sent out hourly to scan the Bellor. Once we're down to a three-hour window, rouse the troops. We will wait behind the beach walls and meet our enemies as they disembark. I want Falcons in avian form and humans with flight harnesses over their armor—just in case they're needed in the air or they need to be pulled out of battle." He glanced at me, and I knew he was remembering my rescue and the wounds it had created.

"Very good, my lord." General Gravenne nodded.

"And ask Commander Varcir if he would join us for dinner," Tae said. "We need to discuss our strategy."

"And perhaps Goblins," I said to Tae.

Tae nodded. "Yes, that had occurred to me."

"Goblins, my lord?" General Smith, the human general, asked.

"I'm uncertain why, but the Goddess compelled us to research Goblins while we were in Varalorre. I need to discuss it with Commander Varcir."

"Yes, my lord!" General Gravenne bowed reverently. Any mention of the Goddess inspired such reverence from the Fae, but especially when it referred to a sign from her.

The men hurried away while Tae and I faced each other.

"It looks as if a day does make a difference," Tae whispered. "We nearly missed the battle."

"But we didn't," I said firmly. "We arrived just in time. There's fate in that, Tae, and I have to believe that's a good sign."

Taeven nodded. "Sit down, my love. Dinner will be here soon, and we'll need our rest. After flying all day, we won't be at our best for battle."

"Perhaps we should stay on the ground?"

"No, I need to supervise from the air."

I started to speak, but he cut me off.

"And don't say that you can stay grounded without me. By my side, remember? That was our agreement."

"What if I can't fly?"

Tae grimaced. "Then we'll fight on the ground. But we will be strongest in falcon form."

"Falcon Lord, dinner has arrived," Nelos announced as he swept in, followed by several soldiers bearing food; one of them was Vanessa.

"Van!" I took the platter she was carrying, shoved it on the table, and hugged her.

"Shane!" She hugged me back. "Welcome home."

"Thanks." I glanced at the food. "And thanks for dinner. Oh, and I've got presents for everyone, but they're gonna have to wait."

"Yeah, I heard about the Farungal." She went grim.

Meanwhile, Tae spoke to Nelos, "Summon the rest of the Guard. Tonight, we'll dine together. The Generals and Commander Varcir will be joining us."

Nelos looked surprised, but nodded and hurried out.

"You may join us too, Corporal," Tae said to Vanessa.

Vanessa gaped at him, then stuttered, "Oh, thank you, my lord, but I've already eaten."

"Then get what rest you can," he said gently. "It will be an early morning and, I fear, a rough one."

Vanessa grinned. "That's every morning for us, my lord." Then she turned to me. "I'll let the others know that you've returned safely."

"Thanks." After she left, I turned to grin at Tae. "And thank you for inviting my friend to dinner."

"We'll have them all for a meal after the battle," Tae offered. "I want to meet them."

Could I get any happier? Doubtful.

"Falcon Lord?" a deep voice preceded a massive man into the tent. A Red Cap to be precise.

"Commander Varcir, please, come in. Join us." Tae waved

a hand at the table even as his knights settled into seats. "Have you eaten?"

"I have, but I never refuse food." He grinned and took the seat beside mine.

I tried not to stare at his damp, red cap, soaked in Farungal blood and kept fresh with a preservation spell. It was kinda their thing—soaking their caps in the blood of their enemies—and it had earned them their name. But technically, they were a type of Goblin. Which made the Commander the perfect choice to speak to about Goblins.

"Commander, we had an unusual incident in Varalorre," Tae started filling his plate as he spoke. "The Goddess led us to a book about the Unsidhe. In particular, she drew our attention to Goblins."

Varcir blinked his ivy-green eyes and leaned forward on bulky brown arms. His head cocked as he asked, "The Goddess wanted you to learn about Goblins?"

"Yes. We were hoping you might have some insight," Tae said as the Generals and his knights came into the tent. He waved them into seats before refocusing on Varcir.

Varcir grunted and heaped food on his plate. "I've got neither out nor insight. Can't imagine why the Goddess would bring Goblins to your attention." He frowned and paused. "Come to think of it, we suffered a huge Goblin loss in the last battle."

"How many were killed?" Tae laid his fork down and focused on the Red Cap.

"Many." Varcir grunted again. "Over forty, thirty-two of which are unaccounted for."

"Unaccounted for?" I asked.

"Bodies missing," Varcir said and shrugged. "Not uncommon. Farungal like Goblin flesh as much as we Red Caps like Farungal blood."

"What?" I growled. "Are you saying that they *eat* Goblins?"

Varcir looked at me as if I were daft. "Yes; I thought I was clear when I said they like Goblin flesh."

"I knew they were monstrous, but I didn't know they were cannibals," I muttered.

"Technically not cannibals," Varcir said casually. "We are two different species."

"I think that's stretching it, Commander," General Gravenne said.

Varcir grunted once more. "True, especially now that we know we are related in a way."

I frowned pensively. "Related and yet they consume Goblin flesh." I looked at Tae. "That must have something to do with it. Why else show us a page with a drawing of the anatomy of a Goblin?"

"I don't know," Tae murmured. "Could be. But what are we supposed to do with that knowledge?"

"Hold on, Red Caps drink Farungal blood?" I asked the Commander.

"We don't drink it, just soak our hats and enjoy the occasional taste." He grinned viciously.

"But isn't Farungal blood poisonous?"

"Only after they've been dead for several hours," Varcir explained. "It's the venom from their fangs and tails—it spreads through their bodies once they die." He cocked his head pensively. "Maybe we should poison the Goblins after they die?"

The entire table stared at Varcir in horror.

"They would want their deaths to mean something," Varcir said defensively. "Perhaps it would be easier to give them the poison and they can take it if they receive a death blow." He shrugged. "If they have the strength left. Hard to know what would be a death blow though, what with their two hearts."

"That would be a fitting payback," Tae murmured. "Killed by the flesh they harvested from a battlefield."

"Serve them right," I added.

"I will offer the choice to my Goblin soldiers," Varcir said firmly. "They can decide if they wish to carry the poison. But, knowing Goblins, I think they will all accept."

Could that be it? I frowned at Tae, then at Varcir. It seemed wise, but I couldn't understand what a knowledge of Goblin anatomy had to do with it. Even Varcir had mentioned the two hearts and for some reason, that felt significant to me. Still, it was the best idea we had and with a fleet of Farungal ships looming on the horizon, we'd have to go with it.

Chapter Forty-Four

It began like any other battle, with the exception that I was on the front line as opposed to the back. I stood beside Taeven in my falcon form, head cocked to peer over the wall of sandbags before me, waiting for my warlord's instructions. Tae stood confidently, head lifted and one falcon eye angled toward the rowboats full of Farungals coming our way.

"Archers!" Tae shouted from his falcon beak.

Our human archery units pulled back their bowstrings and aimed.

"Release!"

Arrows whizzed through the air, hitting Farungals before they'd even made it to land. But there were so many of them. They came like a swarm of bugs, rushing the shore with their shields lifted to ward off the arrows.

"Release!" Tae shouted again.

Another wave of arrows shot past, and that was it for the archers. We couldn't have arrows flying through the air at the same time as Falcon Faeries.

"Swords!" Tae shouted.

Bows were cast aside and swords drawn. With that order, Commander Varcir started shouting, sending his troops into the battle with ours.

"Falcons to me!" Taeven took to the air with a spring of his legs, and I followed him, along with his Falcon Guard.

Battle became a whole new experience from up there. Less chaotic, more precise. I didn't have a lot of training with fighting in Falcon form—as in none at all—but it was as instinctual as shrieking. I picked a target and dove, then my bird took over. Talons the size of human forearms pierced scaled Farungal flesh and rent that hardy skin to ribbons. Barbed tails lashed out but were easy for me to avoid, and their swords couldn't slice fast enough to hit me. I screeched victoriously as I picked them off, one by one, Tae at my side.

Below us, the Unsidhe army joined ours. Leanan-Sidhes hissed viciously, their nails growing with their fury, and gracefully darted through the Farungal ranks, their speed dizzying. Trolls lumbered forward more slowly, but when they reached the front, monsters died, crushed beneath their boulder-fists. Red Caps laughed maniacally as they swung axes and swords nearly as long as a human was tall, slicing Farungals from belly to throat. They didn't pause to soak their caps (though some angled their heads into the spray); that activity was reserved for after the battle.

Around their larger Red Cap cousins, the squat Goblins swarmed, terrifying despite their size. We'd been notified that every single Goblin had eagerly agreed to carry a vial of poison with them. I wasn't surprised; if I'd known there was a possibility that Farungals would cart my body away for a post-battle snack, I would have carried one too. Slightly less terrifying were the Dwarves, with their thick beards and pointed helmets, who swung axes, maces, and hammers nearly as big as they were. Their signature move was to cut a Farungal's legs out from beneath them, then take their heads. Far worse were the Imps, who rushed forward in a tide of laughing little bodies with razor-sharp teeth.

In contrast to the Goblins, Imps, and Dwarves, the Glastigs and Sylphs were breathtaking in their beauty. The Sylphs were ethereal, turning nearly transparent to slip through the Farungal troops and then reverting to solid to strike their blows. Very few Sylphs joined the armies, but those who did were some of the most valuable soldiers around. It was extremely hard to land a blow on a Sylph—like trying to cut the air—but they rarely missed. As for the Glastigs, they looked exactly like what they were—creatures of the forest. A blend of beast and man whose strong hooves could crack bones. In their armor, they were especially stunning, the shining steel gleaming against swarthy skin and dark fur.

It was all going quite well, Farungals falling like flies, until a strange screeching rolled over the battlefield.

Tae turned his head, and I followed his gaze toward a group of rowboats that had just landed on the beach. The creatures scrambling out of those boats were not Farungals. I stared, trying to figure out what I was seeing. They were squat and silvery gray, some with curved tusks, and some had sharp fangs. Vicious claws curved from their thick fingers and spikes stuck out from their shoulders and backs. But it was their eyes that troubled me the most; they were the green of burning death oil. Farungal soul stone magic.

"Goblins!" I screeched in epiphany. "They're the missing Goblins!"

"By the Mother," Tae cursed. "The Farungal have transformed the Goblins with their dark magic and set them against us."

Whatever had been done to those poor Goblins, it made them nearly destructible. They surged forward and spread out to start a wave of slaughter that, from my aerial view, bloomed like explosions. Farungals cheered, then chittered, pushing forward in the wake of their deadly creations. I had wondered why they hadn't been using their death oil and here was the answer; they had a new weapon to test.

Screams peppered the air as soldiers fell to the eerie efficiency of the altered Goblins. Unsidhe soldiers rushed forward, but many were hesitant to strike their brethren and their hesitation cost them. Once those few fatal mistakes were made, they rallied and pressed forward, but the creatures ran them down as easily as they did the humans.

The battle had turned.

The band of altered Goblins did more damage than should have been possible, clearing the way for the Farungal forces to obliterate us. Falcons dove and attacked, but any who tried to strike an altered Goblin was picked out of the air by a little hand and smashed to the ground with impossible, jaw-dropping power. The power of death.

In the seconds it took for the Farungals to gain the advantage, I searched my memories for the information the Goddess had shown me. This had to be why she had presented me with those pictures of Goblin anatomy. Two hearts; strike one and a Goblin goes into a death-like state. That was helpful, but striking either of their hearts was going to be a problem. So, what was the key? What other information had she intended for me to use?

"The armpit," I whispered. Then I screeched, "Strike upward into the right armpit!" I dove at one of the altered Goblins.

"Shane!" Taeven roared, fear tinging his tone, and chased after me.

"Strike upward into their right armpits! It's the easiest path to their heart!" I shouted to our soldiers as I hooked my claw into the armpit of an altered Goblin.

Taeven was screaming above me, but the Goblin I hit stared up at me with startling gratitude. The green glow in his eyes died out as his body went limp, falling into stasis. Instead of letting him go, I clutched the body of the Goblin and carried him to camp. I didn't believe that the Goddess had shown me that book just to give me a way to kill these men. She had done it to save her children—all of her children—and I wouldn't leave this soldier on the battlefield to be trampled.

I laid him somewhere safe and rose back into the air to find myself alone. Knowing that I was in the relative safety of the camp, Tae had gone to rally the troops, shouting orders to strike upward at the Goblin's hearts through their right armpits and to then preserve the fallen. Our armies roared in response, especially the Goblins, and fell upon their altered friends in a huge mass. Glowing eyes winked out all over the battlefield and mutated bodies were gently carried to the safety of the camps. The altered-Goblin threat was defeated in mere minutes, leaving the Farungals fumbling in the middle of a unified force of two very angry armies. To say they were slaughtered would be putting it mildly. Not a single Farungal made it back to the ships.

Chapter Forty-Five

What followed was a massive beach clean-up that I was —thank the Goddess—excused from. The Farungal bodies had to be burned so they didn't poison the land, though the Red Caps did indulge in a good hat-soaking first. Bonfires dotted the beach, the corpses of monsters feeding the flames as our soldiers celebrated, both human and fae, together. Once all the bodies had been added to the flames, our troops set to drinking and eating as if it were a barbecue. But inside the Falcon Lord's tent, the officers of both the Sidhe and Unsidhe camps were gathered to discuss what to do about the altered Goblins. They'd been put in the hospital tent under guard, all of them still in stasis, but they'd be healed soon. Their guards kept a close watch on them, one soldier per Goblin, with the order to stab their charges in the heart at the first sign of awakening. Yes, it was brutal, but we had to keep them in stasis until we figured out how to undo the dark magic the Farungals had worked upon them.

"It's this new Queen," Varcir snarled furiously. "The last King was her brother so she's after revenge."

Tae rolled his eyes, "They've been after revenge from the very beginning, Varcir. It makes no difference. If she hadn't come up with the spell, someone else would have. They are cunning in their cruelty."

"What about your soul stone?" I asked Tae. "Can't it change the Goblins back?"

"It's possible, but with such a large number of Goblins to heal, the amount of magic it would take would be significant. I'm hesitant to drain my kingdom like that."

"We have another option," a man with crimson hair declared as he strode into the tent with a large group of faeries.

I recognized several of them, including the redhead, as warlords. I assumed the people with them were their valorians.

"Vathmar?" Taeven stood up and went to greet his guests. "What are you doing here?"

"As you know, my valorian has been training the others to work with emotion magic," the Wolf Lord said. "So we were together when the Goddess summoned us here. And now I know why she called upon us."

"The Goddess summoned you?" Varcir asked. "She spoke to you?"

"She spoke to the White Lynx." Vathmar waved a hand toward a green-eyed blond with a kind face.

"Hello, I'm Luca," the blond said politely with a wave at the room. "The Goddess showed me a vision of a strange monster and told me to fly to your aid. The Hawks and Owls graciously offered to carry us here."

"So you've got altered Goblins?" another blond, this one more tawny than the last, asked as he stepped forward to take Vathmar's hand. To the Wolf Lord, he said, "Sounds like what they did to our Wolves."

"Yes, Wolf Valorian." Tae nodded respectfully to the second blond. "I thought as much myself. Luckily, we were able to put the Goblins into stasis by stabbing one of their hearts."

"*One* of their hearts?" A dark-haired man swaggered forward. He glanced at the Hawk Lord—a stunning man with long, snowy hair—and asked, "How many hearts do they have?"

"Two," the Hawk Lord said.

"Well, fuck. Lucky bastards."

"Do you think all of you are ready for this, Wolf Valorian?" Yet another blond—shit, there were a lot of them—asked. This one I recognized as the Owl Lord. He had a dark-haired woman beside him and his arm curved around her protectively.

"I'm assuming so since the Goddess led us here," the Wolf Valorian said.

"My valorian has been trained in all but emotion magic. Perhaps he could help," Taeven said proudly as he held a hand out to me. After I took it and stood, he added, "This is Shane Rumerra, the Falcon Valorian."

"Hey." I nodded to the newcomers.

"Hey, man, I'm Ravyn," the dark-haired one with the Hawk Lord said. "Hawk Valorian."

"I'm the Lynx Valorian." Luca reached forward to shake my hand. "It's a pleasure to meet you, Shane."

"This is Sarah," the Owl Lord introduced the woman. "The Owl Valorian."

Then there was Marigold the Jackal Valorian, Julianna the Coyote Valorian, Ryker the Fox Valorian, Tristan the Leopard Valorian, and the Wolf Valorian was introduced as Devyn.

"Welcome to the rapidly growing ranks, Shane," Tristan drawled. "Care to try your hand at emotion magic?"

"I would indeed." I grinned broadly.

"You may be needed too, Falcon Lord," Devyn said. "I'm sure you remember how Vathmar helped me destroy the Farungal soul stones. The connection between a warlord and his valorian is extremely powerful, more than was previously thought. Our warlords amplify our emotion magic and some have even learned to unite their magic with ours. I believe that is the true purpose for the bond the Goddess creates between us. She isn't just turning humans into faeries; she's forging a weapon of multiple parts to be used in many ways."

"Whatever Shane and our Goddess needs, I will gladly supply." Taeven squeezed my hand before heading out of the tent. "Follow me; I'll take you to the Goblins."

Chapter Forty-Six

The bodies of the altered Goblins had been laid on cots in the camp hospital but sectioned off from the other patients by fabric partitions and a line of Red Cap guards. The Red Caps bowed as their commander approached, then stepped aside for us.

"Whoa! That's a lot of ugly," Ravyn whispered, then made a grunting sound when his warlord smacked him in the stomach. "What?"

"Show some respect," the Hawk Lord hissed. "They have been tortured by death magic."

"I do respect them, but it doesn't change the fact that they look nasty." Ravyn waved his hand at the gray creatures. "I'm just keeping it real."

"Keep it quiet as well."

"Can you help them?" a Red Cap asked as he moved away from his charge.

"We hope so, Brelik," Varcir said. "All of you, step aside."

The guards moved to the side of the space as the valorians and their warlords—including Tae and me—stepped forward.

"What do I do?" I asked Devyn, who had taken a spot next to me.

"We've concluded that love is the strongest emotion to use when we don't know what specifically to channel," Devyn said. "Regardless, I think it will be perfect for this because of its ability to transform. Just hold your warlord's hand and focus on the love you share." Then he looked sheepish. "Sorry, I'm assuming you're romantically together."

"We are, and our love will be more than enough to fuel Shane's magic," Taeven said confidently.

I grinned at him before saying to Devyn, "He's my mate."

"Congratulations," Devyn said brightly. "Vathmar is my mate too."

"Uh, Valorians?" Varcir called to us. "You'd better hurry."

We all looked over at the Goblins to see several of them twitching.

"Clasp hands, everyone," Devyn instructed. "Focus on love. On what it means to you specifically. Feel it. Sink into it. Then lift it up and direct it at the faeries before us. See them whole again. See the dark magic burning out of their bodies and souls. Then set your magic free!"

I looked at Taeven, and he smiled softly. The vast sea of emotion that I felt for him opened inside me, surging up to tingle over my skin and lighten my chest. Inside it was a memory of the fear and pain we'd struggled through to get there. Of the obstacles we'd overcome, including the plots of a man who Tae had once thought of as a friend. So many things had worked against us, but our love had been blessed by the Goddess herself and nothing could stop it. I let that gratitude and power fill me and, against the skin of my palm, I felt a responding tingle from Tae.

Taeven nodded to me encouragingly, and I felt that tingle grow. Felt the magic slip into me and magnify mine.

But, out of the corner of my eye, I saw a Goblin sit up, his eyes opening to shine green light through the space, and fear lanced through me. My magic faltered as more Goblins stirred. It became a downward spiral, and I couldn't seem to swim up through the doubt. Couldn't rise back to my love. More emotions hit me—disappointment, shame, panic—and I drowned in them. More Goblins sat up. I could hear Devyn speaking encouragingly to me, but I couldn't focus on the words. I was going to fail. I was going to ruin the whole thing. I shouldn't have been so cocky. How could I have thought that I could do this on my first try? These Goblins were going to pay the price for my hubris. They were—

A warm cheek pressed against mine and through it, I felt a shiver of magic. I opened my eyes and turned to face Tae. He smiled again, not a shred of panic in his eyes, only confidence and love. So much damn love. My love rose to meet it, and everything else disappeared. I went calm under his violet stare. Then he nodded to me—just one sharp nod to remind me that I had a job to do.

I set my stare back on the Goblins and pictured them whole as I gathered my love for Taeven into my chest.

Several Goblins were standing now.

"Hold!" Varcir ordered his soldiers when they started to angle their weapons at the Goblins.

The Goblins stumbled toward us. More roused. Clawed hands clicked and lifted. The glow of green eyes turned the room into a haunted tomb.

I pushed down the anxiety that threatened to rise and prayed, *Please, help me, Goddess. I've got them here, now help me save them.*

Magic burst from me in a brilliant rush, and I screamed with the burning intensity of it. The other valorians and warlords made grunts of effort along with me as shimmers of energy blasted forth from them. They'd been waiting for me, gathering their power so we could release it together. And boy did it make an impact.

The Goblins were blown off their feet as a brilliant light shot through them. Those still in stasis shook with the hit, and then all of them fell into a violent trembling. Horrible shrieks came from their throats, even those who weren't awake, but as they shook and screamed, the spikes retracted from their shoulders and the claws shrank to more natural proportions. Gray skin blushed as color flowed back into it—shades of pale green, rust, and yellow bringing the faeries back to their true selves. The shaking stilled and Goblins began to sit up, opening eyes that didn't glow.

"Well, it's an improvement, I guess," Ravyn muttered. "Ow! Stop hitting me, Dal!"

Chapter Forty-Seven

The Goblins were welcomed back with Red Cap hugs and thumps upon their backs, a few of them succumbing to tears of relief and joy. We were thanked profusely, then offered drinks in Commander Varcir's tent. We could hardly refuse, so Tae and I went with the others and settled onto blankets around Varcir's campfire, just outside his tent, then warily sipped the liquor doled out by the Red Cap commander. It turned out to be quite good and our group began to celebrate in earnest.

Tae made sure there were guest tents available for the visiting warlords and valorians before we started drinking and also made sure to keep his own drinking to a minimum. Even when celebrating, he was still responsible for the camp and couldn't lose his senses entirely. Not entirely but maybe a little.

Taeven and I indulged our exhibitionism a bit, making out like a pair of randy teenagers on our blanket while the Unsidhe camp rejoiced around us, laughing and drinking in the way that soldiers do after a successful battle. The other couples were enjoying a bit of romance as well, but none of them were as . . . enthusiastic as we were. When Tae's hand slid down my pants, someone cleared their throat.

"Oh, shut up, Thorne," the Leopard Lord huffed. "If they want to put on a show, that's their right. And, frankly, I'm all for it. It's been ages since I've seen a good campfire performance. In fact . . ."

"Not happening, Kar," Tristan said dryly.

"But, Tryst, we're celebrating," Kardri cajoled. "At least rub my cock a bit."

"We will celebrate like that in the privacy of our tent."

"Perhaps we should as well," Tae whispered to me.

"Wherever, whenever, Tae," I whispered back. "You sure you want to leave?"

Taeven chuckled, stood up, and held a hand down to me. "I think the middle of an Unsidhe camp is a bit much even for me."

"If you say so." I winked at him.

"I've had tents prepared for all of you," Tae said to our guests. "Just let one of my knights know when you're ready to retire."

Our guests thanked Tae as we strode away, two of his knights falling into place behind us. I teased him all the way back to our tent, rubbing his ass, kneading his back, and even brushing his cock a few times.

"If you don't stop that, I'll make you into the spectacle you're trying to be," Tae whispered to me.

As much as the thought of fucking him in front of an audience excited me, I didn't actually want to be put on display that night. So, I sighed dramatically and stopped. But it didn't matter. We arrived at his tent a few minutes later and as soon as we were past the entry flap, we began yanking off our clothing, using bursts of magic to help us.

One of the brilliant things about shapeshifting is that every change is as good as a shower; filth just falls off you when you shift. So, even though we had just fought in a battle, neither of us was dirty. All Tae smelled of was himself—a rich, amber-like sweetness with a hint of feathers. I breathed it in deep.

"Come here, mate." Tae picked me up and carried me to bed. He laid me down atop the blankets, then covered my body with his. Once he had me where he wanted me, his expression went surprisingly grim. "You scared me today."

"I did?"

"When you dove for that Goblin." He kissed my jaw. "I told you not to leave my side."

"Are you really giving me shit for that?"

"No. Just confessing how scared I was when I saw you plummeting toward that creature."

"I'm sorry," I whispered.

"You did what you were compelled to do. But, sweet Goddess, Shane, I don't want to ever be that scared again."

"You don't have to." I stroked his cheek. "You felt it tonight, didn't you?"

"Our love?" Tae lifted a brow. "I didn't need magic to feel that."

"No, our *power*." I laid my palm on his chest, right over his heart. "We are so strong together. I'm not afraid anymore, Tae. I will stand at the front of your army beside you and face whatever the Farungal send our way, confident in the knowledge that we can do anything together. And with the help of the other warlords and valorians, I know we can end this war."

Taeven smiled. "Be that as it may, I still don't want you leaving my side in battle. Even more so now." He stroked my cheek. "We're stronger *together*. Remember that."

"I will." I wriggled beneath him. "In fact, I'm feeling particularly strong right now."

I pushed Tae onto his back and started kissing my way down his chest, pausing to nibble his nipples. His ardent groans encouraged me and my kisses became licks and then nuzzles as I settled between his thighs.

"Shane, I need to be inside you now," he murmured.

"No, you're going to wait and let me have *my* way this time," I insisted with a grin. Then that grin widened as I spread my lips around him.

We groaned together as his shaft filled my mouth, the salty taste of his arousal spiking my pleasure. I pushed down on that hard flesh, taking him as deep as I could, then called nectar to my hand to rub over the base. Just a little something I'd learned at school.

"Shane!" Tae's hand slid into my hair and squeezed.

I moved faster over him as I ground my cock into the blankets. That plump head was like heaven in my mouth; I could suck at it all night. I licked and laved, then went back to consuming him until he was nearly mad with need. Then I moved downward.

"Oh, fuck!" Tae shouted as I sucked at his velvety sacs.

They tightened in my mouth, and I moaned around them as I brushed my forehead against his cock, loving the way it twitched against me.

"If you don't ride me soon, I'm going to—"

His words cut off as I abruptly lifted his legs and shoved my tongue into his ass.

"Holy Mother!" Taeven cried out.

I shoved my tongue deep, mashing my face against him,

and Tae took his legs from me to pull them back further and open himself to me. I grinned against his flesh and shoved deeper. In and out, plunging into that tightness. It gave me such a naughty feeling, nearly as good as fucking in front of an audience. Then I groaned as I thought about doing this while someone watched us. Pushing the Falcon Lord's legs up high so our voyeur could see Tae's puckered hole as I licked and tongue-fucked it. Oh, yeah, that was a good fantasy; I'd tell him about it later. At the moment, he was a little too anxious for fantasies.

Tae took my face in his hands and pushed me away as he lowered his legs and growled. "Get up here and ride me now, Captain!"

"As my warlord commands." I eagerly climbed up his body to straddle him.

Quickly, I rubbed more nectar over his cock before angling it to enter me. Then, little by little, I worked down onto that thick, long shaft, its girth stretching me deliciously. Rising onto my knees, I began to ride him—his hands at my waist and mine on his chest.

"I love seeing you like this," Tae murmured, happy now that he was inside me.

"And I love riding your big cock." I bent down to kiss him, then pulled back just enough to whisper, "I love bending over for you, and kneeling for you, and spreading myself open for you. I love it when you hold me up and thrust up into me, and hold me down to shove yourself as deep as you can go. I want it all, Tae."

"Maybe not all tonight," he teased me. "But you will have it, mate."

"Whenever and wherever," I whispered.

"Whenever and wherever," he agreed.

And, looking down at him, I felt a shiver of fate roll over me. We had been forged into a weapon by the Goddess, made into something greater than the sum of our parts, but this weapon was wielded with love. Love would sustain us and see us through the war. It would see us through forever. My dreams were now centered around the man beneath me, but that didn't worry me. I could still be myself with him, more than myself. I could be who I was meant to be, and Tae wouldn't hold me back. He would fight for my dreams as hard as he fought for our love.

Whenever and wherever.

A Special Look

Keep reading for a special look into the next
book in the Soul Stones Series:

The Eagle Soul

The Eagle Soul UK

The Eagle Soul Australia

The Eagle Soul Canada

Chapter One

It was hard to be a farmer without a wife. After toiling in the fields all day, I had to make my supper and perhaps get some housework done. But soon, I'd have help. Mary Hillbroke was nearly mine. I'd worked hard to gain her favor and had been courting her for over a month now. I'd saved up and had enough set aside to buy her a modest ring, nice enough to sway her but not so grand as to give her a false impression of what life with me would be like. It wouldn't be easy, but I hoped that she thought I was worth it.

I swung my spade into the hard earth again. Normally, I'd till the soil with the help of my ox, but this patch was in my personal garden, just behind the strawberries, and had to be worked by hand. As the metal hit ground, a shriek caught my attention. It sounded like a bird, but not one I was familiar with. I looked up and searched the sky, then gaped at what I saw.

A giant bird was hurtling straight into my crops.

"Not a bird; a faerie," I whispered and started running toward it.

Then I saw the Farungal.

I stuttered to a stop. The monster was at the edge of the woods that surrounded my farm, watching the bird instead of me. It tracked the path of the faerie then chittered gleefully when it landed hard in my tomatoes. I cursed and ran forward.

The fallen faerie was defenseless, and I couldn't stand there and do nothing while it was slaughtered.

I reached the bird—an Eagle—seconds before the Farungal, who loped forward on thin legs, its back hunched, and claws extended. It saw me and chittered more—the Farungal version of laughter. We'd been at war with the evil Farungal for nigh on forty years, but the magical Fae had come out of their protected lands to help us. And this one would give up its immortal life for us if I didn't man up.

The Eagle flopped helplessly, one of its wings injured, then shifted into a Sidhe. I barely looked at the man as I set myself between him and the Farungal.

"Run, human!" the faerie shouted at me.

"Not happening, mister." I lifted my pickax. "You've defended me for all my life, the least I can do is help you when you're down." I glanced at the way one of his arms hung. "You run. I'll hold him off."

Whatever the Eagle said next was cut off by the chittering of the Farungal, who swooped down with a clawed hand. It happened so fast. I swung my spade and hit the monster in its stomach. It screeched and slashed at my throat. Simultaneously, a stream of fire blasted past me and knocked the creature to the ground. Belatedly, I realized that the faerie hadn't been defenseless at all, only injured. But the immortal Fae heal rapidly, and they always have magic available to them. As my throat burned with pain, I knew I had sacrificed myself for nothing. My only comfort was the sight of the Farungal dying before me. Though, it pained me to know that its blood would taint my crops.

"Damn it all!" I heard a deep voice curse as strong hands lifted me onto a warm, naked thigh, and one warrior palm went to the wound on my neck. "Why didn't you run, you fool!"

I stared up into a stunning face of fae features—exotically slanted and ethereal. Despite the delicate features and full lips, he was overtly masculine, with more muscles than one man should have and a regal brow. His long, black hair fell around me in silken waves, the strands turning blue in the sunlight, and his eyes gleamed as green as a fresh pea. I've always had strange yearnings—urges I'd pushed aside because I knew the hell that awaited me if I gave into them. But there, as I lay dying, I could finally admit that I longed to feel a body like his against mine. I wanted to know what it felt like to kiss his firm lips and run my fingers through his hair.

The Eagle Faerie wore a thick chain around his neck with a triangular stone hanging from it—odd that it had survived his shifting. The jewel began to glow, its neutral green brightening to rival the color of his eyes. Those eyes widened in surprise and then blinked in epiphany.

"Perhaps you aren't so foolish after all," he murmured. "Stay with me, human. The Goddess is calling to us. Can you hear her?"

My eyes widened as the light encapsulated us in a shimmering spear. The man holding me went spectral, his physical form becoming something divine, something unearthly. His beauty increased tenfold—a hundredfold—and I gaped at his glory. It was as if I could see more than the image of him; I could see *him*. Who he was. His honor and bravery as well as his weaknesses. They only made him more beautiful, those little cracks in his perfection. I tried to reach a hand out to touch him, but I didn't have the strength. My body was going cold.

Then the ethereal hand at my throat shifted, moving into my chest. Into it! I felt him there, inside me, and when he withdrew that hand, I knew he had left a piece of himself behind. Warmth flooded me and my throat ached as muscles and vocal cords wove back together. Vibrant tingles rushed through me unlike anything I'd ever felt before, and I suddenly felt so very alive. A cry left my lips, sounding strangely like that of a bird, and the sounds of the world faded around me as if that shriek had called forth silence. Into the silence came a voice and the cry of many beasts.

"I have you now, Aidan," a woman said. "Rest, child. Sleep."

Exhaustion flowed through me, and I started to slip into unconsciousness. The last thing I saw was the man going solid above me, his hand on my cheek and a triumphant look in his eyes. And the last thing I heard was his voice.

"Welcome to your new life, little fool."

Pronunciation Guide

Altarion: Al-tare-ree-on

Daron: Dare-on

Dehras: Day-ross

Nelos: Nay-low-s

Sanasenne: Sah-nah-seen

Siarra: See-air-rah

Shane Ruhara: Shay-n Roo-harr-rah

Taeven Rumerra: Tay-vehn Roo-mare-ah

Tasathor: Tah-sah-thor

Thalsar: Thal-sahr

About the Author

Amy Sumida is the Internationally Acclaimed author of the Award-Winning Godhunter Series, the fantasy paranormal Twilight Court Series, the Beyond the Godhunter Series, the music-oriented paranormal Spellsinger Series, the superhero Spectra Series, and several short stories. Her books have been translated into several languages, have won numerous awards, and are bestsellers. She believes in empowering women through her writing as well as providing everyone with a great escape from reality. Her stories are full of strong main characters, hot gods, shapeshifters, vampires, dragons, fairies, gargoyles... pretty much any type of supernatural, breathtakingly gorgeous man you can think of. Because why have normal when you could have paranormal?

Born and raised in Hawaii, Amy made a perilous journey across the ocean with six cats to settle in the beautiful state of Oregon which reminds her a lot of Hawaii but without the cockroaches or evil sand. When she isn't trying to type fast enough to get down everything the voices in her head are saying while her kitties try to sabotage her with cuteness, she enjoys painting on canvases, walls, and anything else that will sit still long enough for the paint to dry. She prefers antiques to modern furniture, tea to coffee, night to day, and Tom Hardy to Tom Hiddleston. No; Tom Hiddleston to Tom Hardy. No, wait... Tom Hardy *and* Tom Hiddleston to Tom Cruise. Yes, that's it.

For information on new releases, detailed character

descriptions, and an in-depth look into the worlds of the Godhunter, the Twilight Court, the Spellsinger, Spectra, and the Happily Harem After Series, check out Amy's website:

Amy Sumida's Website

Want a free book? Sign up for her newsletter and get a free ebook as well as the latest news on Amy's releases, parties, and giveaways:

Amy's Newsletter

Want more free books? Grab the first books in the Godhunter and Twilight Court Series for free: Godhunter and Fairy-Struck

Would you like to be the first to hear about new releases, win prizes in parties, and get first looks at Amy's book covers? Join her Facebook group: Amy's Imaginary Worlds on Facebook

Join Amy online here as well:
Bookbub

Twitter

Goodreads

Instagram

Check out the playlists for the Spellsinger Series on Amy's Spotify: Spotify

And you can find her entire collection of books, along with some personal recommendations, at her Amazon Author Page:

Amy's Amazon Page

Read more of Amy's books:

The Godhunter Series
The Twilight Court Series

The Spellsinger Series
The Spectra Series